# Edmonia

# Edmonia

BRIANNE BAKER

KENSINGTON PUBLISHING CORP.
kensingtonbooks.com

DAFINA BOOKS are published by

Kensington Publishing Corp.
900 Third Avenue
New York, NY 10022



All Kensington Titles, Imprints, and Distributed Lines are available at special quantity discounts for bulk purchases for sales promotions, premiums, fund-raising, and educational or institutional use. Special book excerpts or customized printings can also be created to fit specific needs. For details, write or phone the office of the Kensington Special Sales Manager: Kensington Publishing Corp., 900 Third Avenue, New York, NY 10022, Attn: Special Sales Department, Phone: 1-800-221-2647.



Library of Congress Control Number: 2025936271

ISBN: 978-1-4967-5487-5
First Kensington Hardcover Edition: May 2026

ISBN: 978-1-4967-5493-6 (ebook)

10 8 7 6 5 4 3 2 1

Printed in the United States of America

The authorized representative in the EU for product safety and compliance
is eucomply OU, Parnu mnt 139b-14, Apt 123
Tallinn, Berlin 11317, hello@eucompliancepartner.com

*For my son*

Dear Reader,

I first encountered Edmonia Lewis's story while planning a syllabus for a writing course, in an academic essay about various artistic depictions of Cleopatra throughout the years. This essay compared William Wetmore Story's sculpture of Cleopatra to Edmonia Lewis's *Death of Cleopatra* and gave a few details about Edmonia Lewis's life and career. I was enthralled to learn about this artist, and while my initial feeling was a sense of wonder at her accomplishments, my subsequent feeling was one of sadness, of regret at never having encountered such a remarkable woman before in my studies. After years of schooling and much coursework purposefully sought to learn about just such hidden figures, my education had still been insufficient to introduce me to this artist.

I began, almost immediately, to imagine what this woman must have felt as she pursued an education in New York and Ohio, as she embarked on her artistic career in Boston, and traversed the Atlantic Ocean to seek greater opportunities and creative freedom in Rome at a time when so many people of her race were enslaved and oppressed across the Western world. It is difficult to make a living as an artist in any era, and would undoubtedly have been much more difficult for a Black woman in the nineteenth century to forge a path in the artistic world than it would have been for many of her contemporaries. I felt an instant kinship with this fellow artist, and began to research her more intently, seeking out any sources I could find that would reveal more of the intricacies of her life. I soon learned, however, that much about Edmonia Lewis's life remains unknown, and what information we do have is oftentimes distorted and obscured by the many embellishments and exaggerations that Edmonia herself perpetuated throughout her lifetime, when speaking with friends or granting interviews to the press. These gaps in knowledge about Edmonia's life did not deter my interest in this figure, but only set my creative mind ablaze, and the fiction writer in me began to work.

While I wanted to maintain some of the confirmed biographical details of Edmonia's life in this novel, such as her attendance at New York Central College and Oberlin College, her exhibit at the 1876 World's Fair in Philadelphia, and her familiarity with distinguished figures like President Grant and Frederick Douglass, this novel is an entirely creative interpretation of those details, and melds them with many other completely fictive events, situations, and characters. Many names, dates, locations, and other historical details have been fictionalized in the service of plot and narrative flow, and the entirety of the dialogue, the interior monologues, as well as the totality of the prose are my own inventions, crafted in an effort to maximize the drama and emotion of nineteenth-century life for modern-day readers.

There is always a temptation to treat underrepresented historical figures as irreproachable and infallible, but by many accounts of the time in the letters of people who knew her and interacted closely with her, Edmonia Lewis was a complicated, if not difficult, and oftentimes, quite mysterious, woman. There were stories of betrayals and broken friendships and mentorships, legal battles regarding some of her artwork, and most intriguing of all, the major scandal that erupted while she was a student at Oberlin College. These accounts only deepened my interest, as I felt that it would be inevitable for Edmonia to experience some measure of controversy while navigating spaces that were never meant for her, while living and working with people who viewed her as subordinate, inferior, and peculiar. In writing this book, I wanted to capture and dramatize many of those facets of Edmonia's existence, including the contentious, as I found they only made her career more remarkable, accomplished as it was under such constant pressure, scrutiny, judgment, and strife.

For a true historical account, I must point the reader to *Child of the Fire* by Kirsten Pai Buick, *The Indomitable Spirit of Edmonia Lewis* by Albert Henderson and Harry Henderson, as well as the many essays of Marilyn Richardson, and *The Petrification of*

*Cleopatra in Nineteenth Century Art* by Margaret Malamud and Martha Malamud, the essay that first introduced me to Edmonia Lewis. These works were invaluable to me as I researched Edmonia Lewis's life, and this novel would not be what it is without the work these historians have done to help unearth the story of this fascinating woman.

Brianne Baker

*"Some praise me because I am a colored girl, and I don't want that kind of praise."*

—Edmonia Lewis

# Part I

# The Student

## 1856–1862

# Chapter 1

THE VISIONS BEGAN WHEN I WAS A CHILD, APPEARING INFREQUENTLY at first, then becoming constant, rapid, relentless, a veritable assault on my young mind. They felt rather more like visitations than visions, the images flashing before my eyes as almost physical, corporeal beings, begging for incarnation, immortalization in some form with more permanence than mere air. The first vision was of my father, a man who had died before I'd ever known him, while away on travel shortly before my birth. He had been a valet, a gentleman's servant, and would traverse the country with his principal, dressed in the finest apparel, as I had been told. I would not have known this first vision was my father had he not appeared before me in this finery, and had he not resembled so greatly my older half-brother, Samuel, with the only other distinction, aside from his attire and relatively advanced age to that of my brother, being a noticeable scar beside his right eye.

One evening, after dinner, on a rare visit my brother made to the small dwelling where I lived with my maternal aunts in the wilds of northern New York, I questioned him about our father's exact countenance, and in particular, the mark I'd seen in my vision. I was careful not to reveal the source of my knowledge, lest he deem my vision inappropriate or unearthly, lest, indeed, he deem me unwell for beholding such illusions.

"Had our father a scar," I asked, touching the same spot on my own face, "just here?"

My brother looked at me strangely, and confirmed that our father did have just such a marking.

"He didn't like to talk much about how he received it," Samuel said, looking into the fire before which we sat. "I believe he got it in a duel during his younger years. He was not a man to accept slights quietly."

Samuel did not belabor the subject, nor inquire as to how I'd gained such knowledge, perhaps assuming that my aunts had told me of my father's visage during one of their usual tales recounted to me at bedtime.

It was not long after this that a vision of my mother manifested before me in the night, and though I had known her no more than I knew my father, her death happening shortly after, and in consequence of, my birth, her demeanor communicated so clearly that of the maternal, her movements so protective, her aura so compassionate, that I knew at once this was who she was. My mother had been an Ojibwe woman, as were her sisters, the aunts with whom I lived, and she appeared before me in traditional dress, her raven hair flowing freely down her back.

"My child, my child," she seemed to say, reaching toward me with outstretched hands. I must admit I was afraid to accept her embrace, as she seemed so insistent upon holding me that I thought she might carry me with her into that celestial world that existed beyond our own. I shut my eyes and tried to return to sleep, but found that it eluded me that night, and came but fitfully for several nights following, as my mother's apparition visited with regularity.

The more I attempted to subdue this vision of my mother, the more she seemed to desire, and even demand, release. I began to sketch her, to give her solidity, using what paper and instruments I could find, but even that was insufficient, as each evening in bed these maternal visions would continue their appearance before me. And so, I began to carve her, to sculpt her, to give her a more durable form than a sketch or a painting, something closer to life itself. I worked with oak, maple, or birch wood, with clay or what fragments of flint I could find. I knew she would not let me rest until I got the sculpture just right, until she, in her ethereal home, could feel pleased by the figure, through my unpracticed efforts, I'd wrought.

I was laboring away on just such a sculpture, having retired to a quiet, and, as I thought, unknown place in the woods during a break from my daily chores with my aunts. My progress was interrupted by two men who approached me, suddenly, from the forest depths, causing me to bolt upright from the spot where I worked, and retreat, slowly, like the prey I then felt myself to be. They were clad all in black, their collars high, their complexions so pallid as to appear almost gray, as if they had sacrificed all sunlight, all recreation, in pursuit of some somber objective.

"You needn't be afraid, child," one of the men said, reaching a thin and pale hand toward me. "We're here to help you."

I had long heard stories of the black-robed men from other members of the Ojibwe tribe, and from such tales I'd surmised that these men offered not help, but a hindrance to the relative freedom with which we lived and roamed on what land had been left to us. These men would want to civilize me, to send me away toward that effort, to steal from me the singularity I'd had since birth, as I'd heard had been done to many other Ojibwe children with whom I'd played and had never heard from again. With that in mind, I fled from that space, and from those men, running swiftly through the woodlands, taking a circuitous route I knew these missionaries, in their restrictive clothing and shoes, could not follow. I was surprised to find, then, that after some moments in what I'd considered relative safety—behind a boulder by a rushing brook whose noise, I believed, would further obscure my movements—I saw my brother leading the black-robed men toward me, ever nearing my hideaway.

"She often hides here," I heard Samuel say, surprising me in his easy betrayal. "Come out now, sister," he went on. "There's no need to run. These men are Baptist missionaries. They mean you no harm."

I shrank still farther into my seclusion, hoping the black-robed men would relinquish their efforts, and yet, my brother continued. "This is Minister Wells, and Minister Smithson. They're here to offer you an education."

"An education in what?" I rejoined after a momentary pause, seeing that these men would not soon leave me be.

Minister Wells smiled at this. I resented his amusement, his seeming assumption that my earnest question could be used toward his entertainment.

"An education in literature, Latin, and grammar," the minister replied, "in history, but most of all in politics, the occurrences of our era, and the ways that strong Christian guidance can lead this country onto firmer ground."

I did not respond to the minister, but still he persisted, speaking assuredly, someone certain that he would receive what he desired, if not by persuasion, then by force.

"Your brother tells us that you are a young lady twelve years of age. Wouldn't you like to learn how to read, how to write?" he asked, daring to step yet closer to me.

"I know very well how to read," I replied, thinking of the ways that I could discern the land, how the rivers and lakes and mountains, the stars and the very air were all as legible to me as if they had been bound within the leather covers of a book. I could see by the mere appearance of this man that he could claim no such knowledge, and yet he deigned to consider me the uneducated one.

"Dishonesty won't do, sister," Samuel said, and he, too, emitted a small chuckle, as if all of my impudence was too juvenile to consider with any seriousness. "You do not yet know how to read, nor write, and you would be a silly girl to refuse this opportunity to learn."

Samuel approached me then, leaving the black-robed men some space behind him, a distance from which they could not hear our short conference. "Come, now," Samuel entreated, "their school is just across the way, in McGrawville. You will not be so very far away. It's even closer to town, so I can visit you there often, if so desired, but I am sure that within just a few days you will have made so many friends, and will have learned about such wondrous subjects, that you would scorn my presence there."

I made no reply, allowing my silence to communicate my vexation. Samuel went on. "They say that their school is called New York Central College, a new institution founded by the Baptists and the abolitionists of this state. They've raised enough funds that you can attend without me needing to pay tuition, nor room and board," he eagerly added.

"I will not go," came my cold reply, as I remained obstinate in my refusal.

"You haven't a choice in the matter," he said, and then, seeming to sense my youthful determination, and perhaps wanting to avoid further conflict, he quickly added, "Surely you know that I would not steer you wrong. This is for the best. This is for your personal improvement."

I did not show any pleasure at this idea of personal improvement, and only said, "I like myself as I am," in the futile hope that this would terminate our deliberations.

"But should you want to always remain here," Samuel pressed, "selling Ojibwe souvenirs to condescending tourists by Niagara Falls?"

I had never known that my occupation with my aunts was thought to be demeaning, and in fact I had always enjoyed the opportunity for the creative release provided through our work, as I would sit beside them and weave baskets and bead moccasins for amazed travelers from across the country, and from Europe. But as I would soon learn that the eyes of Adam and Eve were opened with the first taste of forbidden fruit, so were my own eyes opened at these words from my brother, and I began to see myself, and the life I had lived thus far, in a newer, harsher way, and would never be able to return to the naïveté, the disregard for what the wider world thought of me, that had thus defined my existence.

And so it was with great haste that preparations began for me to attend school, that my farewells to my aunts and the other tribe members were dispensed, that my few belongings were packed and corded and loaded onto a coach. However, it seemed that the only element I could not leave behind were the visions, which plagued me for days before my departure to McGrawville, though now it was not only my mother who visited me, but numerous other unnamed and unknown personages who likewise called out for liberation. I hoped that I would be able to find a mode of expression for these visions within those schoolhouse walls, as I knew that I would not be able to fully concentrate on my studies while they tormented me.

After a coach ride of some miles, we arrived in McGrawville, and I alighted before a building more massive than any I had ever previously beheld. Students bustled about, conversing in groups of twos and threes, all seeming delighted to be at school, comfortable with their place here. Very few of these students, I noticed, resembled me in either color or attire, as they were all of the fairer race, and I stood momentarily petrified before them until Minister Wells ushered me, with much haste, into a small reception building adjoining the main school.

Minister Wells led me down an echoing hallway into a wide, wood-paneled gymnasium. After directing me to join a line of students with whom I shared a greater resemblance, at least in terms of our race, Minister Wells left me there, friendless and alone, standing timidly behind the other young students who appeared equally bewildered. The room smelled of lye soap, and was heavy with the steam of boiling water, the perspiration of the anxious students. I looked around, seeing that the space was divided into stations, with a different woman, appearing to be a nurse, presiding over each spot, taking several other children of about my age behind separate screens to submit to I knew not what procedures. Finally, I myself was directed, by a tall and severe woman, to step behind just such a screen.

"Remove your shoes," the woman said, with no introduction, no preamble. I obeyed her, kicking off the brown moccasins my aunts had given me before my departure. "And your dress," she added, almost as an afterthought, though this instruction left me yet more stunned. Still, after a short hesitation, I did as I was told. The woman then directed me to step into a tub of steaming hot water, and once I complied, she scrubbed at my arms and back until I felt that I might bleed, then moved in front of me and repeated the process. She poured buckets of hot water upon my head, then roughly parted and combed my hair, seeming to closely examine each strand, each inch of my scalp. These procedures completed, the woman dressed me in a frock of all white, then pushed me toward the next station.

"She is clean," the woman told the lady at the next station. "No nits."

"Name?" the next woman demanded, bringing me behind her own screen and sitting me in a hard wooden chair.

"Wildfire," I replied, answering her with the only name I'd been called by my aunts and the other Ojibwe I had lived among. Even my brother, though I knew he was not of the tribe, had always addressed me thus, and it was a name that I appreciated, and felt aptly described my general disposition.

The woman stared at me for a moment as if I were in jest, as if such joking were inappropriate for the solemnity of the occasion, of my enrollment to this school.

"A heathen name," was her terse reply. "It won't do at this institution," she said, writing something upon a piece of paper before her. "And your surname?"

"Lewis," I replied, giving the last name of my father, and my older brother. The woman scribbled upon the sheet of paper. "You'll receive a new Christian name at your baptism this evening," she declared, without waiting for my reply, or my consent. "And your birthdate?" she continued, looking at me impatiently.

I hesitated at this question, for I knew that I had been born around 1844 or thereabouts, as my brother had often told me that I was then twelve years of age. I could not mark the exact date of my birth with any certainty, as in those days, and among my mother's people, such matters were not recorded with paper and ink, but rather, were spread about through tales told around evening fires, or morning washing in the riverbed. As such, I chose the only date I thought the woman might appreciate, one that I had been told held much importance, and was the birthdate of our very nation, in fact.

"July the Fourth, 1844," I declared, with some pride, as if I, too, believed myself to be an inheritor of the ideals espoused on that date.

If I had expected some grand reaction at this revelation, the woman did not give it, and only wrote upon the paper for several moments before ripping the sheet from her notebook and roughly passing it to me. "Hand this to the lady at the next station, just there," she said.

I looked down at the paper, wishing I could make sense of its characters and symbols, to know what sorts of notes the woman had made about me, as her stony visage betrayed very little of her true emotions.

"Move along now," the woman said, dismissing me with a shooing hand, stopping my scrutiny of her notes.

The final station was cluttered with papers and pencils and an array of other instruments that, though I did not then know their names, would soon learn were rulers, protractors, dividers, compasses, and all other matter of tools for drawing and measuring. I found that I could not readily compose myself before this display of strange instruments, so nervous was I at the thought of what was to come.

"Be still, child," the final woman commanded, indistinguishable now from the others, in her stark white frock and tight brown bun. "And look forward, chin up."

I complied, and the woman began to take my measurements, first my height and arm span, then the circumference of my head, the width of my nose, the space between my eyes, and so forth. She carefully recorded each measurement, and as she did so, I looked at the other young boys and girls in the line before me, quietly submitting to the very same close appraisal of their physiognomies by the other nurses. I tried to discern whether they found this treatment as strange, as demeaning, as I did, but I could see only resignation on their faces, evidence that they had undergone such treatment before, that they had long ago learned their bodies were always susceptible to the whims of such people as these nurses and administrators.

"You may go now, child," the woman finally said, interrupting my observations of the other students. "Your phrenology report is complete."

Though I had never before heard of phrenology and had no knowledge of its import or implications, I could tell by the way that she pronounced the word, by the cold and assessing expression she wore as she spoke it, that it meant I was a sort of specimen, a strange and curious study in her eyes, and that my fate at this school was beholden to forces beyond which I had any control.

As the afternoon went on, we students were fed a meager lunch of bread and cheese, and we dined together, seated on the gymnasium floor, though none of us conversed, and not one of us so much as dared offer another a glance, so depleted were we by the morning's physical examinations. At dusk, we children were shepherded out to a wide field overlooking a still and tranquil lake, the first indications of fall just beginning to show on the trees around us. Minister Wells again appeared before me, there, by the lake, addressing all of us young students as we were ushered, by one of the nurses, ever closer toward the water.

"Here at New York Central College, we take it as our creed that all followers of Christ are our brethren, that we are all equal before His eyes," Minister Wells began, looking out at us students solemnly, his voice growing clearer as we drew nearer to him.

"Even you all, of the darker race, are worthy of redemption, of salvation." He paused for a moment to allow these words to take their effect upon us, though it seemed that very few of us children understood his import. "Your people may have wandered for centuries in the wilderness, in the jungles of Africa, or the wilds of North America, worshiping idols and pagan gods, but here, you may find absolution for any transgressions you have committed before, however unknowingly."

Some of the children, seeming then to comprehend what was expected of us, called out their thanks to the minister for this largesse. "And so you will be baptized here," Minister Wells declared, "in the lake, that you might be converted to the faith, and may receive your education at this Baptist institution."

I knew not what it meant to be baptized, but as I saw the first group of children enter the water and allow themselves to be fully submerged, I felt the act was a redundancy of the earlier bathing to which I'd been so rudely and uncomfortably subjected. I stepped out of the line and took a seat upon a boulder nearby, resolving to observe the festivities without partaking in them. Seeing this, one of the nurse women approached me and bid me to rejoin the line of children entering the lake.

"But I've only just had a bath," I protested, unmoving from my perch.

"That was for the cleansing of your body," the woman said, slowly, as if I might not understand her words, "and this is for the cleansing of your soul."

"My soul is quite clean," I replied, still uncertain of exactly what was meant by this term, but sure the woman who had bathed me earlier must have made that organ pristine with her incessant scrubbing. "It has no need of further—"

A girl hastily approached me then, thus stopping my sentence and leaning close to my ear, she began to speak. "A child must not challenge her elders in that way," she whispered, seeming to think herself my keeper, though she appeared to be only slightly my elder. "You'll find yourself in great trouble if you continue on like that."

I observed this young girl for a moment, slightly taller than I, and much thinner, as if many weeks had passed since she'd had a good meal, but the warmth and radiance that emanated from her dark skin and darker eyes rendered this gauntness barely noticeable. Still, despite her seeming warmth, I thought to challenge this young girl on her words as well, but she took me, roughly, by the arm and led me back to the lake before I could do so, instructing me quietly all the while.

"Watch how I behave when they take me into the lake," she said. "Do exactly as I do. Say exactly the words that I say."

With this direction thus dispensed, the girl was swept into the water by a clergyman and led toward the waiting Minister Wells and Minister Smithson, themselves dressed in white robes for the occasion, and submerged waist-deep in the lake water. "Clara Mae Wilder," Minister Wells said, reading from a paper the clergyman passed to him.

I could not then ascertain the exact words the minister spoke to this girl, this Clara Mae Wilder, who evidently thought herself my guardian, but I saw that she nodded her head silently and answered affirmatively the minister's interrogations, then allowed herself to be swiftly and fully submerged within that clear water, and held beneath its surface for some seconds by the ministers' firm grips.

Finally, Clara emerged from the water's depths seeming renewed, refreshed, utterly transformed. She gave first a tentative smile, then a laugh, then a shout with raised arms that so surprised me it caused me to start, and to fear that her emaciated frame might collapse under the effort. Clara's exultations thus completed, she was led out of the lake and back toward the field to watch the remaining baptisms. I noticed that Clara's jubilant countenance had strangely dissipated just as quickly as it had appeared, as she seemed to grow, with each step farther away from the lake, as proportionately dejected as she was formerly joyful.

I could not long ponder this change in Clara's aspect, as it was then, apparently, my own turn to be baptized, as the same young clergyman ushered me forward into the lake with much more force than I thought necessary.

"The child who fled," Minister Smithson intoned upon seeing me, with another one of his unsettling smiles. "And so, you have found your way back to the flock."

I did not return Minister Smithson's smile, and hardly deigned to meet his eye, leaving him with no other choice but to sigh at my insolence, and recommence his words.

"Let me prepare you for what is to come, lest you attempt another escape," he said. "I will ask you a few questions, first, and you will answer as truthfully and faithfully as you can. If your responses are acceptable, I will then purify you in the very lake water in which you stand. Do you comprehend this, child?"

I said that I did, and both Minister Wells and Minister Smithson, appeased by my words, began their insistent questioning, a litany of doctrinal interrogations I found myself unable to fully comprehend, though I answered each in the affirmative, as Clara had instructed me to do. The final of these questions, however, I understood by the ministers' changed tones, was most critical.

"Do you accept Jesus Christ as your personal Lord and Savior?" Minister Wells asked me, with a lowered voice and unblinking gaze.

I had never heard of this name, so I looked out at the other new students gathered at the shores of the lake, hoping to gain some understanding of how I should respond. Each student stared at me with the same expectant gaze that the ministers maintained, until finally, I saw Clara, who gave me a small and almost imperceptible nod, bidding me to answer the minister's question affirmatively. I took a moment to ruminate on the question, as I knew that this acceptance would remove me in a way from the beliefs and lifestyle of my aunts and the Ojibwe with whom I had lived before, and I knew, too, that I would be a person transformed upon entering into this new faith that governed all who attended this school. It seemed to be a decision too profound for a mere child to make on her own, without careful counsel nor the opportunity to weigh the relative merits and difficulties of this new life in McGrawville, but I took courage in that quiet certainty that Clara sent toward me, and I took a breath, faced the ministers, and spoke my affirmation.

"Yes," I replied, in a voice barely above a whisper. The ministers nodded then, evidently pleased by my response.

"I now baptize you in the name of the Father, and of the Son, and of the Holy Spirit," Minister Wells declared, and then, with Minister Smithson laying his hands upon my shoulders, and Minister Wells, his hands upon my forearms, these men endeavored to lower me into the lake water as tradition would bid them to do.

For years in my youth, I loved nothing more than an evening swim in the rivers and lakes that surrounded my home, when the water, thus cooled and calmed, could serve as a balm to my body exhausted after a day's work, or begrimed after much play. This act of entering the lake water, however, felt much different, and somehow, much more dangerous to me, and so I resisted the ministers' hands initially, refusing to be fully submerged, not wanting to be placed in such a vulnerable position by these men whom I did not know, and did not trust. But of course, and at last, I was made to submit to the water's undulating embrace, by the ministers' unremitting force, and I found that I was glad to finally relinquish the struggle.

All grew quiet as the water filled my ears, and as I relented to the experience, the most peculiar sensation overcame me, a genuine shift in my very being that I knew would not easily, if ever, dissipate. I could not name it, could not define it, but it felt as if my thirst had been quenched after a bout of dehydration, as if I had been seated before a feast after many years without proper nourishment, as if I had received a warm embrace after a lifetime of abandonment. Before I could submit this feeling to further analysis, the ministers lifted me from the water, wrapped me in a towel, and immediately began to speak.

"Henceforth, you will be called Mary Edmonia," Minister Wells decreed, without, it seemed, any need or desire for my own consultation on the matter. The nurses and clergymen beyond nodded and took note of my new, Christian name, then a woman approached, wrapped me in a thin towel, and led me out of the water as I contemplated this new identity.

These names, Mary and Edmonia, were so different from the ones I'd heard among the Ojibwe, and I often wondered, in the years that followed, why those ministers christened me thus. I learned that Minister Wells's own Christian name was Edmond, and perhaps this informed his choice of my middle name. But why did he choose to name me Mary, an appellation, I later learned, that could mean beloved, if the minister's motives were generous, but could also mean bitter, or rebellious, which would certainly have aligned with Minister Wells's first impression of me, and might have been given to me in an act of vindictiveness, of retribution. In any case, I only knew that this girl, this Mary Edmonia, was someone quite different from myself, and I felt unsure whether I could truly become this other person, or if I even desired such a transformation. I only knew that the choice of this name was not my own, and was now as irreversible as my presence at that school in McGrawville.

The sound of the crackling fire was all that filled my bedroom that evening, and all the light that pervaded the space, a small habitation that I was to share with Clara and a few of the other girls who had been enrolled in the school's Primary Department. I had quietly observed Clara all evening long as we unpacked our belongings and settled into our modest, almost Spartan accommodations. Though I might have resented being forced to live in such a small space when I was so accustomed to the open air and the vast woodlands, Clara seemed happy, and almost exuberant, to be living in such a room. She hummed as she settled her few dresses and shoes into her wardrobe, as she folded a few blankets and placed them upon her bed.

"Mary, did you have enough to eat this evening?" Clara asked, suddenly stopping her merry tune and turning toward me. "I've wrapped some leftover bread from supper in my apron there, if you still feel hungry."

While I appreciated Clara's concern for me, her almost maternal regard for my well-being, I couldn't wrest my attention from the new name by which she'd addressed me. "You mustn't call me that," I replied, speaking to Clara far more harshly than I'd intended.

"But it is your name now," was Clara's gentle response. "You heard the minister. The sooner you accept that, the better things will be for you."

She came and sat next to me by the fire, where I then worked to untangle my hair that had grown matted and knotted by the lake water. "Here, let me help," Clara said, placing her hands in my hair, and again began to hum as she worked, signaling a mirth I could not understand.

"How can you just bear it all, so easily?" I asked her, swatting her kind hand away and standing up from my spot by the fire. "Obeying everything these strange ministers tell us, quietly submitting to all of their rules and odd treatments?"

"I would not say that I do so easily," Clara answered, slowly. "But that I do so readily, I must concede."

"Why?" I pursued, my petulance even more improper when contrasted with her calm.

She took a moment to consider my question before speaking. "Because this school is better than anything I have ever known," she finally said. "And I should be happy to receive an education, even from such strange people, as you deem them, when so many of our race cannot. Now, sit down, Mary, you must let me help you with your hair."

I did as she bid me, and once I was reseated in front of her, facing the fire, she continued to speak. "You can't possibly understand," Clara said. "I saw your file. You are still quite young and naïve, only twelve years old, while I am a young woman of fifteen and have a better handle on such matters. And what's more, Mary, is that you were living among the Natives when the ministers found you, though you are yet a Negro girl, as am I, or at least you have been categorized so by the administration here. You are freeborn, and so your life has been quite different here in the North. But for those of us who were born into bondage, even the confines of a school are a welcome liberation, a sweet respite from the horrors we experienced down South."

Clara's hands suddenly stopped their movement within my hair, and she seemed to grow contemplative, despondent, speaking as much to herself, or to no one, as she was to me.

"I have no family that I can call my own, no friend with whom I could dwell," she said. "I escaped from Virginia and was rescued in the woods by one of these good missionaries. If I must simply abide by the rules of the Baptists who founded this school to live here, that is no great difficulty for me."

I observed Clara as she spoke, amazed by her composure, her grace as she recounted the dread of her former life. I wanted to ask her about this escape from Virginia, how she managed it, and to learn more about the circumstances from which she fled. Before I could offer any of these questions to Clara, however, a soft rap on the door interrupted us, and brought an unwelcome end to our conversation.

"Put out the fire, girls," came a woman's voice from the corridor. "It is time to sleep."

Clara stood swiftly from her spot behind me, not wanting to upset even that disembodied voice, lest she jeopardize her spot at this school. The absence of Clara's touch was painful, immediate, a mother's hand removed too soon from an infant not yet sufficiently pacified. She went over to her small chest of drawers and removed a nightgown, then slipped out of her baptism dress. It was then that I saw, by the light of the fire, the stripes woven across her back, evidence of those Southern horrors to which she had alluded. I could not help but to stare at this sight, the shock of it, the dissonance of those raised scars on the skin of a young woman so kind. Clara seemed to feel my eyes upon her, as she turned, ever slightly, and only briefly, to meet my gaze, before silently dressing in her nightgown, dousing the remaining fire, and going to her bed.

# Chapter 2

In the morning, I found myself in Miss Keziah King's classroom, in the school's Primary Department, seated beside Clara, to my right, and an energetic young man named Quincy to my left, who could not stop fidgeting in his excitement at the start of the school year, despite Miss King's admonishments. Miss King herself was a beautiful young woman, so young as to appear barely old enough to teach us much, but she carried herself with an air of certainty and authority, her blue eyes fearlessly riveted upon us, her posture tall and confident and erect, a stature that belied her youthful features.

While I still felt quite ambivalent about my enrollment at New York Central College, I found that if I thought of myself as this new person, this Mary Edmonia Lewis, as I'd been so named, it was easier to sit still in my seat, to not wish myself back in the forest, in the ease and spontaneity of my previous life. That abandon, that unrestraint with which I'd lived was Wildfire's behavior, her desires, her impulses, but not Mary's. Mary could be a good child. She could behave according to the customs of this school, and of this town. She could be, in a word, civilized. This Mary became a sort of phantom by my side, guiding me, directing me, observing and correcting my every move. I could almost hear her voice, somewhat lighter and softer than my own, and see her movements, so much more graceful and feminine than what Wildfire's had been. I attempted to embody those attributes, and felt myself almost overtaken by the pursuit, by Mary's presence within me.

At the start of class, Miss King walked slowly up and down each aisle, observing each student, carefully, in turn, taking in our hair, our clothing, our hands and nails and shoes, causing all scattered conversations to cease as she completed her silent scrutinizing. Finally, upon returning to the front of the classroom, she placed her hands on the desk before her and spoke.

"There are those who will say you all are incapable of learning," she said, by way of introduction, and we students held our collective breath in anticipation of her next words. "Unfit for anything but subordination, enslavement."

We all shifted in our seats at this, still silent but visibly uncomfortable at her frank observation, looking around at each other and realizing that our class was composed entirely of colored students, the only ones in attendance at this school. Up until that point, such sentiments had remained implied, unspoken, but Miss King saw fit to tell us explicitly how our minds were regarded by the wider world.

Miss King continued. "But I say otherwise. I will make it my special experiment to see whether you all can learn as quickly as the white students," she said, and then, upon seeing our skepticism at her *experiment*, quickly added, "Yes, if you can learn as well as those of my own race, for I have committed my own life to the abolitionist cause, and have lost both friends and family in that pursuit, as I believe that you all of the darker race are worthy of the very same opportunities and advantages as any other."

Clara and I exchanged a glance. Quincy, on the other side of me, finally stopped his fidgeting, understanding the urgency of Miss King's words.

"As such," Miss King went on, "I must discern the baseline at which you all join this school, the educational foundation you already bring here, if any, upon which we can build. We will begin with a short quiz on the basics of American history, for you cannot hope to challenge or change a system until you know its very core, until you can recite back at your oppressors the very rules they use for your subjugation."

The other students all nodded in quiet acquiescence to this quiz, but I was overcome with a sudden discomfort and anxiety. Miss King took notice of this and considered me for a moment, before moving closer to my seat and speaking to me in a low tone.

"Don't fret, Mary," Miss King said. "It is not what you know now, but how quickly, how efficiently you can improve your knowledge and supply for any deficiencies therein. It is true that many of the students here have already had an opportunity to learn some of the basics of reading and writing as they arrived in McGrawville much earlier than you did, but you will catch up with them, if you apply yourself, and remain focused. Now," she said, speaking more loudly, and addressing the class once again as a whole, "take out the notebook and pencil you will find in your desks, and we shall commence. To begin, please write the name of this nation's first president."

This initial question posed, the other students began to scribble furiously upon their papers, while I sat immobilized by the seemingly simple task. Miss King approached me and placed a hand on my shoulder.

"Just try to write something, anything, Mary," she said. "You must do this for—"

"My personal improvement, yes," I interjected, not wanting another recitation of my purpose in attending this school. "My brother has already told me as much."

Miss King smiled upon me, kindly, before speaking again. "It is not so much for your own improvement, but for the greater improvement of your race," she said. "You can be an example, an emblem, of what is possible for your people when given the chance. A heavy responsibility, indeed, but one that begins with this first day of your education. Do not be nervous, and only remember, it is all for the good of your people."

I nodded my head as Miss King walked away, though I was not quite placated by her response. *Just who are my people?* I wanted to ask her. *Those who see visions in the night, who cannot rest unless they give these visions a physical form? Those who can neither find total comfort nor assimilation with any part of their racial identity?* I knew very well what Miss King truly meant by her words, but still, I could not help but take umbrage at the idea that my mind must be used for nothing more than the advancement of others. This seemed to me a reduction, a simplification of my abilities, an unnecessary restriction to the authentic expression of my very self.

Miss King pressed on with her questioning, assuring the class that spelling and grammar were not as important as getting some idea, any idea, onto paper. I decided to answer Miss King's questions as my genuine nature compelled me to, not through the written word, but through images. And so, when Miss King next asked the class to record the location of the first battle in the Revolutionary War, I sketched a scene of war's carnage, of men and bayonets and horses felled during the combat. When Miss King bid us to write the name of the current president's abode in the nation's capital, I sketched an image of a palatial home, so much more grand than any of us students then in the classroom could imagine as a dwelling for ourselves. When she told us to write the first few words of the Constitution, I depicted, instead, how I imagined that gathering of the nation's founders might have appeared, trying to capture, on their faces, the sort of importance verging on hubris they must have felt in deciding the fate of this new country. On and on I went, my pencil moving much more furiously than the other students', as I found this impromptu quiz much easier to complete when done in this way, more consistent with my disposition, truer to my very self.

At the end of the day's classes, Miss King sighed in evident approval of our labors, as well as her own. "Pass your papers forward," she directed. "I'll have them graded and returned to you all by morning."

She shifted through the papers quickly once she received them, giving each a cursory glance, nodding her head at some, furrowing her eyebrows at others. One paper in particular gave her pause, and I watched as she scrutinized it, until finally, a loud bell clanged from the yard beyond. The students began to gather their books and bags and other belongings, and I did the same, moving toward the doorway to make a hasty and much-desired retreat from that classroom.

"Just a moment, Mary," Miss King said, stopping me in my tread. "The work you've done here, while remarkable," she began, looking down at my work, "which is to say really, truly impressive, with each of your sketches appearing quite detailed and realistic, this work unfortunately does not meet the expectations of the assignment as I've given it."

I only looked down in acknowledgment of Miss King's words, not knowing how to explain my approach to her, to tell her that I understood the world not in words, but in images, and that these drawings were the only real recourse I had for a self-expression I otherwise found not only difficult, but nearly impossible.

"I know that it might feel more natural for you to complete an assignment in this way," Miss King said, speaking softly, tentatively, seeming a bit nervous to broach the subject. "I know that among your people, whether the Africans, or the Ojibwe, these sorts of visual representations feel more sufficient to express thoughts and emotions. And indeed, some civilizations have used pictorial representations to great ends," she mused. "You only need look at the hieroglyphs of Ancient Egypt to see their utility. But I am afraid you will find that such a mode of communication would be inappropriate, not to say useless, to you in polite society."

"I understand," was my barely audible reply, as I felt my skin begin to burn with embarrassment.

Miss King continued. "You know that this is an abolitionists' school, that our mission is to elevate your race, as I have told you."

I nodded my understanding.

"And do you think you can add to such an elevation if you have not the ability to read or to write, to challenge with the pen, with strong rhetoric and debate, what insults and abuses are hurled against you?" she asked.

I wanted to ask Miss King if art could not be as effective as rhetoric or debate, if it could not as quickly and easily penetrate and change the hearts of those who might wish me ill, but she clearly expected no reply, as she continued on without pause.

"Here, I'd like you to take this book," Miss King said, selecting a tattered tome from the shelf behind her. "You must work from it for one hour each night, including weekends. Copy the letters and words you will find within. I will meet with you once a week to go over your progress. With these exercises, you'll find yourself comfortable with writing in no time at all."

I accepted the book from her hands, seeing that it was a book of rhetoric, full of spelling and grammatical exercises, of many words I could not then comprehend, but knew that in time, and with effort, I could make my tools, and my weapons, as surely as was expected of me.

Several months passed in just such a fashion, with us students working diligently toward both a personal and collective improvement, and with my spelling and grammatical exercises leading to great advancement in my rhetoric. Clara would assist me each evening as I worked on these remedial exercises, sharing with me much of the knowledge she'd gleaned from the Bible instruction she'd received since arriving in New York, and using that to help with my writing. She and I grew ever closer as the days advanced, and we formed a sort of trio with Quincy as well, meeting up with him on weekends for games of chase or to run simple errands in town, when such free time was allotted to us, however infrequently. Most of our time, however, was devoted to study, and not frivolity or play. We students of the Primary Department all understood, in the abstract, and based on Miss King's constant reminders, that our purpose was revolutionary, critical, but one night in particular communicated this with a greater clarity than our teacher could ever hope to do.

Much commotion came into my bedroom that night from the

outside, the sound of horses' hooves and a heavy carriage making their laborious journey across the rough path leading up to our residence. Clara and I, both awakened by the noise, ran to the window and looked out, seeing a strange wagoner making his approach. I deemed it to be well after midnight by the height of the moon, and could not fathom what sort of caller would arrive at such an hour, and feared that no such person could bring favorable tidings so late in the night.

We watched from our window as the wagon came to a stop just outside of our lodge, and as Miss King, who kept her own quarters on the first floor of our building, rushed out of the front door to meet its driver, carrying a lantern in one hand and holding her unfastened bonnet upon her head with the other. The driver alighted from his horse, and we cracked open our small window to hear the coming exchange.

"Have you space for three more?" the man asked, his lack of introduction showing that he had at least some familiarity with our teacher.

"We will make the space, if we do not have it," Miss King replied in a breathless tone. "Hurry now, bring them inside."

The man then retrieved three cloaked figures from the back of his wagon, and they shuffled, with much difficulty, toward the front door. The other girls in our room roused from their beds at the sound of the front door closing shut.

"What has happened?" a young girl named Alice drowsily asked, while the others began to chatter amongst themselves and compete for a place at the window.

Clara shushed the girls as she dressed, quickly, in her robe and slippers. I did the same, and in an instant, we were downstairs, with several students from the other rooms emerging and following behind us. Miss King saw us approach, but to my surprise, she met us not with reprimand, but with an urgent and beckoning hand.

"Come, Clara and Mary, I need your help," she said, as the cloaked figures came farther into the house.

"Careful that the youngest doesn't take cold," the wagoner

told Miss King as he ushered the cloaked figures into the front parlor. "They came through the river, and the little one was soaked straight through. I found them sleeping in the woods, so the chill might have set in."

"Sit him just here, by the hearth," Miss King directed. "Mary, fetch more kindling for the fire. Clara, set some water to boil, and fix up some tea and stew. They must be famished. We'll put just a little food in their stomachs."

By this time, several other schoolmates from the house had congregated in the downstairs parlor, until it seemed that the entire residence had gathered as spectators to the scene before us. I went to the kitchen to acquire the requested kindling, then brought it quickly back and placed a few logs into the fireplace.

"Where have they come from?" Miss King asked the wagoner, still looking concernedly down at the youngest boy, who shivered as she positioned him before the now-blazing fire.

"Virginia," the man said, his voice gruff and exhausted by the ride and the chill air. "The oldest told me there were more among their number, but they got separated in the woods. I must depart to search for them now."

"I'll wait up, then, in case you locate them," Miss King said, as she walked with the man back to the front entrance. She shut the door behind him and locked it, then stood with her back upon it for a long moment, breathing deeply as if meditating upon some subject that was far too burdensome for us students to understand. As she worked to think and collect herself, Quincy, having emerged from one of the boys' rooms, sat by the fire to meet our new arrivals.

"What is your name?" Quincy asked the youngest boy, though muteness was his only reply. "Can't you speak?" Quincy pursued, but again, the boy kept his eyes riveted upon the carpet, as if he had not heard the question.

"You must let him alone, Quincy," Clara said, coming in from the kitchen and bearing tea and stew, as directed. "Can't you see that he's frightened?" she asked, in a sharper tone than I'd ever heard her use. Quincy sighed, evidently piqued that his joviality was not being met with approval as it so often was.

Clara turned to the young boy and offered him tea and stew, which he quietly refused. She placed the food on a table, and then, turning back to the young boy and softening her voice, placed an arm around his trembling shoulder.

"I've come from Virginia, as well," she said, and added, speaking quietly, so as not to further upset the young boy, "I, too, escaped from bondage."

She nestled still closer to the young boy as the other two escapees looked on, taking their places at a small table by the fire, nourishing themselves with the food Clara prepared, eating quietly, though ravenously.

"My master was a cruel man, as well," Clara went on, "but he cannot find me here, nor can yours. Here, you have no master, you have no chains. Just look at how well I'm doing here, and you will know that you are safe."

The young boy nodded at this, first looking up into Clara's eyes, then turning his back toward her and snuggling yet deeper into her arms.

"Now," Clara said, leaning her chin onto the young boy's head. "We'll set up a bedroom for you all, and you must try to sleep. Get all of the rest that eluded you in Virginia."

Clara took the young boy in her arms and commenced rocking him, singing softly all the while. I saw by the light of the fire that he was exhausted from his escape, and emaciated from days spent without sufficient food.

I began to cry as I listened to Clara's melancholic song, seeing in her the innate maternal force she had, though she had never known her own mother. I saw, in that moment, all that slavery had wrenched from both her and the child she held, and all of the other students who had come to New York Central College out of bondage. I understood, in a way that I never could before, the gravity of the school's mission, its importance not only as an educational institution, but also as a refuge for those escaping enslavement, and I knew that I no longer had the luxury of believing myself to be singular, for better or worse. I was a part of a collective, a race that needed both emancipation and social elevation, and I would have to use my mind, and my art, toward those ends.

No sleep could I find that night, as the other students went to bed, and Clara and I sat in wait of the other runaways that the wagoner was supposed to retrieve. The man never did return that night with the other escapees, nor did he retrieve them for any of the days and weeks that followed, until Miss King finally told us children that we must not await them any longer. I was haunted by the thought of what might have happened to those runaways, hoping that they might have somehow managed to go farther north, on to Canada, but fearing that their only fate was a return to the Southern horrors they had known before.

My visions returned for the first time in months, phantoms of those escapees, of the pain they had suffered, and might suffer still. I could find no respite from the visions as they returned to me with a greater force than ever before, and so I worked late into the night, by candlelight, making sketch after sketch of these children I had never met, but was sure begged for liberation, depicting the same stripes upon their backs that I had seen upon Clara's, the same pain upon their faces I had seen upon that young boy by the fire. It was the least that I could do for those children, I reasoned, the most effective way I could use my art to show the world what was happening to my people. But I knew, even as I labored over these sketches, working to perfect them until the darkness succumbed to the daybreak, that the visions would continue to torment me until I cast them into stone, until I gave those trying to escape their bondage a memorialization that would last longer, that would communicate more solid humanity, than what my feverish nighttime sketches could produce.

# Chapter 3

New York Central College's reputation began to grow as the months proceeded, and many distinguished figures saw fit to visit the campus, to witness, firsthand, the radical experiment being conducted on our grounds. Many of these visitors graced us with lectures and colloquia, and one lecture in particular struck me in a way that the others could not, as both the message and its deliverer imbued in me an idea I had not yet dared consider.

The speaker was Henry Highland Garnet, a man who himself had been born into slavery and escaped into New York some decades earlier. Clara and the other students who knew the monstrosities of bondage were especially interested to hear him speak, to see what sorts of feats and prominence they might achieve if they continued their studies, as Mr. Garnet had, if they used their newfound and yet tenuous freedom to great ends, as this man did. It was a spring day when we gathered in our small auditorium for the occasion, seated in breathless anticipation for the talk, for this distinguished visitor, with even the doves and warblers in the trees outside of our windows seeming to want a view of this man.

The teachers and administrators all lined the side walls of the auditorium, themselves appearing excited for the lecture that was to come. I saw Miss King among the teachers, smiling broadly and chatting with her colleagues, many of whom I had never met, as they instructed the white students of our institution, and rarely taught in the Primary Department, where the colored students learned. I used the opportunity to observe many of those white students then gathered in the auditorium with us, and noted that they, too, appeared interested in what Mr. Garnet would tell us that day, what knowledge and wisdom he had to bequeath, which would likely build on what their own abolitionist parents were teaching them each day. Finally, after a short delay, Mr. Garnet took his place at the podium as the audience all applauded his presence.

"I'd like to thank the New York Central College administration for inviting me here," Mr. Garnet began, looking down, initially, at his notes on the podium. "Mr. Gerrit Smith, a particular thanks to you for presiding over such a radical institution," he said, glancing then toward the front of the auditorium where Mr. Smith, the school's president, sat. This gratitude thus dispensed, Mr. Garnet took a moment to stare out at us students in the crowd, appearing genuinely affected by our eager and expectant faces.

"I've been asked here today to speak with you all about the ongoing debate regarding repatriation for the colored race," he intoned, "about the ways that Africa, and the country of Liberia, in particular, might be a more suitable home for us all."

There was a collective straightening up in our seats, a held breath that passed across us all as Mr. Garnet broached this topic, one that I would soon learn was quite controversial within the abolitionist circle. "The American Colonization Society has previously made great strides toward this effort, and I will say that I myself plan to make it to Africa one day, to die in the land where my soul should have been born."

I had not yet heard of repatriation, and of course, being still quite young, had not considered the idea of what my own final resting place might be, or whether I would ever want to see the African continent, while life was still mine.

"It is, of course, a contentious subject, one much debated in these abolitionist circles. *Why should we leave America?* the detractors question. *Why repatriate, when we have only lived on American soil, when we are now generations removed from our ancestors who ever knew a life in Africa?* These detractors seem to believe that we colored people in this country might be able to make a home here some distant day, that we might eventually be welcomed into the American fold."

Mr. Garnet meditated for a moment before resuming the idea. "I suppose that by now you all have heard of the Dred Scott decision, recently handed down by the Supreme Court, which declares that no enslaved person can be considered a citizen of the United States."

Mr. Garnet again paused, allowing the import of his words, and of this Supreme Court decision, to pervade the room. "With such a ruling, I have often asked myself, how can any of the colored people in America delude themselves into believing they could ever live more happily here than in Africa? Why should we try to change the way we are viewed here, when we might start a new and ultimately happier life elsewhere? Why should we stay here, in a land where we are so hated, and subjected to such degradation?"

We had learned of the Dred Scott decision in one of Miss King's class sessions, but I had not yet fully considered how it might relate to my own situation, since I was freeborn, nor had I completely appreciated the implications of the decision for someone like Clara or the other escapees.

"But I realize now, as I look out at you all today," Mr. Garnet continued, "at your impressionable, almost ravenous faces, that I simply cannot, in good conscience, tell you that the ultimate step toward your liberty is fleeing this land for another. For the ultimate step toward your liberty is not a fleeing, but a fighting."

Mr. Garnet looked down at the podium for a moment, as if gathering strength for his next utterance. "There are those in the administration here who might disagree with the message I find that I must deliver to you today, but still, I must persist in what I feel that I am being compelled, by some higher force, to tell you all."

Mr. Garnet looked toward the portion of the auditorium where the administration was seated, as if almost apprehensive about how to proceed, unsure whether he would be permitted to speak his next words. "You must fight your oppressors, wherever you may find them," he finally said, "whether they be your masters, when in bondage, or your employers, or supposed benefactors, who still seem to believe themselves your owners, when you find your liberation in the North."

I sat up straighter in my seat, listening then with rapt attention to his words, as he began to speak more quickly, more fervently, warming to his subject, growing more comfortable with his spectators.

"I've written about this before, in my *Call to Rebellion*, a tract that caused my censure by the American Anti-Slavery Society, and by many other members of the more polite, more supposedly *respectable* abolitionist society, besides. The backlash was so fierce, indeed, that I found the need, for many years, to distance myself from some of those early, radical ideas. But I have reached a place in my career where I need no longer heed the disapprobation of the broader abolitionist society. I might vent the innermost feelings of my conscience without fear of total alienation, and so I must tell you students, today, that total resistance is the only recourse for a people so maltreated and so despised. I must communicate that all members of our people who find themselves enslaved should rise up and fight their slaveholders, and if you are free, the slaveholders of your kinsmen, before allowing the submission to yet another day of subjugation."

There was much rustling and some discomfort among the audience then, as Mr. Garnet began to speak the words that were so antithetical to the teachings we'd received at the school thus far. All of our lessons, while progressive, and indeed considered radical by many people outside of the abolitionist circle, were still quite tame when compared to Mr. Garnet's words, and typically centered around themes of passive resistance through the written word, or oratory, in an effort to convince our oppressors of our humanity through the sign of our intellectual capacity.

But this, the idea of a more aggressive resistance that Mr. Garnet brought to the auditorium that day was antithetical to all we had heard at that Christian institution, and I found myself, against my better judgment, beginning to feel enthralled and empowered by all that he said.

"We will not simply leave this land that we have known from our birth for the sake of another continent, where we do not know the terrain, the customs, nor the habits of the people there. We will remain here, in America, and we will fight until we find some sense of retribution for the evils we have endured."

Sudden whisperings from the side of the room caught the audience's attention, and it seemed that all in the room turned toward the source of this upset in an instant. Mr. Garnet seemed to notice this quiet disruption as well and looked over. It was only then that I did, too, and saw several of the teachers engaging in an urgent and whispered conference, several looking concerned. Miss King, in particular, appeared distressed by Mr. Garnet's message, and was speaking quietly, but gesticulating passionately, toward one of the teachers beside her.

"This isn't right," I saw her say, discerning her words by the movements of her lips. "It's against our Christian values for him to speak in such a way. It is only a passive, nonviolent resistance that our students should employ."

Another teacher moved to Miss King's side and placed a hand upon her arm, trying to calm her, but apparently failing in the effort, as Miss King wrenched her hand from the other instructor and recommenced her objections.

A few faculty members then approached the stage and ascended the stairs, whereupon Mr. Garnet gave them a knowing look, seeming to have expected such an intrusion. He spoke quickly then, determined to release his last few words before his premature eviction from the stage.

"You must never surrender," Mr. Garnet declared, "until each slaveholder, until even any person who is *uncertain* as to the question of slavery is vanquished from this earth and made to answer before a Maker who would surely be enraged to see the ways his word has been distorted in the service of this vile system. It is only then that you will be truly free."

"Please, Mr. Garnet," I heard President Gerrit Smith say, as three other male faculty members then forcefully pulled him away from the podium and our young, listening ears. Mr. Garnet finally surrendered and allowed himself to be escorted off of the stage and out of the auditorium, but it seemed that his presence remained in the room, and in our minds, long after his departure.

By the start of the next academic year, I had found my footing, and had completed each of the exercises from the rhetoric book Miss King assigned to me. In due time, I not only equaled my peers academically, but began to outpace them, and was soon assigned additional work, not for remedial purposes, but to keep me engaged as my knowledge increased exponentially, as I spent many nights, when I could not sleep, in assiduous and uninterrupted study. I grew better acquainted with Clara in that time, as well, and with the runaway children who had arrived on that harrowing night some weeks previously, whose names, as they eventually revealed to us, were Deborah, Lizzie, and Nicholas, that previously weak young boy who grew strong and robust and energetic under the close watch and nurture of myself, and Clara, and Miss King, as those new students began to attend classes with us in the Primary Department.

I soon found, however, that I could not be satiated solely by my studies, that despite what Miss King told us students about the importance of rhetoric and debate for the abolitionist cause, I continued to feel that my art was a more critical weapon for me to wield in the greater service of my people. With this in mind, I began to sketch and sculpt many of my classmates, and in particular, Clara and the other runaways who had arrived at our residence all those months before. I felt that they were the perfect representations of all that I wanted to capture in my art, the pain and the struggle of a life spent in a nation that saw no need to deem them citizens nor inheritors of the ideals espoused by its Founding Fathers. I would spend hours depicting my classmates, taking what paper and materials I could find to complete these portrayals, retreating into the woods late at night and on weekends to gather clay or wood to further mold and carve their forms. I grew so immersed in my work, my portrayals of these worthy subjects, that I soon began to overlook the assignments Miss King gave us each week, and in particular, forgot to complete a crucial essay about the relative merits and disadvantages of the approach to abolitionism that Henry Highland Garnet had espoused in his controversial lecture.

"Pass your papers forward," Miss King said at the start of our next class, with an outstretched and expectant hand, clearly excited to read our analyses of Garnet's lecture.

It was only then that I realized the enormity of my mistake in forsaking my schoolwork, and I shrank into my seat as the other students all complied with Miss King's request, passing their papers forward, eager to receive her wise feedback on their work. Miss King walked up and down the classroom aisles as she collected the essays, then stopped at my seat, looking down at me concernedly.

"Mary?" she said, still extending that anticipatory hand. "Your essay, please."

I stalled for a moment, trying to find a way to explain my missing work, knowing that Miss King would not readily accept the true reason, as she had already delineated her belief that the written word was more important than visual art.

"Miss King, I regret to say that I do not have an essay to give to you," I began, in a sheepish tone, grasping desperately for some form of defense. "You see, there were many problems at the library this weekend, and I could not find sufficient paper or ink to complete the work you assigned."

"That is no excuse for neglecting your work," Miss King said, clearly unmoved by my performance. "After all, your classmates have all managed to complete the assignment despite this supposed impediment." She turned to Quincy, who looked at her in surprise as she addressed him. "Quincy, how did you manage to complete this essay, given these purported issues at the library that Mary has mentioned, this lack of paper and ink with which to work?"

"Well, Miss King, there were no troubles at the library whatsoever this weekend," Quincy said, glancing back at me nervously, not wanting to attract my wrath, but wanting even less to displease Miss King, "so it wasn't difficult at all for me to complete the essay. I'd say that Mary would have been able to complete it, too, were she not using all of her time and supplies toward other means."

Miss King turned back toward me and raised her eyebrows at this revelation, this exposal of my excuse for the lie that it was.

"If your explanation was untrue, Mary," Miss King said, speaking slowly, clearly exercising a patience she did not want to extend, "what is the reason that you have failed to complete your assignment?"

I took a deep breath to brace myself as I prepared to explain the true reason for my negligence, with Quincy's swift betrayal leaving me no other choice.

"I have been sketching, and sculpting, instead of writing this essay," I said, my voice low, feeling embarrassed to make the admission, "depictions of my classmates, mostly, as I have felt that this is a better way to spend my time, to aid in the abolitionist cause, than writing mere essays about the ideologies we should adopt in fighting this battle."

Miss King observed me for a moment, clearly displeased that I had challenged her assignment so indelibly, and so publicly.

"And so you feel that you have a better understanding of this fight than I do?" Miss King inquired, clearly rhetorically, though I could not help but to form an answer.

"I feel that, as you are not of our race, you might not understand the best way to advocate for our humanity," I said, realizing as soon as I spoke, by the quiet gasps and shifting of my classmates, that I had quite overstepped my position by speaking to our teacher in this way, but, having begun this refutation, I found that I could not readily cease my response. "I might have spent hours laboring away on an essay about Mr. Garnet's lecture, but no words I could write would communicate the pain of the enslaved as effectively as my artwork. It's a form of the passive resistance for which you advocate, and—"

"Mary Lewis," Miss King interrupted, her countenance shifting into one of disbelief at this challenge to her authority, "you know as well as anyone else in this classroom that I am doing all that I can to help, as opposed to hinder, your people. I have only given this assignment so that you could further analyze Mr. Garnet's words, and strengthen your own writing and thinking. If you do not practice this sort of work, and labor to articulate your thoughts and emotions into strong rhetoric for this cause, you will be completely ineffective in helping your people in this struggle toward liberation. Now, I will not broach any further insolence, and so you will stop your backtalk this instant, lest you be charged with insubordination, an act that is punishable by no less than expulsion, might I remind you." Still fuming, she retrieved a notebook and pencil from her desk, then brought them to me. "Instead of participating in today's class activities, you will write the essay you've failed to complete."

I knew better than to further challenge my teacher on her words, and so I only ceased my protestations and excuses, and decided to capitulate, on the spot, to her commands. I accepted the notebook and began to write, straightaway, the essay that I owed her, though I still felt, all while I wrote, that my art would be a better way to further the abolitionist endeavors, to unleash the stories of my people that had been ignored for far too long.

Months passed without much excitement or controversy to disturb my studies, and I remained on my best behavior following the scolding I'd received from Miss King about neglecting my schoolwork. I knew that with much more misbehavior, I would jeopardize my place at New York Central College, and having completed so many semesters at that school, I knew better than to waste the education I'd already received, and to disappoint my brother, and my aunts, in the process. My brother, as it was, visited me many times during that interval, inquiring about my progress, meeting Miss King and many of my classmates, and seeming generally pleased at the effect the school had taken upon me. I showed Samuel my textbooks and notebooks filled with my schoolwork, that he might see what I'd been learning, how my time had been occupied in the many months since he'd sent me away. I refrained, however, from showing him the many art pieces over which I'd labored for weeks, as I knew he would find such efforts a waste of time better spent on academic endeavors, as opposed to what he would deem extracurricular work. My art, as it was, only existed in the dark of night, when I found some privacy, some solitude, no prying eyes to question my process or its result, no critical opinions telling me what to change or improve in my myriad sketches and rudimentary sculptures.

One night while I sat at my desk and worked on a sketch by the light of the moon, looking forward to many hours of uninterrupted effort, I looked out of my window to see several men, hooded and mounted on steeds, riding up to the front door of our residence. I turned to notify Clara of this occurrence, but seeing how soundly she slept, decided against it, and only turned back to the window to continue my observance, seeing Miss King step out of the front door to meet them, holding a lantern and pulling her shawl and dressing gown close about her.

"May I help you, gentlemen?" Miss King asked as one of the men dismounted his horse and approached her. She was trying her best, I could tell by the sound of her voice, to appear calm, to maintain her composure, though this man was quite tall and broad, towering over Miss King as he neared her.

"Don't need any help," the man replied. He took another few slow, confident steps toward Miss King. "We only need you to hand over Clara Mae Nelson, the fugitive you've been harboring here for some time, though she's been going by the name of Clara Mae Wilder since she escaped the Nelson plantation down in Virginia."

Upon hearing Clara's name, I started, and before I could rush to Clara's side to wake her as I'd originally intended, I heard Miss King's reply.

"I know not of whom you speak," Miss King said, wrapping herself still tighter in her shawl, as if she might protect herself by this action.

The man shook his head. "There's a wagoner down at the tavern done told us everything, miss. Said he often carries runaways here, and that he brought three others from Virginia, not long since. Didn't take more than a moment's questioning for him to buckle." The man shifted his weight to his back foot, moving his jacket and showing—whether inadvertently or purposely, I could not tell—a gleaming pistol on his side, the probable cause for the wagoner's admission, I thought.

"No use in you lying, ma'am," the man continued, speaking slowly, patiently, showing a respect for Miss King that I know he would not have displayed for anyone of my own race. "You're only prolonging the inevitable."

Miss King stammered before finding her voice again. "Sir, if we could just speak for a moment, I'm sure I could clear up your confusion, and—"

"We're not here to converse with you, ma'am," the man interrupted. "And we're not confused in the least. You're harboring Mr. Nelson's property in your house, and he's only sent us here from Virginia to retrieve her."

Miss King took a breath, then began to speak, quickly, her voice quaking and barely louder than a whisper, which seemed to be all that she could muster. "New York is a free state and—"

"We have the right to pursue Mr. Nelson's property, even in a free state. You know that as well as I do," he said.

Miss King, though her voice seemed to grow more tremulous with each word, pursued her case. "The recent personal liberty laws state that you cannot seize these children without a trial by jury."

The man, seeming to have exhausted all reserves of patience, even for someone he deemed a lady, pushed past Miss King and into the anteroom, as another man dismounted from his horse and followed closely behind him.

At this, I moved away from the window, ran to Clara's bed, and shook her with a violent force. "Clara," I whispered, "you must wake up, now."

Clara blinked heavily, then stared at me with a dazed expression as she finally roused from her deep slumber.

"There are men here to take you back to Virginia," I said, in near disbelief that these were the words I had spoken, that this was the news I carried to my sweet Clara.

At this, Clara shot up in bed, the terror on her face unlike anything I had ever seen. "Mary," she said, her eyes wide, her cold hands tightly gripping my arms, "you mustn't let them take me."

I stood immobilized for a moment, petrified at being so suddenly thrust into this role of guardian, protector, a role that Clara herself had previously occupied. We groped about for a suitable hiding place, deciding finally on a spot beneath her bed. I moved all manner of chests and trunks and storage that lay underneath her bed, and together, we worked to nestle her as close to the wall, and as far away from our bedroom door, as we could manage. These exertions awakened the other few young girls who slept in our room, and though I tried to hush them back to sleep, they demanded explanation for the noises that woke them, and refused to return to their beds until I did my best to placate them. Finally, with Clara hidden beneath the bed, and as I believed, in relative safety, and with the other girls in my room returned to their own shallow slumber, I decided to go downstairs, to try my best to hinder and thwart those men in their efforts, for as long as I could.

By this time all other inhabitants of the house had gathered near the parlor to surmise the source of this commotion, unwilling to miss the rare opportunity for excitement, for a change in our typically rigid routines, unaware of the abhorrent source of this disturbance. Miss King turned to face all of us students who gathered downstairs as the two men began to search through each first-floor room, then to ascend the stairs, two at a time, still hunting for their elusive prey. I was, perhaps naïvely, confident these men would not discover Clara as she was secure in the hiding place we'd made beneath her bed, and so I did not immediately pursue them upstairs. Miss King, it seemed, had already relinquished her authority to these men, though not to us students, as she tried to exert what force she had left upon us.

"Go to your rooms," Miss King said, and then, seeing that none of the students obeyed her, added, in a yell, "now."

The others all complied, scared into submission by this alien tone issuing forth from Miss King's usually quiet and subdued voice. I remained where I stood despite her command.

"I said go to your room, now, Mary," Miss King repeated after a moment, and an evidently unsuccessful attempt at gathering herself.

I had no intention of obeying her, but even before I could show my insolence, my resolve, the men returned from upstairs, carrying a thrusting and screaming Clara between them, then heading for the front door and out toward their horses and the other waiting men.

I began to run almost involuntarily toward those men, feeling as if I was being carried by some force beyond me to stop them, to defeat them. In any other moment, I would have understood that I was no match for men of their size and stature, for men who were armed, no less, but I could not stop myself from pursuing them, believing that my fury alone might be sufficient to defeat them and liberate Clara from their clutches. Miss King grabbed me by the shoulders as I fought to run toward them, stopping me in my tracks before I could reach my beloved Clara.

"No, Mary," Miss King said, shaking me until I was forced to wrench my eyes away from the scene and fix them on her. "They have the power to take you, as well. They will say that you are a runaway like Clara, and will sell you down South. It will come down to their word against yours. You must," she added again, with a desperate force to subdue me, "be quiet, now."

A shrieking tore through the night as the men forced Clara into the back of their covered wagon, drowning out the sounds of Miss King's next words.

I turned to face Miss King and began to speak quickly, desperately, in a last attempt to incite her to help Clara.

"You are no less than an agent to these men if you do not stop them, if you do not implement everything in your power to protect us students in your charge," I said, speaking before I lost the nerve.

Miss King looked at me for a moment, as if in disbelief that I could speak to her in such a way.

"I will never again view you with any deference or respect if you do not retrieve Clara from those brutes this instant," I said, "If you do not unleash upon those hateful men all of the ire and vehemence that you are showing to me, in this moment."

Miss King, having then grown truly incensed, grabbed my face and exerted a compressing force upon it I didn't know she possessed.

"You will hush that talk this instant, Mary," she admonished, her voice panicked and shrill. "How could we hope to defend ourselves against those men? They are armed, and we are not. To try and release Clara would mean the loss of our very lives. You will go inside now, this instant," she finally declared, aggressively pushing me back toward the house.

I finally obeyed her, but then I understood in a new way, with an almost blinding starkness, that even those teachers who were supposed to protect us might fold in the face of even the slightest opposition, and that while we students were in our classes writing and debating, the fugitive slaves among us faced the real consequences of the ideologies that the freeborn treated as mere declamations. I recognized then that no lessons Miss King taught had prepared me for the reality of those men, and no books I had read nor essays I had written were sufficient to stop Clara from being recaptured, returned to a fate too wretched for me to imagine, though imagine it I did, night after night following her capture, until I thought that I might be driven mad with the remembrance. I knew that something much stronger was needed to force such hateful men to recognize our humanity, and I felt, once again, that I must use my visions, my art—that innate ability I had once thought of as a curse, but now understood to be a benediction—to tell the stories of what happened to my kinsfolk, to give humanity to those who were treated as mere beasts, to expose the truths that might go ignored without the sort of artist that I would become.

# Chapter 4

This motivation carried me through the space of several years, during which time I pursued my studies with an assiduity, a singularity of purpose and determination unlike any I had felt before. I might have hoped this time would lessen the pain of Clara's capture, would help to redirect my anguish into this new-found purpose for my art, but I found that I could hardly begin to embark on this new objective with any real success.

Each attempt I made to immortalize Clara in one of my art pieces seemed to fall far short of my intentions, to exist as but a mockery, a mere caricature of the beautiful girl I had come to know. I grew much more isolated during this time, choosing to take my meals alone in my room as opposed to in the dining hall with my peers, to go to the library or return to my own quarters directly after classes instead of convening in the yard for laughter and congenial diversions. I could not understand how my peers could simply carry on with their lives after such an atrocity had occurred, how they could still find opportunities for laughter, for frivolity, when we had been shown how tenuous such liberation could be. As such, I was not kept abreast of the latest happenings around the school, as I had been when Clara was my closest companion, and so it was with great surprise I heard the salacious news that had recently begun to float among the students, as I passed by a group of my laughing and whispering peers outside of our dining hall.

"Oh, Mary, haven't you heard?" a girl named Henrietta asked, stopping me as I walked, her brown eyes wide with excitement. "It's the most scandalous affair," she said, seeming thrilled at the words she would next deliver. "Professor Allen has run off with Meredith Kingsley."

I recoiled my head at this news, trying and failing to fully understand Henrietta's words. Though I did not know Meredith Kingsley personally, as she was quite a bit older, and attended the more advanced classes as an undergraduate in the college, I knew that she came from a devout family who had taken Professor Allen into their home when he needed a place to stay upon first moving to McGrawville. Professor Allen, for his part, was a brilliant man—or at least I believed him to be, as I had never attended his classes myself—and taught Greek and rhetoric to the older students at the college. He was one of the few colored instructors at the college, and had never been involved in any sort of misbehavior or scandal before, at least from what I knew of him. I must have appeared dumbfounded as I processed Henrietta's words, as I found myself unable to properly respond to her, or to share in the group's entertainment.

Quincy, who was among the gossiping group, took the opportunity of my silence to ask me, gleefully, "Can you believe it?"

Before I could answer him, Henrietta went on. "Now Meredith's parents can no longer believe their little girl is so naïve, so innocent," she said. "With her rosy cheeks and her golden curls, not when she's run off with that old, ungrateful brute, as they see him." She laughed as she considered this, and the reaction of others. "Can you imagine what the Southerners will say about this school, now?"

"Oh, they'll have a grand time with this one," Quincy said, on the verge of laughter as he mused. "They'll say this institution is nothing more than a cover for intermarriage and amalgamation, a sullying of their perfect white race."

The group's laughter continued for several moments, during which time I struggled to process their words, before I was finally able to gather myself and speak. "Do you have definitive proof of this affair?" I asked, unsmiling and curt.

"It has been said they are married and on their way to Liverpool as we speak," Quincy replied. "Little Frederick in the lower school saw them down by the port, boarding their ship headed for England. Is that proof enough for you?" he asked, still smiling and pleased with his supposedly incontrovertible evidence.

I stared at the group for a moment, ready to disabuse them of the notion that this news would give me any similar enjoyment to their own.

"That doesn't prove a thing, only that you are silly enough to believe in such nonsense. And even if this were proven to be true, should you all delight in such an occurrence? Should you laugh as if this is some high comedy?" I asked, being met only with my peers' surprised stares at my indignation, when they had expected only to find fellow mirth.

"You are all unbelievably foolish if you do," I went on, speaking to my classmates as if I were their teacher, their moral leader, though I was much younger than most of those gathered. "We are meant to be improving ourselves and advancing the position of our race, and all you can care about is this absurdity?"

With this, I turned to leave the ridiculous group, shaking my head and dismissing their gossip as the mere frivolity I believed it to be. I went to the library that day to try to continue my studies, and attended my classes the next day as usual. However, as the days went on, it became clear that their gossiping was correct, and the reverberations of this misdeed between instructor and student would extend far beyond simple schoolyard conversations.

On a Monday some weeks later, we students were all gathered in our seats, as punctual as had been our practice up to that point, and yet Miss King was not at her usual post before us, seated at her broad wooden desk. We students waited for nearly twenty minutes before Miss King made her tardy entrance, and when she finally arrived, her face was splotchy and scarlet, her eyes and nose inflamed as if she had just barely composed herself from a torrent of tears.

"I didn't think I'd be able to face you all today," were the first words Miss King spoke, as she placed her bag and books upon her desk. "You all have been my joy for so long, my special pride."

Her voice wavered as she continued on, finally looking up at the class and fixing each of us with a sincere gaze in turn, even looking upon me with much warmth, though I had provoked and defied her so many times over the years that I had known her, and our relationship had never quite recovered since Clara's capture. "I'm in awe of all that you've accomplished in just a few years," she said, "but it appears that now, our journey together must come to an end."

There was much outcry and clamor at these words, so much that Miss King was unable to continue delivering her announcement.

"Are you leaving the school, Miss King?" Quincy asked, in disbelief, as the other students continued to vent their lamentations.

After several failed attempts to calm the commotion, Miss King finally managed to speak above the noise. "It is not that I am leaving the school," Miss King said, "but that the school itself will soon cease to exist."

My classmates again began to clamor and protest, but all seemed to fall into silence around me as I realized the import of Miss King's revelation, of what it would mean for this school to close, the only place where someone like me could hope to receive an education, to eventually gain the sort of platform and position necessary to help advance my race.

"I'm sure that by now you all have heard the rumors of Professor Allen and Meredith Kingsley," Miss King continued, her modesty forcing her to once again avert her gaze at the mention of such an affair. "And I must tell you now that those rumors are, indeed, true."

I avoided the glances of several students at this disclosure, though I could feel their eyes searing into my profile, each student vindicated, it seemed, by Miss King's confirmation of their eager gossip.

"We can debate the propriety or impropriety of intermarriage," Miss King said, "as we know that many opposers to abolition believe that intermarriage would bring about the very downfall of civilization, it seems. But in any event, we must agree that it was not appropriate for Professor Allen to engage in a relationship with his student. We teachers are meant to protect and guide you students, and certainly any sort of romantic involvement precludes such a mission. This affair has strained, and perhaps even trampled upon, the very core tenets of our Baptist institution, and has caused many donors to lose faith in our mission here."

Miss King sighed and took a moment before going on, the room momentarily quiet, clinging fiercely to her words. "But it is not my task today to speak with you all about intermarriage, about racial amalgamations, nor forbidden relations," Miss King declared. "It is only my task, dear students, to tell you that this institution, and the radical experiment in which we all have engaged, has lost all of its funding because of this affair, and you all must depart from this space in only two weeks, by semester's end."

There was a great disturbance in the room at this revelation, much clamor among all the students as we all tried to reckon with this idea, to determine how we could leave the school so quickly, and what complicated arrangements this would require. The runaways among us were especially distraught at this news, and rightly so. Without such a school, such a haven, how could they survive, how could they manage to outpace their pursuers, to maintain what tentative liberation they had known?

"Let this be a lesson to you," Miss King recommenced, "that even one misstep, one inkling of impropriety, of any behavior less than pure perfection, is enough to end all of your progress, and your education, and hopes of success in this country."

This lesson that Miss King hoped to impart with the school's closing was imprinted indelibly upon my mind. I was just short of fifteen and still quite impressionable at that time, and this affair between Professor Allen and Meredith Kingsley, and the subsequent condemnation of New York Central College, its dearth of funding, its hemorrhaging of its remaining finances, was more of an admonition, a warning to me, than an instruction. It was a clear signal that I would need to be pristine, faultless, and above reproach everywhere that I went from then on, regardless of whether I could ever hope to enroll in another school or not. I only feared that I would not be able to maintain the guise of this pristine and faultless person, as I always found myself wanting to challenge authority, to go my own way, ever since the day Minister Wells and Minister Smithson found me in the woods. But I knew that I would have to wear the mask of another person moving forward, of a calmer and tamer young lady, someone who did not have wildfire raging through her bones, and countless visions plaguing her mind.

In a few days' time, Samuel traveled to McGrawville to help me pack my belongings and move out of my residence. He could see that I was distraught at the school's closing, and seemed to want to lift my spirits by performing an inordinate happiness of his own, smiling and thrilling over past schoolwork I'd done, reports and exams and essays that he'd found buried in the deep recesses of my desk as we sifted through my possessions. It was so strange to be in that space with Samuel after all that I'd endured, so uncanny to be with him and act every part of the girl that I was before I'd attended New York Central College, when in reality, I was a young woman transformed, a metamorphosed, and increasingly melancholic, being. I did not tell Samuel about the struggles I'd had during the three years I'd spent there, nor did I divulge that my closest friend at that school, a girl I had come to consider my sister, had been wrenched from me, as it was yet too painful for me to broach such subjects. But yet and still, being my brother and understanding some central part of myself that he held in his own being, Samuel could sense that I was disquieted, and so he made it a point to treat me to a special dinner at the inn where we stayed before our departure from McGrawville. Samuel supped heartily that night, eagerly tucking into the pot roast and potatoes and rye bread before us, though I could not bring myself to partake in this feast.

"You should eat something, Mary," Samuel said, momentarily looking up from his own half-eaten plate. "You've hardly touched your roast."

"I'm not hungry," I replied, somewhat haughtily, pushing the plate away from me and sitting back in my chair.

"You don't know when you'll next find a meal so fine," he insisted, reaching across the table and pushing my plate back toward me. "Eat."

"How can you expect me to eat when my school, the place I have called home for some years, that *you* bid me to attend, has closed down?" I inquired, sounding more like a petulant child than the young woman I then believed myself to be.

Samuel allowed me to have this moment of self-indulgence before speaking yet again. "This is the subject I want to discuss with you," he said. "There is an opportunity for you to attend another school, Mary—a proper college. One that has been established for some years, and cannot lose its endowment from one scandal, as has been the case with New York Central College."

I looked up from my untouched dinner, intrigued by his words. "What school would that be?" I asked, my interest piqued.

"Oberlin College, in Ohio," he said. "They have recently agreed to allow women and colored students to enroll there."

"Ohio?" I repeated. "But, Samuel, that is halfway across the country," I protested. "We have no family there, no one I can call a friend."

"I know of good people there, Mary," Samuel returned, seeming prepared for this objection. "The Reverend Keep, who sits on Oberlin's Board of Trustees, has written to Mr. Gerrit Smith that he would be glad to accept any students from New York Central College, given their grades are acceptable, and they have the money for tuition and board."

"And have we the money for tuition and board?" I asked, not

knowing from whence Samuel could procure the funds for such a monumental move.

Samuel nodded, still chewing and evidently enjoying his food, slicing into another piece of his pot roast. "I've been setting money aside for you," he answered. "For just such a purpose."

"You have?" I returned, not much pleased by the idea that my brother had been making such arrangements without my consultation.

"I knew you'd need an education beyond what New York Central College could give you," he said, "even if it hadn't lost its funding. I knew as well that Oberlin was the only school that would accept our people, and so I have been following its doings all this time."

"I don't want to go to Ohio," came my definitive reply. "I want to stay here in New York, where I can be with you, and my aunts."

Samuel shook his head. "And that is another matter we'll need to discuss, Mary. I will not be living in New York much longer," he said. "I will see you off to Ohio, and then I will make my own journey west to California."

I stared at Samuel as he continued to divert his gaze, staring down at his plate, the table, the floor, anywhere but my own eyes. "Are you in earnest?" I asked, staring at my brother for so long, and so forcefully, that he had no choice but to finally meet my gaze.

"Quite so," Samuel replied.

"You will travel to California for what purpose?" I asked, addressing him as if he were an impetuous child rather than my older sibling.

"I will set up my own business there, still working as a barber, but to service the Gold Rush crowds," he said. "I've been told by many friends this is the way to make a fortune, if not directly by what gold is left there, then by catering to those people who seek it. I believe that within a few years, I will have earned enough money to keep both myself and you settled for decades to come."

I considered this for a moment, unable to refute the appeal of a fortune made at the western edge of America. "Then I will stay here with my aunts without you," I finally offered, a last attempt at maintaining the life I had always known.

Samuel again shook his head.

"They, too, are leaving New York," he said. "They're heading up to Canada, to claim a plot of land that awaits them there, having been set aside in an act of reparations to the Native populations who were previously displaced from that region."

"Can I not join them?" I asked. "I would like to see Canada, to roam freely there as I did before school. Perhaps that will yet be a better country for me than this one, as I—"

"I'm afraid that you cannot go with your aunts up to Canada, Mary," Samuel interrupted, wanting to disabuse me of the notion before I could carry it too far. "The land they will claim cannot be shared by you." He sighed, then looked off into the room around us, searching the air, it seemed, for a proper explanation to offer me. "It's a complicated matter, but suffice it to say that the Canadian land they seek can only be claimed through patrilineage—the blood of the father—and as our father was no Ojibwe man, but as clearly of the African as you or I, your presence there would impede their objective, and so they cannot take you with them."

It took me a moment to process his words, and still, after considering for some time, I could not accept them, could not tolerate the idea that I would be sent to a new state, quite alone, and as I saw it, unprotected.

"Where would I live?" I finally asked, regaining some modicum of my composure.

"The Reverend Keep's wife runs a boarding house, just for girls. It is there that you'll lodge and make your new life. I've already written to them to secure your residence there."

I was silent at this for much longer than etiquette and decency would allow me to be, but I simply could not justify my brother's words with any response more solid than a low and incensed exhalation.

"What do you make of this, Mary?" Samuel finally asked, when my silence could be tolerated no longer.

"Does it matter what I make of it?" I retorted. "It seems that this has all been decided for me, and I have no say in my own fate."

Samuel sighed, then returned to his food. "It is for your best. You will understand that one day, even if you do not now."

I pushed away from the table, the sound of my chair legs dramatically scraping against the floor the only reply to Samuel's words. Samuel, much to my annoyance, only quietly continued his dinner, seeming to savor each morsel the more once I had quitted myself from the table. Finally, after several moments of silent dining, Samuel thoughtfully wiped his mouth with a white cloth napkin, folded it, and placed it upon the table. He then excused himself from the table to return to our quarters upstairs at the inn.

I started to pace the room, collecting my thoughts and processing all that Samuel had told me. After some time of silent though frenzied contemplation, I began to accept my fate, and came to believe that a separation from New York might give my mind brighter ideas on which to focus, and might bring a renewal both of person and of purpose. I convinced myself that a move to Ohio and a furtherance of my studies would be just what I needed to grow, both as a young woman, and as an artist.

The day of my departure for Ohio arrived much more quickly than I'd anticipated, as I was allotted only a matter of days to gather myself and my belongings, and dispense with all final farewells to the acquaintances I had left in McGrawville. Despite my best efforts at protracting my time in New York, and when delay was no longer possible, Samuel woke me early on an August morning and told me it was time to prepare for my trip. We left our small dwelling before sunrise and took a coach some miles into the city, and though we had allotted ourselves much time for the trip, the coach ran into various issues along the way, slowing our progress so much that I began to entertain hopes my trip might be rendered impossible, and I could spend but a bit more time with my brother before embarking upon this monumental move. We did, however, finally make it to our destination, and by the time we reached the train station, we had to rush as quickly as we could, Samuel holding my lone suitcase, and me lagging behind him, struggling to keep apace with his quick and determined stride. He would not have me miss my train, so eager he was to be rid of me, or so I thought then in my youthful view of the opportunity he had arranged for me.

"You've got to stay close, Mary," Samuel said as he walked, glancing back at me. "We're in the city now. No dallying."

My heart raced as we pushed through the crowds, making our way to the ticket counter, with me hardly able to observe or enjoy my first time in a train station.

"One ticket to Oberlin, please," my brother said, as we approached the clerk.

"One-way or round-trip?" the clerk inquired.

"One-way," my brother responded, taking his wallet from his pocket and procuring his last few bills for the clerk.

The clerk eyed the two of us, as if to surmise how we could afford the fare for such a long trip, until finally, begrudgingly, he stamped the requested ticket and slid it to my brother under the glass window. Samuel handed me my ticket, and I stared down at the words stamped upon it, feeling a sudden jolt as the reality sank in that I was truly leaving New York, the land I had known since my birth.

My brother noticed my expression, then stooped down to meet my eye before speaking. "Don't look so afraid," he said. "You've completed years of school now, and you're sufficiently prepared for this next step."

"I don't know that I am," I said, my breath catching in my throat at the thought of our separation, of the momentous task then before me. "I don't know that I can manage this transition on my own."

"You mustn't speak that way, Mary," he said, "not when so many people are taking a chance on you, when the Reverend Keep and his wife have done so much to arrange for your stay in Oberlin. Any hesitation could be read as ingratitude for what they've done."

Samuel looked at the large clock at the center of the train station, then continued on, wanting to dispense as much final advice to me as he could before my departure. "Now, I want you to appear confident when you're on that train. You're fifteen now, and you can handle yourself as well as anybody else. When the conductor asks for your ticket, hand it to him straightaway. If he inquires what your business is in Ohio, tell him you're heading into Oberlin to attend the college there."

I nodded my understanding as Samuel pressed on. "And if the conductor says that no colored girl can attend a school like Oberlin College, what do you do?"

"I show him this," I said, removing the designated letter from my pocket, a short note that Reverend Keep had sent to us, with his signature, confirming my place at Oberlin, and in his wife's boarding house.

"Very good," Samuel said. "Anyone based out of Ohio will be familiar with the Keep family, and will know that you have a legitimate place there, in their boarding house. Now, we must head to the platform. Your train will leave shortly."

As we walked away from the ticket window, I was overwhelmed by the uncanny sensation that we were being followed, stalked and pursued like prey, and when I turned around to determine whether my premonition was correct, I saw two men trailing us, one pointing our way.

"Samuel, do you know them?" I asked, finally pulling my eyes away from those men, but feeling their gazes upon us all the while.

Samuel turned to see what men I had mentioned before speaking. "I've never seen them before, but it seems that they want trouble. Keep your head down, Mary. Carry on as you were."

We began to walk faster, though I could feel that the men were still pursuing us, and after a moment, I could hear their hastening footsteps approaching close behind us.

"Stop right there, boy," the first man said, placing a rough hand upon my brother's shoulder. "Not another step."

Samuel complied, and I did as well, not daring to walk on without my brother.

"What's your name, boy?" the first man demanded, towering over Samuel.

"Samuel Lewis, sir," he said, showing this man a deference he did not deserve.

"No, I don't think that is your name. You look mighty familiar to me," the man speculated, scrutinizing my brother's entire person. "Don't he look familiar to you?" he asked, in his distinct Southern drawl, turning to his grizzled companion.

"They're the runaways we read about. Seen posters about you two all the way up here from Georgia," the second man averred, and in one swift motion, he grabbed my brother by the wrists and twisted them behind his back. Samuel tried to resist, but another man came and helped the first to restrain his arms. The two men subdued Samuel, one pushing him to the ground and the other kneeling upon his back, pressing his face into the cobblestones, sending my suitcase, which Samuel had previously held, into the dust in the process, my possessions scattering across the earth.

"Let him go," I screamed, but the men ignored my pleas. I called out for someone, anyone of the surrounding crowd to help us, but the other travelers merely looked on in vague curiosity, with barely an interruption in their strides, seeming to take it for granted that my brother and I were indeed deserving of this maltreatment we were experiencing.

"You've got the wrong person," Samuel insisted. "I work as a barber. I have no master."

"Well, there's a five-hundred-dollar bounty on your head that says otherwise," the second man said, disregarding my brother's words.

Samuel continued to resist and pursued in his protestations. "Please," Samuel begged, his strength beginning to give way under the crushing force of the man's knees upon his back. "Check the papers in my back pocket."

The men made no move to do so, but only continued in their

struggle to keep Samuel on the ground. I stepped toward my brother to retrieve his identification papers myself, to show them that Samuel was telling the truth. I took Samuel's identification papers from his pocket and thrusted them toward one of the men, who promptly snatched it from my hands and shoved me onto the hard ground, soiling my traveling dress, disheveling my hair, and upsetting my countenance. Only then did the man give the identification papers a cursory glance, and this superficial act completed, tossed them onto my brother's back.

"It isn't him," the man told his accomplice with a tone of disappointment at their thwarted reward, and the two men walked away from us without an apology, without saying another word, their cruelty toward us so casual, so accepted even here, in the city, that they felt no need to even offer an explanation for their maltreatment.

I hastened toward my brother and helped him to his feet, trying unsuccessfully to wipe the dirt from his suit jacket, to straighten his clothes and place his hat back upon his head.

"Are you badly hurt?" I asked, touching a hand to a scrape on his forehead.

"I'll be fine," he replied, taking out a handkerchief to wipe away the blood that began to drip down his face. "We've got to get you on your way."

"On my way?" I asked, incredulous at his insistence. "I can't leave you here like this, in this condition," I said, observing his disheveled clothes, the indignity of what just occurred. I thought then of Clara, of my impotence in the face of her own violation and capture, of the ways that her own fate might have been saved had I not been so timid, had I gone against Miss King and acted in accordance with my own inclination. "I *refuse* to leave you here like this," I declared, pulling Samuel still closer to me as I protested. "What if those men come back? What if they hurt you all the worse next time? You are in need of my help, Samuel. That much is clear."

Samuel shook his head and removed my hands from his neck, finally beginning to regain some semblance of his composure, and to shake away some of the embarrassment he clearly felt. "The way that you will help me is to continue with your education, to show everyone our capability, our humanity. It is only then that we can hope to escape such maltreatment from people like those men."

I could not countenance this deceptively straightforward instruction, could not pretend that I was someone so simple and amenable as to easily execute such a command.

"What if I'm not good enough to do that?" I asked, and internally added, *What if I'm* incapable *of doing that? What if my visions and disturbances and terrors and imaginings preclude any possibility of success at Oberlin, or wherever I may go afterward?*

"That isn't an option," Samuel returned, "and so you will be good enough. You'll abide by the rules of Oberlin College, and of the Keep house. You'll keep your head down, stay focused, and complete your studies well. There will be people in your new home who try to distract you, who try to diminish you, but you won't let them. You'll make me proud, Mary, just like you always have."

Before I could offer a word in reply, a train horn sounded across the platform, and we were required to hasten toward the train doors before embracing one final time.

"I'll send word to you once I'm settled in California," Samuel said. "You'll have an address where you can write to me if you need anything, anything at all. You mustn't ever hesitate to contact me if any such need does arise." My brother considered me then with an expression he had never before fixed upon me. "I love you, Mary," he said, and though I could remember many occasions when he had told me that before, I had never yet heard him pronounce the words with such an ardor, such an earnestness, and I was greatly affected by his intonation.

"I love you, too," I managed to reply, though I feared that my words were drowned out by the sound of the other travelers hastening toward the train doors, the hiss of the engine, the insistent and repeated blasting of the train's horn. I finally boarded the train, took my seat, and watched from the window as Samuel's eyes grew misty, his face forcefully contorted into the mask of a smile, though it was apparent that he wanted to relinquish himself to the sorrow that brewed within. It was then that I realized my brother might have been just as frightened as I was, just as uncertain as to the sort of fate that might await me in that distant locale, at my new school that purported to be progressive, but might be just as hateful, just as exclusionary as the majority of our country at that time. I held my hand up in one final wave, one ultimate goodbye that cemented the reality of our separation. I knew not what would await me in Oberlin, but I knew that I must endure all that came my way.

# Chapter 5

I arrived in Oberlin on a September morning, the air cool and the birdsong sweet, incongruous to the anxiety I felt roiling within me. My hands shook terribly as I clutched my lone suitcase, standing before the Keep boarding house, its lodgers, all girls of my own age, milling about its front garden. They appeared to me as beautiful as the foliage around them, speaking and laughing with an ease I could never have, a mirth I could never know. For some time, I went unnoticed as I stood there by the front gate, so engrossed were these girls in their own conversations, until Mrs. Keep stepped onto the front porch and addressed me, causing all eyes then in the garden to fix themselves upon me.

"Ms. Lewis, you're late," Mrs. Keep said, her demeanor firm, but not unkind.

"I'm sorry, Mrs. Keep, it's just that the stagecoach—" I began, in an effort to absolve myself, but she interjected with a raised hand and closed eyes.

"There's never an excuse for tardiness, Miss Lewis," she said, thus closing the conversation. "Come along, now. Classes begin shortly, and you'll want to settle your things."

I walked closely behind Mrs. Keep through that household's vast hallways, past the front parlor and drawing room, and through the kitchen, where we encountered a housemaid, a girl who appeared to be of my own age and race. She reminded me, uncannily, of Clara, as if her very spirit inhabited the young girl before me. I gave the maid a smile, which she did not return, so perturbed she seemed to be by my presence. It seemed, by her face, that she thought I disrupted the natural order of things, that I should not be a lodger in the Keep house, but a worker there. Suddenly remembering her manners, however, the housemaid returned my gesture, and gave me a quick, deferential nod before returning to her chores.

Mrs. Keep spoke swiftly as we walked through the house, delineating several rules I was to follow as a tenant.

"Breakfast is promptly at six each morning, dinner at six each evening," she said. "You're to take your lunch at school. You've missed breakfast for the day, but you might find some leftover bread in the pantry if you're quick about it. We do keep a housemaid for general upkeep," she said, gesturing back toward the kitchen where the young girl continued her work, "but she only tends to the common areas, and you are to complete your own personal cleaning, your room, your laundry, your own dishes and the like. As such, Saturdays are for chores, and Sundays are for church. Recreational activities take place on Friday evenings, but may involve no booze nor boys if you're on this property. Is that all clear?"

"Yes, ma'am," I said, though in truth my nerves made it difficult to remember all she told me, and I hoped that a fellow lodger might review these rules with me at a later time.

"Very well," Mrs. Keep said, as she led me up a wooden staircase and down a long corridor. "Your room is just here."

Mrs. Keep knocked twice upon its closed door, then opened it before receiving an answer. Two girls stood within, silhouetted against a bow window, whispering conspiratorially and examining some unknown object held between them. Upon our entrance, one of the girls, taller and fairer than the other, hid this object within the pocket of her voluminous skirt, a swift maneuver that seemed to evade Mrs. Keep.

"Girls, this is Mary Lewis, the new roommate I've mentioned," Mrs. Keep began. "She's enrolled in Mrs. Dascomb's Young Ladies'

Course, along with the two of you. Mary, this is Sarah Miles," she said, gesturing toward the first girl, "and Gemma Ennes," she added, now pointing to the taller one.

"A pleasure to meet you both," I said, to no reply. While Sarah seemed to pay me little heed, the taller girl, Gemma Ennes, fixed upon me a cold, assessing gaze. I recognized this look, one I had been subjected to before, not unlike the looks of those nurses on my first day in McGrawville, the close scrutiny of an anatomist infuriated that I defied all categorization, a colored girl, evidently free, in clothing just as fine as her own. I felt so exposed under Gemma's gaze that I wanted to flee, to cling to Mrs. Keep as if I were the child I no longer was, as if she were the mother I no longer had. Knowing that such a move would be inappropriate, however, I only stood my ground, and began to unpack my suitcase.

"Must she room with us?" the first girl, Sarah, asked.

"Your room has the spare bed, Sarah, so indeed, she must. I trust there will be no trouble between you three. Now, Mary, unpack your things and settle in. You'll all be down at the bell to leave for class."

With this, Mrs. Keep moved toward the door, but I felt that I could not let her leave without some expression of my gratitude.

"Thank you, Mrs. Keep, for your generosity," I said, as she stood with her hand upon the doorknob.

Mrs. Keep seemed genuinely touched by my thanks and gave me the first kind look I'd received all morning. "Of course, Mary. You're as welcome here as any other."

She left me then, alone with my new roommates, as vulnerable as prey to its famished predator.

"You know there's no use ingratiating yourself to her," Gemma said, continuing to stare at me with her merciless examination. "She'll still evict you if you break any of her rules."

Sarah gave a sharp laugh at this in evident agreement. "And so, you mustn't let her know when you're breaking her rules," Sarah added, removing from her skirt pocket the previously hidden object, a small silver flask engraved with someone's initials.

"Have some," she commanded, proffering the flask toward me. "It'll stop that awful trembling in your hands."

I was embarrassed that she noticed my shaking hands, my nervousness, my uncertainty in this new abode, and I wanted nothing more than the repose I was sure would come with one small sip from my roommate's flask, that certain warmth to which I'd grown accustomed at the few secret parties I'd attended while at New York Central College. Before I could succumb to this temptation, I remembered myself and the strict rules of the Keep house, and wondered whether my roommates were testing me, setting me up for trouble on my very first day. I made a show of stepping back from the flask in my roommate's hand, glancing toward the grandfather clock in the corner, and remarking that it was still quite early in the morning.

"It's only wine," Sarah said, seeming to divine my thoughts. "Just take a little. It'll make the day's classes go by much more quickly."

"I'm quite alright, thank you," I replied, then added as further explanation, and in an attempt to close the subject, "I don't drink."

Sarah shrugged and took a sip. "More for us," she said, and after Gemma had her share, Sarah placed the flask deep within her wardrobe, where it could remain undiscovered by Mrs. Keep.

"It would appear we have a proper lady on our hands," Gemma said, a look of vague amusement on her face as she resumed her observation of me.

"Indeed, we do," Sarah agreed. "Never knew a colored girl could be so genteel, wearing such fine dresses, speaking so well. You can see by her hands she's never done a day of real work in her life."

"No, she wouldn't have done any work," Gemma added. "She was never a slave. Mrs. Keep told us as much, remember, Sarah? Her people are freeborn blacks. Isn't that right, Mary?"

Her tone in speaking these words arrested me as I unpacked. I disliked the way she pronounced the word *blacks,* as if the word itself were an epithet, something beneath her lips to utter.

"My father's side are all freeborn, yes," I finally managed to respond. "My mother's people are the Ojibwe, of northern New York, and Canada."

Gemma gave a mirthless smile. "From such unlikely beginnings to a college education. Your parents must be very proud of you, indeed."

"I can only hope they would be," I said. "I never knew them."

"Who sends you here, if not your parents?" Gemma inquired, acting every part the interrogator.

"My brother, Samuel Lewis," I replied, feeling a pang of sadness as I mentioned his name, an acute sense of our distance, the farthest we had ever been apart since I was a child.

Sarah raised her eyebrows, seemingly intrigued by this detail. "He must make good money to afford the tuition here."

"He does well for himself," I confirmed. "He works as a barber. He'll be opening his own barbershop soon in California."

"An enterprising man," Gemma observed. "Glad to know he's putting his freedom to good use."

"My father says soon you'll all be free," Sarah added. "Says there's a war coming that will bring this whole dreadful system of slavery to an end."

"Then may the war come soon," I replied, as I continued unpacking my things, wishing to end the subject.

"So, it is violence you invite," Gemma pronounced, her tone accusatory. I paused as she said this, remembering Miss King's admonitions, and how even the hint of a rebellious nature would be received in polite society. I remembered, too, however, how abhorrent, how painful it was to simply accept the maltreatment this country seemed determined to give me, and how I had silently vowed to never allow myself to accept it, or to see those I loved subjected to it, either. It was from that remembrance, and from the words of resistance in Mr. Garnet's lecture all those years ago that I next spoke, quite without proper thought or care of how my sentiments would be received.

"If that violence would bring about the freedom of my people," I said, "then I would welcome it, wholeheartedly."

Sarah and Gemma both stared at me then, surprised at my frankness, with Gemma especially seeming discomfited by my resolve.

"You're in favor of war's bloodshed?" Gemma pursued, speaking in a tone of disbelief, if not disgust. "Its death and destruction?" She shook her head without breaking her gaze, as if to remove her eyes from my person would be a risk too great to take. "I never thought I'd share my room with a person so cruel."

"Oh, Gemma, you mustn't be too hard on her," Sarah defended, turning then and addressing me. "Gemma is just upset that her grandfather would lose everything if slavery were abolished. Gemma's father might be an abolitionist, but her grandfather is not, and she has richly benefited from his great wealth. With slavery's end, Gemma would inherit nothing, and then her dresses won't even be as fine as yours, a colored girl's."

Sarah laughed at this idea, but Gemma remained unamused, looking at me all the while.

A loud bell clanged from downstairs, inciting my roommates to gather their things. I did not move from my spot, and only continued to slowly unpack my belongings.

"Aren't you coming?" Sarah asked, her hand on the doorknob, her eyes fastened on me. "You don't want to be late for the first day of classes."

"I'll be right there," I replied, still taking my time. "You two needn't wait for mc."

Sarah shrugged at this and followed Gemma, who didn't seem to need such permission, out of the door.

I watched as my roommates left the room, waiting until their footsteps receded, until I surmised, from the silence that fell across the residence, that all other lodgers had exited the Keep house. Once I confirmed that I was truly alone, I went to Sarah's wardrobe and removed the flask she had hidden there, unscrewed its top, and took a long, satisfying drink of the wine she had stored within. In so doing, I felt the dissipation of some portion, though not all, of my anxiety at coming to this new town, to this new state, at being the interloper in my new boarding house. With another sip, feeling that I finally had enough relief and clarity to face the day, I grabbed my bag and left the bedroom, heading forth to the first day of my true education.

I took my seat at the back of Mrs. Dascomb's classroom, where I might listen to the day's lesson unobserved by the other girls. Since my days in Miss King's class, I had realized that I learned best that way, when I could freely write and sketch as the teacher spoke, when I could allow my mind to wander, following any personal strands of interest to their conclusion in the safety of my seclusion at the rear of the room. My classmates all laughed and talked amongst themselves before the class began, my roommates chief among them, regaling the others with stories of their summer vacations, their trips to the Continent, their courtships and cotillions, all exciting occurrences that thrilled me as I listened, and as I rendered hasty sketches in my notebook of the events they described.

"Girls, settle down now," Mrs. Dascomb said, after allowing some time for the girls to converse, and finally assuming her place at the front of the room. "You'll have plenty of time to talk after class. We'll begin with attendance."

Mrs. Dascomb commenced to call each girl in turn, who primly confirmed her attendance in class. I observed Mrs. Dascomb as she completed this task, noting her more diminutive stature when compared to Miss King, her less delicate features, her harsher voice. She seemed to be kind enough, and certainly she must be a good woman, I thought, to dedicate her life to teaching at such a progressive institution, but still, there was something in her that felt less genuine than Miss King, less wholly devoted to the cause of abolitionism. Perhaps, I thought, it was simply the demographics of my classroom that made me feel this way, as unlike my classes at New York Central College, I was the only person of my race in this Oberlin course. As such, I could more easily compare Mrs. Dascomb's treatment of me to the other girls in the room, could note each smile and wink she bestowed upon the others, but withheld from me. Finally, after some time, Mrs. Dascomb came to my name for attendance, last on her list and a clear addendum to her roster.

She paused before speaking. "Mary Lewis?" she called, looking up and directly at me.

"Present," came my meek answer, my embarrassment intensified by the attention of all the students in the room.

Mrs. Dascomb smiled at me, more out of condescension, I observed, than kindness. "It says here that you're joining us from New York Central College in McGrawville."

"Yes, ma'am," I confirmed, retreating further into my unease.

"Well, you may find that our curriculum is a bit more advanced than what you might have learned there," she said, with a patronizing smile, "but I'm sure you'll adjust to the rigor here, as all of you girls will, regardless of the education you might have received before."

I nodded and looked down at my desk, embarrassed that Mrs. Dascomb knew my previous school to be insufficient. I hoped that no one else in the room knew about New York Central College and its scandal, had no knowledge of its radical experiment, nor the ways that this experiment had failed. While I remained grateful for what learning I'd received while in McGrawville, I knew that it would fall far short of what was expected of me there at Oberlin, having been established so many years before, having received such a greater endowment, such greater esteem than New York Central College.

Mrs. Dascomb continued after a moment's pause, an interval filled by my classmates' close examination of my person, and my roommates' quiet entertainment.

"There was a time when people thought that the female mind was unfit for academia," Mrs. Dascomb said, "but the country is changing now, and you girls are evidence of that. You young ladies are among the most fortunate women in this country. Nowhere else can a girl earn a degree in higher education. You are participating in a storied tradition that goes back to antiquity, the time of the ancient Greeks and Romans."

Mrs. Dascomb began here to lecture us on the marvels of

those ancient men, and the ways that, though we might not ever achieve their levels of genius, we might strive to approximate their successes, to exist within the orbit of their intellects, their skill.

"What you learn here will enable you all to be better daughters, wives, and ultimately, mothers to the children you will bear," she said. "Your future husbands will be grateful that you have minds that, if not equal to their own, might still serve as a basis upon which they can sharpen their own thinking. Your children will be indebted to you for the education you will give them, without the heavy cost of tuition nor the need to travel from home. You girls will become absolute amazements to the relatives who have sent you here, shining beacons to the offspring you will bear, and will always be, without a doubt, the pride of your spouses, who can show the world what suitable partners they have found."

All girls in the classroom seemed to thrill at this idea, especially at Mrs. Dascomb's last words, mumbling amongst themselves excitedly, each seeming to have a particular beau in mind to fulfill this matrimonial role. I had no young man in mind for such a station, so my thoughts were instead occupied by the ways that I might emulate the work of the ancient Greeks and Romans, or supersede them in their efforts. Mrs. Dascomb showed us sketches of their architecture and artwork, their vases and reliefs and sculptures, and I believed that I could create something similar, if given the chance. Indeed, I felt that I had already come close to the work these ancient artists and writers had completed, especially when considering my relative impediments in completing my own art.

I had many thoughts to offer as the day's lessons went on, as I realized that my education at New York Central College had not been so deficient as I might have thought, since I knew the answers to many of the questions Mrs. Dascomb posed to the class. But I found, much to my chagrin, that my knowledge was unnecessary, or at the very least, unheeded, as Mrs. Dascomb called on all of the other girls who eagerly raised their hands, but persisted to ignore my own raised hand, though I extended my arm as high as it would go, and after a while, took to shaking my hand about as if it were on fire. I could not determine why Mrs. Dascomb neglected to call on me, whether this neglect was born of a desire to spare me any embarrassment if I gave a wrong answer, or if she simply, truly, failed to notice me. This neglect did not deter me as I continued to take notes throughout the day, to listen carefully to the class discussion as it went on around me, to accept and study eagerly the class syllabus when Mrs. Dascomb finally distributed it at the end of the day, a document showing our upcoming readings and assignments, class projects and learning objectives, though one subject, I saw, was notably absent.

At day's end, as the class was dismissed, I lingered in the classroom, waiting for all the other girls to quit that space, not wanting anyone to hear the question I had saved for Mrs. Dascomb. I approached our teacher as she erased the chalkboard, seeming to assess herself on the success of the day's lessons, meditating on the areas where she, and we students, might improve.

"Mrs. Dascomb, do you have a moment?" I began, finding that even this small inquiry required great reserves of courage. I found myself ever grateful for that morning's sip of liquid fortification.

"Yes, Mary," Mrs. Dascomb replied, again looking down upon me with more than a hint of condescension, as if wondering where I found the nerve to address her after the class session's termination. "How may I help you?"

"It's just that I noticed here," I said, gesturing toward my class schedule, "on the curriculum, there aren't any art classes. I do see history and Latin and French, grammar and composition, piano and voice, dancing and etiquette, but no more."

I spoke almost against my own volition, feeling that the urging I'd experienced since childhood, those visions that always appeared before me, compelled me to address this topic with my teacher.

"Does that present a problem for you?" Mrs. Dascomb asked, looking at me impatiently.

I considered her question and how I might answer it, knowing that I should not reveal the truth of my artistic inclinations and yearnings, the whisperings, the compulsion I felt that forced me to question our coursework and its lack of creative pursuits.

"It's only that I used to create art," I persisted, "with my aunts, by Niagara Falls. We would make clothing, blankets, baskets, and other souvenirs. It was said that my mother was especially skilled with painting and basket weaving. I'd like to continue that sort of work here at Oberlin. I don't see why I should abandon it now."

"Yes, your Ojibwe kin," Mrs. Dascomb averred, seeming to have been briefed on this part of my history as well, and unimpressed by the detail. "The art classes are not a part of the Young Ladies' Course, Mary. If time allows at semester's end, we may do some sketching, perhaps watercolors, but that will suffice for our purposes. Any additional art classes would only be a strain on your time, and a distraction, if you will."

I continued, refusing to readily accept this answer. "But if I guarantee that I will still promptly complete my other coursework, and—"

"What purpose would art serve toward you being a better help-mate for your eventual husband?" Mrs. Dascomb asked in exasperation. "It would only detract from your household duties."

"I suppose I desire more than simple household duties," I said, knowing that I might be straining Mrs. Dascomb's patience, but unable to drop the subject.

"Then you will be a teacher," Mrs. Dascomb answered, and then, sitting down and addressing me for the first time with genuine regard, said, "You know, Mary, Rosetta Douglass completed the Young Ladies' Course not long ago. She herself is a teacher now and quite fulfilled by the work. Surely, if that is sufficient for *her*, daughter of a famous orator, it should do for you."

I looked at Mrs. Dascomb, thinking, but not saying, that I'd rather be like Rosetta's father, Frederick Douglass, traveling and speaking before the world to advance the abolitionists' cause, than a mere teacher. I realized, of course, that such an admission, such an insult to her admirable career and life's work, would not be permitted, and so I held my tongue, and only looked down at the floor in response.

Mrs. Dascomb sighed, seeing that I would not easily abandon this matter. "The art department building is just across the way. You can speak to Professor Westbrook there and see if he will allow you to sit in on a class. I must say I doubt that he would approve of such a request, but I suppose it can't hurt to ask. You can tell him I sent you."

I gave Mrs. Dascomb my fervent thanks, and before she could reconsider her recommendation, I hurried from the room, and toward Professor Westbrook's art studio.

The art room was expansive, smelling of paints and turpentine, of clay and ink and fresh reams of paper, all the tools necessary to unleash the farthest reaches of my imagination. I stood just beyond the classroom door, admiring all that stood within. Professor Westbrook was inside, rinsing paintbrushes and sculpting tools in a wide, deep sink. I felt nervous to approach this man, but knew that I must take this initial step toward satisfying my artistic yearnings, toward slowing my visions and night terrors, and so, with another breath, and a steeling of my resolve, I made my entrance.

Professor Westbrook started upon seeing me. "Who are you?" he demanded, his brusqueness taking me aback.

"Professor Westbrook, my name is Mary Lewis," I began, speaking as quickly as I could, lest I lose all nerve, all resolve, before communicating my intentions. "I just moved here from McGrawville, in northern New York. I'm enrolled in Mrs. Dascomb's course, and I was wondering if I could—"

"Yes, I know all about you girls in Mrs. Dascomb's course," he interrupted. "What is it that you want from me? Out with it."

Unnerved, but undeterred by his tone, I persevered. "I'd like to pursue a course of artistic study while I'm here at Oberlin. As art courses aren't offered in the Young Ladies' Department, I was hoping that I might sit in on some of your classes—simply to observe, nothing more."

Professor Westbrook, far from being impressed by my aspirations as I'd hoped he might, turned on me with a fierceness so sudden that I nearly went to flee from the room.

"You ought to be content with what you have," he said. "The Board is doing quite enough in allowing you to attend this institution, and I dare say that not all of us faculty are altogether pleased with that decision. You needn't press on an open wound by demanding even more than what you have been given."

Professor Westbrook locked his art supplies in a cabinet then, and, without so much as a final look in my direction, quitted the classroom, leaving me standing there shaking and, as I thought, quite alone.

"He shouldn't have spoken to you that way," said a voice, ushering forth from the back of the classroom. I started and turned, seeing a young man of about my own age, tall with dark hair and kind blue eyes, collecting several books at his desk. "I'm sorry," he said, speaking with a distinct brogue, an accent I'd come to recognize after acquaintance with some of the Irish immigrants who attended New York Central College. "I didn't mean to frighten you," the young man went on, "I've only forgotten some of my books," he said, lifting them as evidence.

"I'm not frightened," I replied, though my trembling hands and unsteady breath belied this assertion. I hid my hands behind my back.

If the young man noticed this, he had the manners not to comment, as he only went on with his next thought.

"I'm a student here. Ronan Clarke," he said, extending a hand. I accepted it and introduced myself in turn.

"Perhaps I can be of help to you," he said. "I'm quite advanced in my artistic studies. I might enjoy playing the role of professor."

I hardly knew how to respond to this, the first genuinely kind offer I'd received since my arrival in Oberlin.

"That would be generous of you," I began, slowly. "Exceedingly so. And what would I owe you in return for such a kindness?"

He gave a quick shake of his head as if wanting to disabuse me of any suspicion. "I would expect nothing in return," he said. "I'm only looking to help, I suppose." He considered me for a moment, then added, "I wouldn't be anywhere near where I am if someone hadn't helped me along. I guess I'd just like to do the same for someone else."

I could hear in his last sentence all of the pain he must have experienced in this country, the mistreatment that I knew his people endured here, some of which I had witnessed back in New York. I could see, likewise, in his clothing, which was nowhere near as fine as a young college gentleman would be expected to wear, that he was an outsider, of low stature when compared to his classmates, and that he had perhaps left all hope of comfort back in his old home, across the Atlantic. I wanted to ask him how he found himself at this school, if his path here had been as peculiar and circuitous as my own, but he went on before I could inquire, speaking quickly, almost nervously, as if he wanted to continue his offer before all nerve abandoned him.

"We'd have to meet when Professor Westbrook isn't around, of course," he said. "Nighttime would be best, when the campus is closed, and we wouldn't risk discovery. We could access the classroom through the window, just there," he said, pointing to the back of the room.

I looked to where Ronan pointed, then returned my eyes to him, trying to discern, in their depths, whether he was someone I could trust. I remembered Samuel's warnings to me before I'd departed New York, his cautioning me to avoid all misbehavior while I was in Oberlin, as I could expect to be under much harsher scrutiny than my classmates. Entering the art classroom after hours without permission, and with a stranger who might well mean me harm, no less, would certainly qualify as such misbehavior, and could destroy the carefully curated image I was expected to maintain. I knew that I should decline Ronan's offer, but before I could voice my refusal, I heard myself speaking, almost involuntarily, my acceptance.

"I would like that very much," was my eager reply.

Ronan seemed pleased by my answer, and held my gaze for a long moment. I recognized in him a certain restlessness that I knew well, an inability to neatly fit into one place, into a prescribed societal position. I wondered if he, too, experienced the same sort of artistic visions that I did, or at the very least, if he could be someone who would help unleash those of my own. Finally, propriety bid me to look away, and so I wrested my eyes from his. We set a time to meet later in the semester, and I departed the classroom, though my mind remained there, with Ronan Clarke, for some hours afterward.

# Chapter 6

Excitement pervaded the Keep house some weeks later, on a Friday evening, as all of its lodgers, save me, prepared for a ball. My roommates giddily rummaged through their wardrobes, considering and discarding dresses with a stunning rapidity until they landed on those gowns best suited for the night, those that were most likely, it seemed, to please the young men who would be in attendance. I sat still in the midst of this, the eye of this feminine storm, slowly and distractedly turning the pages of some book, pretending not to notice the unignorable activities before me.

"Oh, Mary, I wish you could join us," Sarah said, as she sat Gemma in a chair before the vanity mirror, placing rouge upon her cheeks. "It promises to be quite the evening."

"I've got plenty of work to keep me busy," I rejoined, without lifting my eyes from my book, determined to project an air of unconcern.

"What enjoyment could she find, in any case?" Gemma asked, dismissively. "Who would invite her to dance?"

Both girls seemed to earnestly consider this, then said, simultaneously, "Jack Pemberly."

By their laughs I surmised this boy was a preposterous suggestion, even less suitable for courtship, in their estimation, than I was. I did not show any sign that their remarks might have been hurtful, and refused to dignify their insult with any response. My silence was no deterrent, however, as my roommates' teasing continued, uninterrupted.

"But to be sure, I suppose it is best that you stay here," Gemma went on. "The whole point of this ball is to find a husband, after all, and no one of your kind will be there."

"I don't want to be married," I retorted, sharply. "I aspire to something greater."

This rejoinder evidently annoyed my roommate, as she answered, testily, "Do you hear that, Sarah? Our aspirations are too low, at least in Mary's estimation."

"Wouldn't you say the same, if you didn't have any prospects?" came Sarah's swift response. My roommates again dissolved into a forced, shrill laughter.

*So, it is a row that we'll have,* I thought, and I shut my book, sitting up straighter in my seat. Before such a battle could commence, however, several girls appeared at our open doorway, all attired in their finest gowns and jewels.

"Make haste, you two!" a short girl demanded, her auburn curls bouncing as she spoke. "The carriages have arrived."

My roommates grabbed their gloves and silk purses, and then, with a condescending petting of my head, Sarah said, "Farewell, studious Mary. Don't work too hard."

It took some effort to refrain from grabbing the patronizing hand that petted my head and wrenching its wrist, crushing its delicate bones, making its owner cry out in pain and supplication for mercy. With deep and purposeful inhalations, however, I managed, and only sat quietly as my roommates rushed out of the room with their friends toward an evening of galivanting, dancing, and joy.

As I sat in the room alone, calming myself, the sounds of a broom sweeping in the hallway grew nearer and nearer. I looked up and saw the housemaid diligently executing her work, and wondered how long she had been outside of my door, how much of that uncomfortable scene with my roommates she had observed.

How desperately I wanted to speak with this young woman, to forge some connection with the only other girl of my race within these walls. It might have been that this desperation was evident upon my face, that the housemaid felt the same desire to connect with me, for in the next moment, she stood before my doorway, halted her sweeping, and said, "That debutante ball is not the only party in town tonight, I'll have you know."

So surprised was I by her sudden address, so unsure that it was not some mental invention on my part, that I did not immediately respond.

"I'm Josephine, by the way," she said, extending a hand toward me. She seemed to think twice about this gesture, then wiped her hand upon her apron before extending it again, deeming me a lady too fine to easily accept her greeting. "We haven't had a chance to properly meet yet."

I took Josephine's hand in mine and shook it gratefully. "I'm—" I began, but she interjected.

"Mary Lewis. I know," she said, to my surprise. "A lot of us folks on the south side of town have heard about you. We've been keeping up with your progress. We've never seen someone like you before, a college girl."

This candor unmoored me. "Thank you," was the only response I could muster, before realizing that I was unsure whether her words were meant as a compliment, or simple observation.

"You seem to be in need of a friend, Miss Lewis," Josephine offered, warming to her theme, stepping yet farther into my room. "A true friend. Not like these roommates of yours."

I felt exposed by her frankness, her sharp assessment of my situation. "I suppose a friend would be better company than these textbooks," I agreed.

"I suppose so, as well," she said, and then, gesturing for me to stand, added, "let's be on our way then."

"Now?" I asked, looking at my books, the work I needed to complete by the start of the next school week.

"Now," Josephine replied, definitively. "We've a bit of a walk to the south side of town, and we don't want to be too late. In any case, we must seize the opportunity we have now, while Mrs. Keep and the others are away, to find our own enjoyment."

I was not opposed to the idea of attending a party with this new acquaintance, though I felt unprepared for such an outing. "But I have nothing to wear," I responded, gesturing toward my plain dress and shoes.

Josephine considered my attire, a yellow calico frock and simple amethyst necklace, a gift my brother had given me some years ago. "What you've got on now is the finest thing anyone on my side of town has ever seen," she declared. "You mustn't fret. Off we go then."

With this, Josephine grabbed my hand, and she, leaving her cleaning, and I, my studying, we set off from the Keep house and toward her own neighborhood, south of town.

After a walk of some miles through the brisk open air, through broad fields and expansive woodlands that spoke to the unsettled nature of that frontier state, we arrived at an old, abandoned barnyard. Even from its exterior, I could hear the strains of music, of drumbeat and banjo strum, wafting from its windows. As we neared the barn, I heard much talking and laughter, a certain joy and abandon not even the girls of the Keep house, on that night of their own extravagant ball, could attain. Josephine excitedly led me inside of the barnyard, where I saw dozens of revelers drinking and dancing together to the music.

"Come along now, don't be timid," Josephine said, feeling the tension in my arm. "Who knows when you'll next have an opportunity like this, so secluded they keep you in that boarding house, with your books and your studies. You might as well enjoy yourself. Now," she said, gesturing toward the crowd, "that's Joey Bucknell, and his brother Tim. They work in the lumberyard. And over there is Cora Redding. Her parents run our general store. Titus Jones and Jeremiah Lawson, just there, work as farmhands," she said, pointing to two young men pouring drinks for their companions, as I tried, and failed, to keep up with all of these names.

"It seems you've forgotten the one name worth mentioning,

Josie," came a voice from behind, startling me. "I'm Cade Bronson," said a young man, with a look of earnest expectation, as if he had somehow been anticipating my arrival, "the only man here you'll need to know."

I stared at this young man for a moment, taken aback by his boldness, not breaking my gaze until Josephine hit him roughly on the arm, as the beat of the music still continued beneath our encounter.

"How can you be the only man she needs to know when you're just a silly boy?" she inquired, with much playful disdain. "And I told you not to call me Josie," she added, with a scowl and another push. "I'm not a little girl any longer, and I'll have my full name, Josephine Campbell. Now, Mary," she said, again turning to me, "you're to pay him no mind at all."

"Surely she'll have to pay me some mind," Cade said, undeterred by Josephine's admonishment, "in order to dance with me."

He extended his hand toward me and waited. So unused was I to such forwardness that I only stared at his hand for a moment, entranced by the attention. I had never before been invited to dance, and had never had much opportunity to interact so familiarly with any young man aside from my brother, and Quincy, on the occasions we were able to converse while at New York Central College.

"Will you?" Cade asked again, moving his hand closer still toward my own, and it was only then that I realized how rude I was being in my delayed response.

"Oh, go ahead then, Mary," Josephine said, with an exasperated sigh toward Cade, and a playful nudge at my shoulder. "You might as well appease him. He won't wait forever."

My verbal capacities seeming to abandon me, I could make no reply, but only took Cade's hand and allowed myself to be led onto the dance floor among the others. It seemed that all eyes then fell upon us, and I noticed not a few jealous stares from some of the ladies on the dance floor. I understood from their looks that Cade was much admired among their set, as well he should have been, I thought, given his stature, his fine features, his natural ease and confidence. We began to dance to the music, a bit awkwardly at first, as I could not seem to follow the fluidity of his movements, could not meld what I'd observed among polite society, what I'd been taught were appropriate movements for a lady, with those of the crowd around me.

"You don't have to be that way, here," Cade said, speaking into my ear to be heard above the music.

"What way?" I asked.

"So . . ." He seemed to struggle for the right word, being careful, evidently hoping not to offend. "So stiff. So prim and proper."

I drew back my head to observe him, to try and discern his meaning.

"You're among your own people, here, Mary," he said. "You can be yourself."

"Am I not being myself?" I inquired. It was almost a genuine question, as I had no real sense of how he expected me to behave, of how I would behave were I not placed in such peculiar circumstances. I had spent the last several years learning how to comport myself in polite society, to mold myself into a shape that might better fit the expectations of this country, and here this young man was, so easily dismissing all I had practiced.

Cade shrugged his shoulders and pulled me yet closer. "I suppose I just imagined you'd have to act differently up at the college, trying to impress all of your benefactors. And I guess I thought you might not know how to turn it off, to be at your ease."

I nodded and leaned my head against Cade's shoulder, feeling seen and understood in a way I hadn't anticipated.

"How do you manage it, anyway?" he asked, as the music shifted to something slower, softer, and we changed our own movements accordingly.

"Manage what?" I asked.

"To be forever surrounded by people who disparage you, to be without your own kind. Josephine has told me she sees you there at the Keep house, and how alone you always are. It's one of the reasons she wanted to invite you here tonight," Cade said, leveling me with his words, and confirming my suspicion that he had somehow expected my attendance at this party.

I took a moment before responding. "Whenever I feel alone, I just think of my brother, and my aunts," I told him, after some time, "and all of the people who are expecting me—depending on me—to succeed."

"A lot of pressure," he said. "I believe I might lose my sanity in your position."

"You would adapt," I said. "A person can get used to anything with enough time."

"Not anything," he said, looking off, seeming to recollect something painful. "There are things that cannot be quietly endured. Things that can make a person go mad. But you might be among the fortunate ones who will never have to learn such a lesson, firsthand."

I wanted to tell Cade that I perhaps understood this better than he might have thought, that my time in McGrawville, and the loss of my closest friend there, had engrained this message in me. Before I could respond, our conversation was interrupted by a loud bang, then another, and yet another, until it became clear that gunshots were ringing out in the night. A few partygoers began to run, with the sound of screaming pervading the air. Several hooded men entered the barn, yelling out names unfamiliar to me, along with epithets and slurs hurled like weapons. Cade threw one arm around me and pulled me from the dance floor, then ran to throw his other arm around Josephine, who still stood at the periphery of the crowd, almost rooted to the spot in her fear. Cade led us quickly toward the back door, pushing through throngs of people, confusion and panic filling the space. As we approached the barn door, more hooded men appeared, blocking our exit. Cade pushed us to the ground and out of the men's sight.

"The loft window," he said, breathing heavily, "it's the only way out."

Before Cade could utter another word, before he could issue

any further directions, panicking partygoers rushed past us and between us, separating me from Cade and Josephine.

I tried my best to move through the crowds, the chaos, but my feet felt leaden, my limbs heavy and useless in my fear. Somehow, I made my way up to the loft window, and without hesitation, I climbed out of it, hanging by my arms, my booted feet dangling over the earth below. With a deep breath, I let go, and fell to the ground. By the time I righted myself, got my bearings, and began to run in the direction of the Keep home, I heard footsteps behind me, growing nearer and nearer, and men's voices shouting at me, telling me to stop running, to surrender. A hand grasped at my dress, then another at my head, the fingers firmly gripping at my hair, yanking me back and onto the ground. I tried to escape, but to no avail, as the man had me in a chokehold, ripping my amethyst necklace from my throat in the process. I screamed and flailed like a wild animal, desperate, kicking my legs until I felt my foot land a solid blow against the man's head. He released me, and I turned around to see another group of men still accosting the partygoers at the barn. A few of the men had Cade by the throat, then grabbed his hands and tied them behind his back.

"We've got him," the man said, as they led Cade away into the night. Not daring to see where they were taking him, I ran in the opposite direction the entire distance back to the Keep home, tears streaming down my face as I realized that even my new home would be no refuge, that any mirth or enjoyment my people dared to find would be wrenched from us just as surely as we sought it.

I did not want to risk discovery upon my return to Keep boarding house, and so I dared not enter the residence through the front door. Sarah and Gemma were awake when I climbed through the bedroom window, almost as if they had been awaiting my return, as if they knew, or indeed sensed, that something was amiss. They sat up in their nightgowns and watched me closely as I moved to my bed, sitting down and removing my boots. I didn't speak to them at first, but even in the darkness, they could see that I was aggrieved, scratched and disheveled.

"Mary, you're bleeding," Sarah said, gesturing toward my neck.

I burst into tears at this, and Gemma approached me, swiftly. I thought she might embrace me at first, comfort me somehow, but she instead placed a firm hand over my mouth, stifling my cries.

"You'll wake the others," she said. "You must calm down. You're perfectly safe, now."

"What happened?" Sarah asked. She sat on the bed beside me and put a hand on my back.

I shook my head, unable to speak.

"How can you expect us to help you if you don't say something?" Gemma demanded.

"I was—we were—chased," I began.

"Chased by whom?" Gemma asked brusquely.

I shrugged and threw up my hands. "Bounty hunters," I said. "Slave catchers. I don't know exactly, it all happened so fast, and someone caught me, he tackled me to the ground, and—"

The tears returned. Sarah handed me a handkerchief.

"Where did this happen?" Gemma asked.

"South of here—" I began.

"The colored part of town," Sarah interjected.

"Now you should have known not to go to that part of town, not to socialize with such people, but you did it anyhow," Gemma lectured. "I've half a mind to tell Mrs. Keep what you've been up to. Associating with fugitive slaves, partying, dancing, drinking. I can smell it on you, you know."

"Please, don't tell Mrs. Keep," I begged, between sobs.

Gemma leaned closer to me, her face mere inches from mine. "We're doing well to let you stay in this room with us, but I will not abide by you hanging out with those people and bringing their filth back into this room. Mrs. Keep promised us that you were nothing like those people, but if that proves to be untrue, I'll see to it that you are banished not only from this room, but from this school. Do I make myself clear?"

"Yes," I answered, finally managing to slow my tears. A sudden fear then compounded my sorrow, the thought that Gemma would indeed tell Mrs. Keep where I had been that night, that I would be evicted from the Keep boarding house, and expelled from the college, with nowhere to go, no means or ability to travel either to Canada to seek my aunts, or to California, to reunite with my brother. I knew then that I would have to be careful never to anger Gemma any further than I already had. I would have to tread lightly around that girl, lest she see fit to upend my whole life, and any academic progress I had managed to make.

As my roommates returned to their beds and drifted off to sleep, I remained awake, still reeling from the events of that evening, feeling an unmitigated rage at the treatment my people endured. I sat up in bed watching my roommates, resenting the peace with which they rested, the calm and certainty they took for granted, a repose that would never be my own.

# Chapter 7

That rage was still resident within me when I arrived at the art classroom, many weeks later, to complete my first lesson with Ronan. It was well after dark, when all was still and quiet on Oberlin's campus, the only time that we might safely convene, so I could learn the subject that had been forbidden from me, and hopefully ease my mind after weeks of torment and separation from my artwork. Though I wished for the ability to focus on my craft, to take full advantage of this rare gift to learn from such a generous young teacher, I could not bid my mind to concentrate, so preoccupied was I by the constant slights from my roommates over the previous weeks, the unceasing mockery, the insults that had increased in severity since the night I returned from the party.

"Is something the matter?" Ronan asked, noticing my distraction as he pulled textbooks from Professor Westbrook's shelves. He looked at me with such genuine, undisguised care that I nearly unburdened myself of all that had occurred with my roommates in the past few weeks, of all of the unprocessed anguish I harbored when thinking about the plight of my people. Since I could not yet discern what sort of a person this Ronan Clarke truly was, I only shook my head, and denied that anything was the matter.

"I'm quite alright," I lied, trying unsuccessfully to rid my face of all betraying emotion.

He seemed to identify this for the untruth that it was. "Whatever is bothering you, be it trivial or otherwise, you must use it," he said. "You must put it into your art. Now," he said, turning to a page of a heavy artbook and showing me a daguerreotype of a marble sculpture, "this is Michelangelo's *David*, one of the great works of the Italian Renaissance. Perhaps you've encountered it before." I had not encountered that sculpture before, but I nodded my head as if I maintained, indeed, some measure of familiarity with the piece. "We'll do something simple to start," Ronan said. "I want you to try and replicate his eyes, the furrow of his brow, the ferocity of his gaze."

He passed me a hammer and chisel, then sat me before a moderately large block of what he explained to be steatite.

"It's a cheaper stone than marble," he said, "so it won't matter if you make a mistake. Easier to manipulate, too, which is just as well, given your small stature. Go on now, make an attempt."

I gripped the sculpting tools, appreciating their weight, the coolness of their iron, feeling powerful as I wielded them. It was with much relish that I struck the steatite block, hitting it again, and yet again, pleased as I saw it growing closer to the shape of the eyes I sought to sculpt, thrilling at the tumult as chunks of stone fell to the floor.

"There you are," Ronan said. "That's just the way to do it. You must think of yourself as simply releasing your subject from the stone. It already exists within it, you see. You are simply its liberator."

I nodded in eager agreement, surprised to hear Ronan describe the act of sculpting in just the way I'd always thought of it, as an act of liberation, of an incarnation for the visions I always saw. I continued my work with assiduity, though growing more conscious of Ronan's close attention, all the while.

"You've got a natural ability for this, it seems," Ronan said, "and you cannot go wrong emulating the work of the greats."

"I have some experience with sculpting," I replied, thinking of all the work I'd done through the years with clay and carving wood, "though I have only practiced the craft as an autodidact, thus far. I should mention, though, that it is not only emulation I'm after." I paused for a moment and observed my work before speaking my next words. "I have ideas of my own that desperately need release," I said. "Visions that will not let me rest until I give them that liberation of which you speak."

Ronan observed me. "Visions of what kind?"

"Of my own people," I replied. "Those who have been forgotten, subjugated and enslaved. I dare say we deserve immortalization as much as any other."

My eyes wandered as I remembered Clara, and all of the fugitives I had met while in McGrawville. I thought, too, of Cade, my brief acquaintance with him those weeks before, and the fear in his eyes as our innocent gathering was disrupted by those hateful men. I felt it was only more urgent now for me to use my skill to sculpt such people, to show the world our struggles, our humanity.

"Indeed, you do," Ronan answered. "You would surely find many worthy subjects among your kind."

I went on, seeming not to hear his words, but determined to give my thoughts a full articulation. "It seems that all I am taught in school is about the genius of other races, about their humanity, and how they had the foresight to set their ideas down in ink or in stone, while my own people, with their oral traditions, and their ephemeral—so it is said—art, can only hope to be forgotten."

Ronan seemed entranced by my words, watching me closely as I spoke.

"I will see to it that my people are never forgotten, that we are elevated to the status of the ancient Greeks and Romans," I said, "and I will use my art to do it."

I picked up my tools and resumed my work, hammering at the steatite with yet more force, more determination, and more ruckus, again delighting in, and feeling cleansed by, the noise. The sound was so loud that we did not initially notice the nearing footsteps emanating from the corridor, the sound of rustling, of jingling keys.

Ronan placed a sudden hand on mine, stopping my work, and it was only then that I heard the heavy step in the hallway just beyond the classroom. "That must be Professor Westbrook," he said, as the footsteps neared, and we heard a key in the door.

"He can't know that we're here. We would both be charged with trespassing, and surely expulsion would be the result. Come on now, make haste."

Ronan threw a sheet over the small, incomplete sculpture, slid it beneath his desk, then extended a hand toward me and led me to the window at the back of the classroom. He opened the window, bracing against its loud creak, then climbed out of it, and held out a hand to help me down. I jumped down from the window with Ronan's assistance, and just as we heard Professor Westbrook entering the classroom and rummaging around, the two of us set off running in the direction of the woods, where we might evade notice.

We ran for several moments, though I struggled to keep up with Ronan's quick pace, and soon found myself tripping over my long skirt and falling down onto the woodland ground, wrenching my knee as I did so. Ronan stopped and turned around as I languished there amongst the soil and leaves, holding on to my knee and rocking back and forth against the radiating pain.

"Are you alright?" Ronan asked, stooping beside me.

"It's my knee," I responded, still clutching my leg. "I've twisted it."

"Here, take my hand," Ronan said, helping me to stand. He slipped his arm around my waist and guided me forward, deeper into the woods. "My house is just this way. We'll get something to mend you."

We made our way forward, slowly, through the forest, with nothing but the moon to attend us. After some time, we came upon a small log cabin, so dark and nondescript as to be almost indistinguishable from the surrounding woodlands. Ronan led me to the front door and opened it, but I hesitated, assuming that his family would not approve of a colored girl in their home.

"Only my father and I reside here," Ronan said, understanding my hesitation. "He's away on a hunting trip, and won't return for another week. You needn't fear discovery, if that's what stalls you."

I still felt quite nervous to enter Ronan's home, to be there with a young man, unchaperoned, unseen, but needing the help for my knee, and with no other recourse or remediation, I went with him inside of his house.

Ronan's home was quite modest, surprising me in its cramped quality, its notable absence of a necessary feminine touch. It seemed that only the bare minimum was present in terms of furniture or objects, with no superfluous item or piece of decoration in sight.

"It's a modest lodging, I'll be the first to admit," Ronan said, as he closed and locked his front door. "But I'm proud of it. My father and I constructed it ourselves, in fact. Come, I'll help you to my room."

I tensed up for a moment, however briefly, as I feared to venture any farther into Ronan's house. Stepping through his front door was one matter, but going back into his room seemed to be another altogether, and I felt once again that I might be leading myself into danger by being alone there. It was too late, however, for me to make a retreat, as I could hardly walk on my own, and Ronan could certainly take advantage of my vulnerable position, if he so pleased. I felt, then, that I must go with him into his room, though I quaked with anxiety and the pain from my knee, and wished I might have something to palliate me.

"Have you ever been alone in a man's home before?" Ronan asked, unable to ignore my continued reticence. He lit a candle to help guide our way as we moved still farther into the house. I might have taken umbrage at the question, as I was sure Ronan would not inquire this of any other woman in polite society, but would only assume that she had not ever been in such an improper position before. Instead of showing my slight offense at this question, however, I decided to answer him back with a slight barb of my own.

"Is that what this is?" I responded, as he helped me into his room and onto a chair beside his desk. "I thought a man's home might have a beer, perhaps a whiskey," I said, hoping also to quell some of my fears with this note of levity.

Ronan looked at me askance, amused, and not disquieted by my request.

"For the pain in my knee, of course," I added, though in truth, I wanted it more to ease my nervousness.

"Of course," he said, adopting my mischievous tone. "Let me see what we have." With that, Ronan left me in his room alone, with nothing but the candlelight to attend me.

As Ronan searched in his kitchen for a drink, I looked around his room, intrigued by the chance to have a glimpse into his mind, and already feeling relieved, comforted at the prospect of a libation. I was perusing the contents of Ronan's desk, flipping through his history books and novels, when he returned to the room with a drink of whiskey in each hand, passing me one that I gratefully accepted. As I went to replace his books on the shelf, a small portrait of a young woman fell out of one, attached to a sprig of dried pink roses, a clear gift from someone Ronan was courting.

"Gemma," I said, not even realizing I'd spoken aloud until Ronan, too, looked at her portrait as it fell to the floor. Ronan stooped to retrieve the portrait and replace it in the book from which it fell.

"Do you know her?" Ronan asked, as he placed the book back on his shelf.

"She's my roommate at the Keep house," I said, still startled by the appearance of her likeness in the room. "And who is she to you?"

"My intended," came Ronan's quiet, and somewhat sheepish, response.

I must have reacted sharply to this, for he added, quickly, and almost apologetically, "she can be a difficult person, I know."

I showed my agreement. "And yet knowing this, you still intend to marry her."

"It's more complicated than you might imagine," he said.

"And I'm sharper than you might imagine. You must enlighten me," was my harsh return.

Ronan sighed as if already tired of the subject, as though he had needed to defend this choice many times before. "She comes from powerful people—influential."

"Rich," I returned.

"In a word. And as you can see," he said, gesturing around his small cabin, "I don't."

"Surely there must be other ways for you to earn a living and improve your station," I said, perhaps showing more of my disdain than I intended.

"Surely there must," he repeated. "What would you suggest?"

"Your art. You seem to have a real talent for it," I said, "a real knowledge of the craft, as I can see from what you've taught me thus far."

"It's not much more than a hobby, I'm afraid," he said. "No money to be made from it."

"The greats have managed to do so," I responded. "I believe that I would manage to do so, if given the chance."

"And if there is any justice in the world, you will be given the chance to prove yourself as an artist," he said. He took a moment to observe me before speaking again. "It's no wonder the other girls leave you be," he said. "You've got ambitions that would put them to shame. They only think of being wives and mothers, what dress they'll wear for their societal debut. But you—you're different. Your disposition compels you to pursue something higher."

We stared at one another for some time after he said this, neither of us knowing how to proceed, how to acknowledge what was then brewing between us. I was filled with a certain warmth, then, something fierce, and surely shameful, but impossible to ignore. I could see by Ronan's expression, by the clench of his jaw, and a certain fire on his face, that he felt a similar sentiment, and that he, too, understood its danger.

"We must now tend to your knee," Ronan finally said, needing to disrupt the atmosphere, to puncture any delusions either of us might have begun to harbor in that moment. I consented to Ronan's touch, enjoying his close attention, savoring this small rebellion against my roommate, this quiet venting of my rage, though I knew that it would take far more for my resentment against her to be quelled.

# Chapter 8

How long can a wound fester? For what stretch of time might disease go ignored before the patient in question must either amputate that plaguing member or succumb to its fatal blow? So it was that the troubled American nation, whose citizens had, for so long, existed under a diseased and depraved slave system, ultimately found the need to dispose of that system by no less than the very act of war. This war found its first expression at Charleston Harbor, in South Carolina, when Confederate troops fired upon Union soldiers at Fort Sumter. Though the Confederacy gained victory in this first battle, my hopes for the Union cause were not diminished, for I knew from my studies that war could be long, and the road uncertain, but that ultimate victory could still come to those forgotten and oppressed.

Even those in the midst of war must find a way to survive, to endure, and must find some method of diversion to maintain their sanity. Josephine visited me frequently in those days, providing just such diversion, sitting with me in my room when Sarah and Gemma were away. Neither she nor I had heard from Cade in the months after that nighttime attack, but one morning, she brought news of him as we convened together over tea and surreptitious food that she saved for us from the kitchen. Cade had managed to escape from the slave catchers' wagon the night of the party, shortly after they'd captured him. He had hidden, Josephine explained, in the woods for weeks, not daring to venture out even for food or water, but subsisting on whatever nourishment he could find there in the wilderness. Though Cade feared that he might not ever be able to return to town, and might need to spend the rest of his life in hiding since the slave catchers had discovered him, he had finally found the courage to return to Oberlin after many weeks, traveling to his home with his aunt Grace in the dead of night.

"His aunt Grace burst into tears when she saw him," Josephine said. "She thought that he was dead. We all did, I suppose. But he is alive, and he is well, and now that the war has begun, he is no longer afraid to venture out into town. He believes the war will bring about true emancipation. He's already started planning all the things he'll do once he's truly free."

I was amazed to hear of Cade's escape, and found myself all the more intrigued by him, his bravery, his determination. So it was that I found myself thrilled to hear Josephine's next words.

"It seems that his plans involve you, Mary, you might be pleased to know," she said, her tone growing more spirited. "He wants you to join him for dinner, at his home with his aunt Grace. He asked me to tell you directly as soon as we next spoke."

I was surprised by this request, and indeed, immensely pleased. This would be the first time I'd had dinner with any young man other than my brother, a first proper act of courtship, and I relished the opportunity.

"He's quite taken with you, Mary," Josephine said, eyeing me as if to discern some hidden meaning in my countenance. "Do you return the sentiment?"

I considered the question, and knew that in truth, I was taken by Cade as well, though I did not feel comfortable making such an admission to Josephine just then, and so I maintained my silence, allowing my coyness alone to serve as response.

"He's a good person," Josephine told me, between sips from her teacup, undeterred by my quietude. "He's endured much hardship in his life, and saw his own mother die by the hands of their slaveholders when he was only a child. It was only by means of his escape from that Kentucky plantation that he is alive today," she said, "And now, he deserves a respite."

I took a silent sip from my own teacup, then placed it gingerly upon my desk as Josephine gazed at me.

Josephine continued, not breaking her stare. "Perhaps you can provide just such solace for him. But I must tell you, Mary, that you shouldn't embark on any sort of a courtship with Cade if you do not truly see a future with him. He has already dealt with enough pain and loss in his life. I wouldn't want you to become another source of sorrow for him."

I nodded my understanding of Josephine's words. She seemed to care for Cade as she would a brother, as I cared for my own dear Samuel. I knew it would not be appropriate for me to tell Josephine what my roommates had said, that they had instructed me to stay away from the colored part of town, and had made terrible comments about many of the fugitive slaves who lived there, Cade among them. I did not then care about my roommates' insults, their disparagements and verbal abuses, and only asked Josephine to send word that I would join Cade for dinner as requested. In just a few weeks, I found myself walking the long route south toward his home, nervous for our first meeting in quite some time.

Cade's home was small, of rough-hewn wood, with peeling white paint and a sagging, thatched roof, a stark contrast to the expansive and well-maintained Keep home to which I had grown accustomed. I sat beside Cade at the dinner table, still a bit winded from the long walk to the south of town, but glad to be near him for the first time in many months.

"Are you warm enough?" Cade asked, observing me nervously.

"I feel fine, thank you," I replied, though he stood up and went to the fireplace anyway, moving and resettling a few of the logs.

He returned to his seat beside me. "We get a draft here sometimes, and we had to use most of the firewood to make dinner, so . . ." He looked embarrassed, struggling for the right words. "My apologies."

I wanted to place my hand on his arm to reassure him, to tell him there was no need to apologize. Such a gesture, though, seemed far too intimate, suddenly, as his aunt Grace emerged from the kitchen with our meal, interrupting our private moment.

"I do hope you eat tripe," his aunt said, spooning food onto my plate before receiving a response. "The hen got loose this morning, and this was all I could get at the market. It's not much, but it's what we have, thank God," she said.

"I quite enjoy tripe, thank you," I replied, accepting the plate. "I'm not too particular when it comes to food."

"You aren't as exacting as I might have expected for a young woman of your caliber," Aunt Grace said, approvingly. "Cade tells me you live at the Keep home, and take classes at the college," she observed. "Must be nice, living like that, like a proper young lady."

"I'm grateful for the unique opportunity I've been given," I conceded, without offering much more in the way of describing my life at Oberlin. Aunt Grace looked at me then, seemingly surprised by my measured and somewhat cool response. I was hoping to escape, that evening, all thoughts of school and the stresses I experienced there, but it seemed that Aunt Grace would not easily let me do so.

"What are you learning there, at the college?" she asked, as she piled food upon her nephew's plate.

"Greek and Roman history mostly," I said. "Some grammar and composition, Latin and French, music and poetry. Lots of dancing and etiquette classes for a societal debut that I will never have."

"And do you enjoy all of that?" Aunt Grace asked, with a genuine curiosity as she sat down to her own plate of food.

"I enjoy learning of Roman history, I suppose. Marcus Aurelius and his wisdom. Caesar and his assassination. Spartacus and his rebellion."

Aunt Grace smiled and sat up excitedly in her seat. "*Spartacus,*" she repeated. "Don't you sound just like a book? And do you think all of that learning will really help our people? Can you use those lessons to help with the emancipation efforts?"

I considered her question before responding. "Perhaps not the dancing and etiquette classes, so much, but the writing and history lessons are quite important," I said, thinking of all the times Miss King had told me as much, back in McGrawville. "Really, though, I believe it will be my art that helps our people the most. I'm a sculptor, you see," I said, surprising myself in the confidence with which I asserted this, "and I believe the pieces I create will help the world to see our stories, our humanity."

Aunt Grace smiled at me before turning and speaking to her nephew. "Cade, you'd better not let this one get away."

"I don't intend to," Cade said, glancing over at me. "She's a part of the reason I even found the courage to come back to this town."

Aunt Grace sighed, this comment seeming to deflate her excitement and wrench her back to the reality of her nephew's situation. "I still fear it was unwise to return," she said, looking now toward Cade. "When you escaped your plantation and made your way here, I promised myself that I would always keep you safe, that I would always guard you as if you were my own son, as your mother would have wanted me to do. But I don't know that I can do that here, in a border state, especially now with the outbreak of war. If the South were to win, your life, all of our lives, will be too wretched to imagine."

"She worries too much," Cade said to me with a teasing tone, and a searching glance toward his aunt, hoping, it seemed, to comfort her, to alleviate some of her fears.

"She seems to have a right to do so," I returned. "What I saw that night of that party, the night you were captured, was quite shocking, Cade. I've never seen such horrible treatment, such hatred unleashed upon our people."

"It's a sheltered life you've lived then," Aunt Grace said. "You should be quite grateful for that."

Cade clenched his jaw at the memory of that night. "I went through hell to make it to a free state," he said, quietly, seeming to be physically transported back to a much darker time. "I fled from Kentucky in the night, chased by overseers and their dogs, all to set foot on this Ohio ground, to make it to Aunt Grace's house, as my mother always told me I should try to do. Yet even here," he observed, "I'm still treated as a slave. It's enough to make you want to kill," he said, looking down at the table. "And I will, if given the chance. I'll enlist with the Union forces as soon as our people are allowed to do so. I'll take up arms. I'll ensure that any slaveholder I encounter has a horrible end. I'll ensure that the man who took my mother's life meets his own death."

Aunt Grace shifted in her seat, uncomfortable in the face of such unmitigated anger. "Cade, that's quite enough," she said. "You must have forgotten that you are in the company of a fine young woman, a proper lady. Surely, she's unused to such harsh language."

"It's quite alright," I assured. This seemed to surprise Aunt Grace, who raised her eyebrows, then looked down at her plate and quietly sliced her food. I turned to Cade then and addressed him directly. "You might speak as you wish. You can always say what you feel, around me."

Beneath the table, Cade took my hand and held it tight.

Cade held my hand once again some months later, in the gloaming as he walked me home, through the long and winding roads toward the Keep boarding house. We had just finished another one of our frequent dinners at his home with his aunt Grace, something that had become a regular and indispensable occurrence for us as the weeks passed, and as we found it increasingly difficult to spend time away from each other. I came to feel as comfortable in Cade's home as if it were my own, as myself with him and his aunt Grace as if I had known them both for my entire life. It seemed that hardly a day could pass without my needing to see Cade, and I grew so reliant upon him for my own personal contentment that I became nervous about what this might mean for my studies, and my art, for all that my brother expected me to achieve while at Oberlin College. I knew that Cade was becoming more serious about his relationship with me, and the more that I wanted to return this gravity, the more I felt myself pulling away, almost subconsciously sabotaging our growing intimacy. It was in this attitude that I approached our conversation that day as Cade walked me home, as he attempted to broach a subject that had clearly been on his mind for quite some time.

"I plan to make my way up to Canada after the war," Cade said, looking forward as we walked, too nervous, it seemed, to meet my eye while broaching this subject. "Regardless of what the war's outcome might be, I feel that I could make a better, and freer, life there in Canada. And I want you to join me, as my wife."

"I have my studies," I said, thinking of Mrs. Dascomb's course, yes, but also of my art. In the previous months, I had advanced quite far in my lessons with Ronan, and the idea of abandoning Ohio, of leaving that unique opportunity behind, was impossible to me. "I have begun to learn much about art, about sculpture. I could hardly find the circumstances for that in Canada, I should think. Surely you don't believe I can just forsake that?"

"I'm not asking you to forsake your studies," Cade said, finding the strength to look toward me then. "You could finish your course here, then move up North with me, to a land of true liberation."

"And what would I do there?" I asked. "Simply bear your children and tend to the home?"

"Would that be such a punishment?" he returned. "Most women might be happy to have a home to call their own, a family to raise."

"But I'm not most women," I replied. "You've said as much yourself. Different expectations have been placed upon me. My brother hasn't sent me here for courtship, but for education, and advancement, not only for myself, but for our people."

"A family can be a noble aspiration in itself, Mary," he said. "Especially to those of us who have had our families wrenched from us. Matrimony could be an act of radical advancement for someone who has been denied it for so long. All I ever wanted when I was a kid was a home to call my own, to have my parents there to raise me. Now I want to create a family with someone special, someone like you."

"I don't know if I can be that person for you," I replied, with much regret. "You mustn't place such expectations upon me. You should find someone else who can fulfill that station."

Cade fell into silence then as we walked, with only the sound of our footsteps on the gravel to ease the tension. I felt some guilt at rejecting him so totally, and remembered Josephine's counsel all those months ago that I must not hurt Cade, and yet, I knew that it would be much more cruel to encourage in him any notions I believed to be impossible. But still, even then, in all of my youthful conviction, some small portion of my mind was troubled by the thought that I was making a mistake in denying Cade, the only young man who might feel a true love for me, or for the woman he thought I could be.

"How was the dinner?" Josephine asked, once I'd returned from that latest meal at Cade's home. It had become our habit to discuss each of my dates with Cade, as Josephine still viewed him as something of a surrogate brother, and thrilled at hearing each detail of our progressing relationship. She sat comfortably upon Gemma's bed for our conversation, her legs folded beneath her and each of us with a mug of my roommates' secret wine in our hands, as the girls were away with their families for the evening. "You must tell me all that happened."

I wanted to share with Josephine the confusion I felt in my mind, the simultaneous attraction to, and repulsion from, the vision of a family Cade had presented to me. I wanted to ask her if she thought I was wrong to reject Cade, if she believed I should have taken more time to consider his proposition, but I felt that even Josephine, who had come to be my dear friend, might not understand my predicament. My situation was yet strange to her, as she had observed on several occasions, and so I wondered whether she would even understand my reticence, my thought that a domestic life would necessitate the certain end of any hopes I harbored for an artistic career.

I hadn't the chance to pose such questions to my dear friend, however, as Gemma unexpectedly returned from her family's home at just that time, and saw Josephine and I convened in the bedroom.

"What is she doing in our room?" Gemma asked upon her entrance, speaking only to me and not to Josephine. "And daring to sit upon my own bed?"

Josephine bolted up immediately, offering her sincere apologies, but Gemma continued to ignore her, and turned only toward me.

"Mary, what did I tell you about socializing with such people?" she asked, her voice all the more threatening for its quietness, its evenness. "You have the housemaid sitting in our room as if she's worthy of such comfort, as if she's one of us. And yet you know that she is not."

I was silent at this, knowing that to contradict Gemma was to risk my status in the Keep boarding house.

"Tell her to get out," Gemma then demanded, staring at me, unblinking.

I was paralyzed at the instruction, unsure of how to proceed.

"Tell her to get out," Gemma repeated, more firmly now, taking another intimidating step toward me.

"Josephine, it's best if you leave now," I quietly said, obeying my roommate in a show of weakness and fear. Josephine looked at me briefly in disbelief, seeming to truly see me for the first time, the coward she believed to be lurking within. With my eyes, I tried to communicate my regret, but the message seemed to be lost in the discomfort of the moment, for it was only a look of bitterness, of seething hatred that I saw upon Josephine's face. She looked at Gemma as if she wanted to strike her, took a step toward her as if she truly might, then seemed to think twice, turned, and silently left the room. I considered chasing after Josephine, apologizing, begging for forgiveness and absolution. I thought about reprimanding my roommate, insulting her in turn, and somehow finding the strength to stand up for my wounded friend. But I did none of those things, and only remained seated at my desk once Josephine left the room.

Gemma set her belongings upon her desk, placed her silk gloves and hat into her wardrobe, then removed the pins and floral hairdressing from her hair slowly and quietly before her mirror. She moved to her bed, examined it, then ripped its blankets and sheets away as if she dared not sit somewhere the housemaid had so recently been. After settling herself upon the bare mattress, she looked at me.

"It will be your responsibility to wash that bedding," she said. "It shall be done before tomorrow evening, or else I'll need to notify Mrs. Keep of what has been happening here without her knowledge."

I did not immediately answer Gemma, and so she stood up from the bed, quickly approaching and towering over me as I sat at my desk.

"Mary, you will answer me when I speak to you," she seethed, grabbing my face and forcing it toward hers.

"Yes, Gemma," came my forced reply. "I will tend to your bedding first thing in the morning."

Evidently satisfied, Gemma returned to her side of the room, took out a novel, and began to read. I remained at my desk, quietly took out a notebook, and began to sketch a series of images of Gemma and Sarah feeling all of the pain that they mercilessly inflicted on me, day after day. I hoped that my sketches might have a purgative effect, but yet and still, I found it to be an insufficient balm for my wounds, and so I stowed the pictures away deep within my wardrobe, where I was sure they would not be found.

I arrived at my next lesson with Ronan, still feeling unsettled after my interaction with Josephine and Gemma. It was impossible for me to reconcile the kind young man standing before me, setting out sculpting tools and textbooks, risking his own status at Oberlin just to help me learn, with the cruel young woman he called his fiancée, to whom he would, immediately after graduation, commit his life. I could hardly look at Ronan during that evening's lesson for fear that my true emotions would be too easily legible on my face, that I might lose all composure if he asked me what was wrong, if he could somehow divine that I was upset.

"I should think you would need to speak to me for us to have a successful lesson," Ronan finally said, after I had neglected to return his salutation or respond to his assignment for the night. "Or at the very least meet my eye."

I continued to avert my gaze, though I did finally speak to him, however curtly.

"I do not want to emulate the artists of the Renaissance this evening, nor of the Antiquity," I said. "I have brought my own sketches from which I must work."

Ronan readily accepted, and even seemed pleased by this idea. "That is just fine, Mary," he assented. "Here, let me see your sketches, and we'll discuss the best method by which to sculpt them."

I passed him the requested pages, pieces I had labored over long into night over the previous weeks, and watched as he flipped through them, his countenance growing suddenly inscrutable, illegible. I could not simply sit without hearing some pronouncement on my ideas, whether positive or otherwise, and so against my will, I said, "Well, do not only stare at them. You must tell me your thoughts."

"I think," he began, still flipping through the pages. "I think that these sketches are unlike anything I have seen before."

"And is that to their recommendation?" I inquired, now growing nervous, desiring, as any pupil might, to please my teacher.

"Indeed," he exclaimed, and then selecting one sketch in particular, said, "we'll try to sculpt this one."

It was a sketch of a fugitive slave, his hands and feet still fettered, but his head turned to the sky in a small yet determined display of hope. I had been thinking of Cade as I sketched it, and Josephine, too, believing that I could render some small tribute, some peace offering, however imperfect, and offer it to them the next time I dared venture to their part of town. Most of all, though, I had been thinking of Clara, and the runaways who had arrived when I was in McGrawville, especially the young boy, terrified and trembling by the roaring fire.

Ronan seemed to sense the importance of this project, and he asked, "Is this modeled after someone you know?"

"Someone I know, yes," I replied coolly, an image of Cade flashing across my mind. "Someone who wants to make me his wife."

Ronan took a moment to process my words, taking my cryptic response for the bait it was meant to be. "And what have you answered him?" he inquired, looking a bit troubled at the anticipation of my answer.

"I have told him that I cannot be his wife," I said, "that I cannot be anyone's wife."

Ronan seemed to be relieved by this answer, but before he could grow too comfortable, I pressed on.

"You see, I am a woman of principle," I said, finally deigning to meet his eye. "I would not simply agree to marry someone if I could not truly commit myself to that union, if I had any doubts, any reservations, whatsoever."

Ronan clenched his jaw, understanding, and resenting, my meaning.

"What would you have me do, Mary?" he asked, surprising me with his sudden anger. "Shall I end my engagement to Gemma? Shall I simply forego all that such a union would mean for my family? And what if I did?" he demanded, standing up before me. "Would that mean I could make you my own?"

I was silent, growing quite nervous at this display of unmitigated rage, but determined to maintain my own composure, even if only to provide a contrast to his own agitation.

"No, of course I couldn't," he said. "You and I could never be joined together in marriage, and so why do you concern yourself with who I will make my wife?"

"I concern myself because I care about you," I said, "and I know that Gemma is not only unkind, she is unsafe," I continued. "I have seen how she treats those who defy her, who even mildly displease her, and I fear that one day, she will treat you the very same way."

These words seemed to appease Ronan, as he paused, and took a steadying breath.

"You needn't worry about me, Mary," he assured, sitting down now beside me and taking my hand. "I can look after myself. I've done it for quite some time since coming to this country."

When I made no move to speak, he continued on. "You must know that I would change this system if I could," he said, "But I cannot. I come from lowly people. We can hardly find the resources to change our own station, much less the country. And so, I must act as expected, and marry as expected, to try and help myself and my father. But you," he said, taking up my sketches then and showing them to me. "You possess a determination, a vision I could only dream of having. And so, you mustn't be preoccupied by me or what I will do, whom I will marry. You must work," he declared then, passing me the hammer and chisel and turning me toward the steatite I was to sculpt. "You must stick to your principles, to your ambitions, and it will bring about freedom, if not for your people, at least for yourself."

Though I did not want to admit it just then, I knew that Ronan was right in all that he told me, and so I took up the sculpting tools and began to work with a new alacrity, and a renewed sense of purpose.

Christmastide arrived with its usual pomp and cheer, the townspeople all busy with their shopping and preparations, a stark contrast to the isolation I then felt. Without family of my own in town to partake in the festivities, I spent much time alone, wandering through the streets like a phantom, a mere spectator to the joy around me. I had tried, unsuccessfully, to mend my friendship with Josephine by going to her part of town each day to seek her, as she was on leave from the Keep house for the holidays. My efforts were to no avail, as it seemed that both she and Cade wanted little to do with me any longer, the traitor who had so disappointed those I most wanted to impress.

The Oberlin College Christmas Ball was to be the event of the season, a way for the students to decompress after the long and arduous semester, and my peers all relished the opportunity for fun. With no beau of my own, with no friends to invite, I watched from some distance as the other students entered the banquet hall, walking in twos and threes and much larger groups, all smiling and laughing and ready for the dance. I walked closer toward the building where I could look through one of the large French windows, seeing the walls and doorways and stairwells all festooned with holly and pine, the lavish food spread upon a broad oak table, the wide dance floor and string quartet to provide entertainment for the night. I was thinking of how much I wished that I might join in the merriment, the holiday glee, when a voice from behind interrupted my thoughts.

"Mary, where have you been?" Ronan inquired, walking toward me, leaving a group of his friends standing before the banquet hall entrance. "I've searched for you all week," he said, and then, lowering his voice and leaning in closer to me, added, "you missed yesterday's lesson."

It was true that I had missed our last lesson, choosing instead to venture to the south of town once my roommates were asleep in the hopes that I could find my distanced friend.

"I had . . ." I hesitated, not knowing how to explain the delicate nature of the previous day, another unsuccessful attempt at reconnecting with Josephine or Cade. "Business to attend to, in the southern part of town."

Understanding that I would not divulge more about my day, Ronan continued, though I could see that he would press me on the subject at a later time.

"Professor Westbrook saw the sculpture you've been working on," he said, looking eager to share this information, "your emancipation sculpture."

I thought of that unfinished work, that attempt to sculpt my own people, to give us honor and import by setting our likeness into stone. I had not taken much time to work on it since I'd first embarked upon it, finding the sculpting too painful as more days passed without a word from Josephine or Cade. To have it mentioned to me that evening of the Christmas Ball felt like a sign, a portent or an omen, that I should take up the work yet again.

"He questioned me about the sculpture," Ronan continued. "He declared he'd never seen anything like it before. He wanted to know its source, its inspiration. I thought about telling him I'd done it in order to preserve our secret, to protect you from accusations of insubordination, but he seemed so impressed by the work that I knew I had to tell him the truth. He said that your vision, your approach, is remarkable."

I hardly knew how to respond to this, so surprised was I by the idea of my work being seen, and indeed admired, by anyone other than Ronan. The thought of Professor Westbrook not only assessing, but also approving of my art, made me reel with excitement.

"He wants to work with you, Mary," Ronan said, his eyes bright. He grabbed my hands in his excitement, seeming not to care about how this move could be perceived by his friends who observed us from a short distance. "He told me to send word to you directly."

I held Ronan's hands tight, wanting to thank him for the news, but was interrupted before I could respond.

"Ronan, what are you doing?" a chilling voice inquired from the night.

Ronan turned then and pulled his hands from mine. Gemma left her group and approached us swiftly, like a child who has seen another take a favorite toy.

"What matter do you have to discuss with Mary?" she asked, saying my name as if it were almost too ridiculous to pronounce. "You might as well hold a conversation with a dog for all the enlightenment you can hope to gain with her."

Several of the others in her group laughed as she said this, like courtiers showing deference to a queen. My face grew warm, my breath shallow. Ronan didn't answer Gemma, but only turned to me to ensure that I was alright.

"Come along now," Gemma said, reaching out a gloved hand and gesturing for Ronan to follow. He hesitated, which seemed to enrage her, a flash of indignation passing across her eyes, a look that was so swift, so fleeting, that perhaps only I could discern it after so much time of living in such close quarters with her.

"Ronan," she repeated, more forcefully now. "You will come along with me, now."

Ronan didn't move, still staring at me, not wanting, it seemed, to part from me.

"I'll be fine," I assured him. "You can leave me here."

After some time, Ronan turned away from me, reluctantly, an apology legible in his eyes. He took Gemma's extended arm, then led her into the banquet hall, where they joined the other students and took their own place upon the dance floor. I watched from the outside as they mingled, as they danced. I remained there at the window for quite a while, much longer than appropriate, watching these students, this joy in which I could not partake, feeling every part the interloper, the strange being they all felt me to be.

When I finally managed to wrest myself from that place, I went almost involuntarily to the art room, as if my feet knew where I needed to go, though my brain could not quite process what I should do next. I began to hammer away at my work in progress, the emancipation sculpture, initially like an automaton, then increasingly with more purpose, a woman determined, a woman overcome. I unleashed upon that sculpture all of the aggression I could not express in polite society, seeing in it my only opportunity for retribution, revenge, striking it once for Gemma's cruelty to Josephine, then again for her cruelty to me. I struck it yet again for the abuse of the enslaved, the mistreatment of the fugitives, for the unfairness of my position, my inability to be truly myself anywhere I might go. I thought that these actions might calm me, but they only whetted my appetite, only left me with the desire for a vengeance more total, a retribution more true. I wanted upheaval, I wanted a change, and I would create it, if it would not freely come.

# Chapter 9

The winter recess between semesters was always a quiet time, a welcome respite from our academic rigors, and a chance for me to gain greater focus on my sculptural studies, when most of the other students were away, and I could use the art supplies left over from the school year. Very few of the Oberlin students remained in town at that time, and the Keep house was much quieter than it typically was during the semester, as only a handful of girls remained there for the recess. I appreciated the relative solitude, and wished only that it might be total, for I resented the presence of my roommates, who had remained at the house for an extra day to go on a special sleigh-riding trip through town with their beaus. I sat at my desk quietly working on a sketch as my roommates prepared for this outing, trying not to think of the time Gemma would spend with Ronan that day, time I felt he could better spend with me, helping me to set my latest sketches into stone, to prepare for the lessons I was to have with Professor Westbrook once the spring semester began.

"Promises to be a cold one today," Sarah said, sitting upon her bed and lacing her heavy snow boots.

"All the better for our sleigh ride," Gemma replied, standing before her vanity mirror and fixing her braided hair.

Sarah nodded. "If we aren't half frozen by the time we arrive. How long is the journey into Lorain?"

"It'll take all morning," Gemma answered. "But we'll have our beaus to keep us warm."

Sarah's voice grew playful, mischievous. "I can think of something else that'll keep us warm, too."

She removed a bottle of wine from the inner recesses of her wardrobe, shaking it playfully before Gemma's face.

Gemma hesitated a moment before Sarah uncorked the bottle. "I have a better idea," Gemma said, and then turning to me, she called, "Mary?"

I paused in my sketching, then turned to face her.

"Could you mull this wine for us?" she asked, thrusting the bottle toward me. "Add in those cloves and cinnamon, like you do with your tea."

I hesitated, considering her request before answering. I still felt some fear at the prospect of refusing her, believing she would convince Mrs. Keep to evict me from that home, revealing my secret excursions, my former unchaperoned outings with Cade, should I ever go against her wishes.

"I suppose so," came my reluctant reply.

I accepted the wine bottle from Gemma, then walked over to our small potbelly stove. I procured the requested spices and herbs, then placed a pot upon the stove, moving quickly so as to return to my artwork. As I labored by the stove, Gemma moved to my desk, leaning over it and observing my latest sketch.

"That's a wonderful portrait, Mary," she said, her tone surprisingly earnest. "Did Ronan help you with that?"

I stopped stirring the wine and looked at my roommate as she stood there, holding my sketch aloft.

Seeming to notice my bewilderment, Gemma said, "Ronan told me you've been doing artwork together. I know all about it, so there's no use in any denials. It's alright, Mary," she claimed, then added, "Really, it is. I harbor no bad feelings toward you."

I met Gemma's eye, trying to discern whether she was in earnest, but I could determine nothing, so empty and even was her gaze.

"You seem to have a real talent for art, too," she said. "Ronan certainly thinks so. He says that your sculptures are magnificent, singular, and that even Professor Westbrook wants to work with you."

This seemed to pique Sarah's interest, as she turned from admiring herself in the mirror and asked, "Professor Westbrook is going to teach you?"

"It appears that he has offered to, yes," I said, not wanting to go deeper into the matter.

"Well, I should believe that other girls might be as good at art if given the chance," Sarah complained. "Why should you receive such special treatment?"

Gemma smiled at Sarah's protestation, as if pleased to have laid the foundations for this small rift. I hastened to finish the concoction I stirred, then poured out two mugs and passed them to my roommates. Sarah took a large sip before waiting for it to cool, but seemed not to mind the heat of the mulled wine.

"Oh, Mary," she exclaimed, "you must try this. It is absolutely divine."

She held her mug out to me, but Gemma placed a hand between us, stopping Sarah from moving farther toward me.

"She doesn't imbibe, remember?" Gemma returned. "We mustn't corrupt her. And in any case, she has work to complete—this wonderful sketch."

Sarah shrugged and took another sip. "More for us," she said. She finished the remainder in her mug, then refilled her cup from the pot on the stove, taking another large sip as she turned to stare out of the window. Gemma sipped her drink slowly, gingerly, staring down at the mug as if curious about its taste. She opened her mouth as if to speak, but Sarah interrupted her before she could say anything else.

"The boys are here," Sarah sang out. "Come, come, Gemma, let's not make them wait."

She and Gemma hurried to finish their dressing, donning leather gloves, woolen hats, and thick scarves. Before leaving, Gemma picked up her mug of mulled wine and drank it down quickly in large, insatiate gulps, then placed the mug roughly back upon her desk. Gemma and Sarah then departed from the room without another word or glance in my direction, ready to be free and upon the snow.

I moved to the bow window and looked down at the scene at Ronan, and at Sarah's beau, Daniel, as they helped my roommates into the carriage, their elation and excitement undisguised, on full display. I hoped that Ronan might remember I remained in that room alone while he went out with his intended, but he appeared too invested in the day's trip up to Lorain. Only Gemma seemed a bit distracted, preoccupied as she took her place in the carriage among the others. She looked up from her seat then and saw me watching from the window, locking eyes with me before I could move away from my perch.

I offered Gemma a small smile, a quick wave, but was met with only a blank stare in return, a look that left me as cold as the frigid air outside.

The day carried on as it normally would after my roommates' departure. I was grateful to be rid of their prying eyes, their disparagements, the stifling atmosphere they created in our room. In celebration, I decided to have a bit of the mulled wine left unfinished in the pot upon the stove. The wine helped me to work more easily, made my hand obey my thoughts more readily, made the sketches I created seem to come alive, to breathe, to smile at me, to serve as my companions. Before I realized it, I was quite buoyant and joyous, feeling a relief and calm I had not experienced in much time. Not wanting this feeling to dissipate, I mulled another large pot of wine, taking the last bottle from Gemma's wardrobe and finishing it without thinking, making sketch after sketch that I was excited to show to Professor Westbrook once our lessons began, sketches I knew I would soon be able to set in stone. After hours of cheerful work, and satisfied with my efforts, I cleaned the bedroom, ridding it of all evidence from my day of solitary drinking, then settled into my bed, and drifted off to sleep.

Sometime later, I was awakened by the sound of a loud banging on the front door downstairs, running footsteps, frenzied voices. My head pounded as I sat up in bed, the room spinning around me until my vision resolved itself. All was dark apart from the silver glow of the moon through the curtains, the dying flicker of a candle on my nightstand. Unease consumed me as I realized that I was quite alone, my roommates' beds empty, still freshly made and untouched since their departure that morning. The clock on the wall read well after midnight, several hours past the time they should have returned.

I heard a man's voice reverberating from the floor below, speaking in a tone unfamiliar and irate, so different from the usual soft sounds of the girls' boarding house.

"Where is she?" the man demanded, "Mary Lewis?"

My heart raced at the sound of my name, at his heavy bootsteps growing closer, ascending the stairwell just beyond my door.

"Sir, please, I'm sure there is a rational explanation for this," came Mrs. Keep's pleading voice, but it seemed that her begging was to no avail. In an instant a hand rattled my doorknob, and the man forced his way inside of my space, leaving me with no time to get out of bed, to gather my thoughts, to properly dress in anything other than my nightgown. Mrs. Keep rushed in behind him in a small and futile effort at my protection. Through the doorway in the corridor, I saw the few housemates who remained over the winter recess peering in to see the cause of the commotion.

"What did you give my daughter?" the man yelled, approaching me. I cowered in a corner of my bed, pulling the blankets up around my body.

"Your daughter?" I asked, my breath unsteady as the stranger moved ever closer, towering over me.

"Gemma Ennes," he replied, "Don't feign ignorance."

I shook my head at this revelation, having never met my roommate's father, never expecting nor receiving an invitation to her home in the time we had lodged together.

"Mr. Ennes here says that Gemma is ill, Mary. Gravely so," Mrs. Keep said, her voice steady despite her trembling hands. "Sarah Miles is sick, as well. Both girls say that you gave them something before they went out today, a drink of some kind. It would appear that they've been," she hesitated initially, unwilling to speak the word, "poisoned, Mary. The doctors say their symptoms are consistent with cantharides ingestion. It's best to just be honest now."

"I've given them nothing," I said, the words leaving my lips quickly, before I could reconsider, a primal act of self-preservation. I thought of the mulled wine I had served them, but knew I could not admit to this, as it would seem incriminating, and no alcohol was allowed in the Keeps' strict boarding home.

Mr. Ennes ignored my protestations. He moved toward my dresser and flung the drawers open, one by one, rummaging through my items, searching for any evidence of wrongdoing, throwing dresses, shawls, and corsets onto the floor, hurling profanity and epithets along with my clothing.

"Cantharides, Spanish fly," he said, continuing to toss my items about. "Where do you keep it?"

He moved next to my vanity, and then to my desk, smashing perfume bottles and mirrors, scattering my jewelry, my journals, my sketchbooks, with all manner of papers and drawings flying across the room. Dissatisfied, Mr. Ennes went to my wardrobe, flinging the doors open, and at this, I leapt from the bed, terrified at the thought of what he might exhume from its depths.

"You've no right to go through her things," Mrs. Keep said, stepping between Mr. Ennes and my wardrobe as I gathered my possessions from the floor. "Miss Lewis has stated her innocence. We must take her at her word."

"Her word?" he repeated, his face inches from Mrs. Keep's. "What should her word mean to me? She comes from a deceitful and conniving race, I see that now. I've been a fool to listen to the likes of you, the abolitionists around town. Her people are not fit to live among us. They are violent and depraved. I should have never agreed to let my daughter live with someone of her kind."

"Mr. Ennes," Mrs. Keep said, placing a firm grasp on each of his arms. "Your emotions are getting the better of you. You must remember yourself. I know you to be a good man, a Christian man, and often a supporter yourself of the abolitionist cause.

We cannot accuse Miss Lewis of such a horrendous crime without any evidence, without so much as a motive."

Mr. Ennes wrenched his arm out of Mrs. Keep's grasp. "If you won't take this seriously, Mrs. Keep, perhaps the police will. I've half a mind to ride there tonight and inform them of what's happened."

"You are well within your right to do so," Mrs. Keep returned, trying to maintain her composure. "But I must ask that now, you leave us ladies be. This is quite enough agitation for one night."

Mr. Ennes hesitated, his jaw and fists clenched, his chest still heaving with anger. After what seemed to be an eternity, he relented and turned toward the bedroom door. Before departing, he turned toward me, his face contorted, disgusted, as he stared at me.

"You won't get away with this," he said. "You'll pay for what you've done."

He walked out of the room and back down the stairs, pushing my housemates aside as he did so. The other girls lingered for a moment, whispering amongst themselves and glancing in my direction.

"Girls, return to your rooms," Mrs. Keep instructed, and the girls, after some moments, reluctantly complied. Mrs. Keep lingered in my room, her hands still trembling as she reached up to smooth her hair. I walked toward her and released the feelings I'd been bottling, crying and clinging to her desperately.

"Mary," she began, speaking slowly and extricating herself from my grasp. It was only then that I saw, despite her defense of me, that Mrs. Keep was uncertain of me as well, and perhaps even frightened by me. "These are serious accusations from your roommates, and you were indeed the last person with them before they left today. Is there anything, anything at all, that you aren't telling me? You know that you can trust me."

I hesitated for a moment, grasping for any sliver of memory from the day. Vague images appeared before my eyes, my roommates excited about a sleigh ride with their beaus, their careful selection of clothing, the primping and preening before their departure, Gemma's observance of my sketch, her request for me to mull their wine. I felt there was something else, some detail that eluded me, gnawing and persistent at the periphery of my mind.

"I'm in earnest," I insisted, feeling the sting of tears return to my eyes. "I would never hurt them. I would never hurt anyone," I said.

"Why, then, would your roommates fabricate such an accusation against you?" she asked.

I shook my head. "Perhaps they are simply mistaken. Perhaps something else, someone else, caused their illness."

Mrs. Keep sighed and dropped her head. "You should know that Mr. Ennes is a powerful man, Mary," she said, lowering her voice. "And should he take this to the police as he has threatened," she paused, drawing in her lips as if considering whether she should speak her next words, "I believe it will be best for you to secure legal counsel straightaway."

I balked at this instruction, this escalation of my situation. I felt that seeking legal counsel would seem like some sort of admission of wrongdoing, would be a move that only a guilty party would make.

"There's a man here in town," Mrs. Keep went on, before I could air my protestations, "a Mr. John Mercer Langston, who takes on these sorts of cases, usually pro bono." She moved to my desk and scrawled his name and address on a sheet of paper. "You must go to him in the morning, first thing."

I accepted the paper and read the attorney's name. Mrs. Keep placed a hand on my shoulder, then stared into my eyes as if the answer to this mystery were inscribed there, as if she might be able to read my guilt or innocence by means of clairvoyance. After considering me for another moment, and with a final squeeze of my shoulder, Mrs. Keep left me alone in my room.

I paced back and forth for quite some time after that, feeling like a caged animal. I took out pen and paper and dashed off a letter to my brother telling him of all that just occurred, knowing that he would be the only person I could truly count on to believe me, and planning to mail the letter off to him as soon as I could.

When I was certain the rest of the house had gone to sleep, when not another floorboard or mattress creaked, I went to my wardrobe and opened its doors, exhuming the wooden box I kept buried deep within, what I'd feared might be discovered by Mr. Ennes as he ransacked my bedroom. I opened the box and removed first the series of sketches I'd created in my anger, of Gemma and Sarah and the revenge I imagined I could unleash upon them. Then, I removed a folded letter, its script and prose so familiar to me after repeated readings of its contents that I might have recited the entire note verbatim. It was a letter from Ronan, sent to me shortly after our encounter outside of the Christmas Ball. He wrote of his remorse for not staying with me that night, and detailed his increasing affection for me, such affection that was starting to become, as he said, unignorable.

*Could I but think of a way for us to be together,* he'd written, *for Gemma to be removed from my life, and from yours, for us to live as we might if we were of one race, as we know ourselves to be of one mind, our contentment might then know no bounds, our happiness would be the envy of all.*

I had been shocked to receive such a note, and knew not how to respond to his admissions, and so I only hid it away for a time when I might know the right words to reply. I knew that the discovery of this letter and my sketches would seem to provide motive for this alleged poisoning, would appear to implicate me beyond all doubt. And so it was with shaking hands and held breath, grateful that these papers had gone undiscovered, I held them over the candle flame at my nightstand and watched, one by one, as they all turned to ash.

# Chapter 10

At sunrise, without delay, I sought out Mr. John Mercer Langston's law office, walking swiftly all the way, my dark shawl pulled close around my head lest any of the townsfolk who had heard of the recent accusations should see me. Attorney Langston's clerk ushered me inside quickly, looking around behind me to ensure I had not been followed there. The clerk led me into Attorney Langston's office, where I found him engrossed in a heavy legal tome, looking pensive and concerned.

"Miss Lewis," he said, seeming to expect my entrance. He closed his book and stood up. "Mrs. Keep sent word that you'd be visiting me today. Attorney Langston," he introduced himself, extending a refined hand that I shook, gratefully, in my own. "Please, take a seat," he said, gesturing toward a large leather armchair across from his desk.

I took my seat and looked around his office, noticing his populated bookshelves, the array of diplomas framed on his wall, most prominent among them declaring his graduation from Oberlin College. Noticing my observations, Attorney Langston turned and looked at the diploma himself, saying, "Yes, I'm a graduate of Oberlin College myself, as you can see," he said. "A great service they are doing our race by allowing us to attend, I suppose I should say, when so many other institutions will not. And yet, attached to such goodwill is much hardship. I'm quite aware of the sort of treatment our people must endure there to gain our education."

I nodded, thinking that hardship might be an understatement for what I was then enduring.

"Now, I've been briefed on some of the details of your case, but I'd like to hear it from you, directly," he said. "Miss Lewis, I'm going to do all that I can to clear your name of these charges, but this is going to require complete honesty on your part."

"Yes, sir," I replied, though I knew that pure honesty would be difficult.

"To begin, I'd like to ask you about the accusation made against you. Your roommates allege that you served them wine on the morning in question. Is there any truth to that?"

I took a steadying breath before answering. "Yes, that is true. I served them wine before they departed for their sleigh ride."

"They said that you did not partake in this mulled wine," he noted. "Is that correct, as well?"

"I did not drink any of the wine while my roommates were present," I said, "though I partook later in the day, after they left," I admitted. Attorney Langston did not seem shocked or upset at the admission, but only nodded his head as he continued on.

"And did you grow ill from this wine, Miss Lewis?" he asked. "The girls report that they were heaving, retching, and had difficulty breathing once they were a few miles into the trip. Did you experience any such symptoms?"

I thought of the wooziness I'd felt after imbibing so heavily throughout that day. "I had a bit overmuch perhaps, and so my head did ache much throughout the night, but nothing that would suggest a poisoning."

Attorney Langston looked up at me over the rim of his glasses after jotting this down. "Are you in the habit of drinking much, Miss Lewis?"

I hesitated, thinking of how I might soften the truth in an effort to project an image of innocence, of a young girl unused to the soothing effects of alcohol, of someone who would never go against the reigning societal expectations. Remembering I'd promised full honesty, however, I answered Attorney Langston truthfully.

"At times, yes," I answered him. "It can be quite uncomfortable, this position I'm in, the only colored girl in my classes, and living at the Keep home. Drinking is the only solace I can find sometimes, being so far away from any family of my own. It helps me to decompress."

"And yet you are aware that alcohol use is against the rules of the Keep home, and of the college, that being a Christian institution?"

"I am aware of this," I affirmed. "My roommates are, as well."

I watched as Attorney Langston wrote this down, nervous that this admission might later be twisted against me should these accusations escalate into an official lawsuit. Attorney Langston cleared his throat, then peered back up at me.

"I'd like to ask you about the nature of your relationship with your roommates, Sarah Miles and Gemma Ennes. The general belief around town is that you've harbored much resentment and jealousy against these girls," he said, eyeing me curiously. "They've both said this to their friends and family, on multiple occasions. Is there any truth to such allegations?"

"I suppose I envy them for their wealth and social status," I confessed. "I would like to have the freedom from worry that these girls take for granted."

Attorney Langston nodded, then further pursued the point. "And a certain young man—Gemma Ennes's intended—a Mr. Ronan Clarke. Miss Ennes has alleged to several friends that you might have carried on an illicit, some would say *illegal*, relationship with him. What do you say of this?"

I shook my head. "I say that it is untrue," I declared, a sudden vision of Ronan's letter flashing through my mind.

Attorney Langston stared at me, seeming not to fully believe my assertion. "Do you have any relationship with him at all?" he continued.

"He has helped me with my art, that is all," I said, hoping that my voice did not waver. "We share a passion for sculpture, and have bonded over that subject."

I watched as Attorney Langston wrote this in his journal, waiting for his next response.

"Such a detail will be quite incriminating to a jury," he said. "It would give you a clear motive for wanting to harm Miss Ennes, especially if you felt that she might have been an impediment to your relationship—however *platonic*—with Mr. Ronan Clarke."

"There are many people who might want to harm Gemma Ennes," I rushed to say. "She is an unkind person, rude to most people she meets, haughty and disrespectful, even to those in authority. She believes that her wealth and status give her a right to condescend. Her father might claim to be an abolitionist, but she comes from a long line of rich slaveholders just across the border in Kentucky. She hates those of our race, and hopes that our people might remain enslaved. She has said as much to me, directly."

Attorney Langston said nothing for a moment and only silently nodded as I spoke. "I understand this, Miss Lewis," he said. "I am quite familiar with the Ennes family, and their reputation in these parts."

He looked at me with some sympathy then, considering me for several seconds, seeming to understand fully what a strange situation I'd lived in since coming to Oberlin. After some time, he seemed to come back to the present. He glanced at his clock and went on then, apparently needing to conclude our consultation.

"My clerk, Benjamin Stewart, and I will begin building your defense, in case any criminal charges are ultimately filed against you," he said. "I'll go into Lorain and interview potential witnesses, and will speak with your roommates' physician there to get further details on their case, and to analyze any evidence they have saved from their alleged illness. And on your part, Miss Lewis," he proceeded, "is there anyone you suggest I should consult with? Anyone who might have been a witness to the scene that morning, or anyone who could testify as to the content of your character?"

I thought for a moment. Ronan was the most credible witness I could think of to attest to my character, but I feared that if Attorney Langston spoke with him, if he were asked to testify under oath in court, he would falter under cross-examination, and admit that our relationship had risen beyond anything our society deemed acceptable.

"I haven't many friends here," I said. "The housemaid Josephine was the only girl in that house I might have called a friend, and might be able to testify on my behalf as a character witness. She has been witness to many of the slights I've endured by my roommates," I said, though I knew that Josephine would not want much to do with me since my failure to defend her against Gemma. Thinking of this, I added, "She has endured many of those slights herself."

"A colored girl?" Attorney Langston asked.

"Yes," I replied. "The only other one to ever occupy the Keep boarding house."

"Is she freeborn?" he pressed, jotting down all that I told him.

I hesitated for a moment, realizing that I had never ascertained whether Josephine was free, or a fugitive, as so many of the other colored people were in her part of town.

"I am not certain," I replied, shaking my head.

"If she is not legally emancipated, she won't be permitted to serve as a witness in the Lorain County Court," he quickly returned. "Is there anyone else?"

I shook my head, thinking of Cade, but knowing that he, too, would be barred from testifying, and even if he weren't, that he would not want to defend the character of a girl who had so easily dismissed his proposal of marriage.

Attorney Langston sighed and removed his glasses, massaging the bridge of his nose in a small show of the stress he then felt.

"We have a difficult task before us, Ms. Lewis, but that is not to say it is impossible." He closed his notebook and set his pen upon his desk, then arose as if to underscore the importance of what he would say next. "You should be well aware, Ms. Lewis, that public sentiment is currently against you, and many townspeople are increasingly calling for your arrest. They are incensed that you are still walking freely through town. They say that you are a danger, and even many people in the colored part of town say they are unable to trust you, that you have conducted yourself as if you are above them, set apart from them. This being the case, I want you to refrain from socializing with anyone, anyone at all, in the coming days. You are to remain in the Keep home at all times as my clerk and I work to build your defense. If this situation is still ongoing once the spring semester begins, you are to take a leave from your classes. This is the only way that we can assure your safety until we are able to clear your name."

"I understand," I replied. In truth, I had no desire to go anywhere other than my room and sit there in safety and isolation as my roommates were away, supposedly convalescing in their homes. Where else would I go? To whom would I confide? If all thought me suspect, if so many believed me to be a criminal, I would make my home in the shadows, in solitude, as I had so often done.

# Chapter 11

I followed the directions Attorney Langston had given me, and kept myself far from my housemates and the townsfolk for many days following our meeting. I only left the Keep home for absolutely necessary errands, and to mail at the general store in the south of town my letter to Samuel, explaining my situation and the difficulties that had recently befallen me. I found that my housemates were all too eager to keep their distance from me as well, moving far away from me when I went to visit the washroom, never speaking when I ventured into the kitchen to grab a buttered roll and coffee for breakfast. So it was with great surprise that a knock came upon my door one morning a few days later as I sat quietly in my room, laboring over a sketch. I opened the door to find Mrs. Keep standing before me, her countenance concerned, her voice grave.

"Attorney Langston has been injured, Mary," she said without preamble, revealing her purpose as soon as she stepped into my room. "He was in Gemma's hometown in Lorain to interview the doctor who examined her and Sarah."

"Yes," I said. "He told me that he would go there for just such a purpose."

Mrs. Keep nodded. "It appears that Mr. Ennes accosted him outside of a shop there. He had his rifle; he pointed it at Attorney Langston and took his shot. Another man was there and saw what was taking place. He intervened just in time, pushing

Mr. Ennes's rifle up toward the sky at the very moment he took his shot. Had it not been for this man, Mary, Attorney Langston would not be alive."

This news was quite jarring, and I needed a moment to process it. Mrs. Keep allowed me this interval, then continued on.

"Attorney Langston has been quite disturbed by this event, to be sure, and is mending from a nasty fall he took after the rifle went off. He sent word to me, however, that he will be fine, and will still serve as your attorney, should your case go to trial."

I must have looked somewhat relieved then, for Mrs. Keep found the need to quickly add, "I should let you know, though, Mary, that he was unable to secure any witnesses to testify on your behalf while he was on travel," she said. "All of the townspeople there in Lorain are quite hostile to your case, and seem to stand by everything that Gemma and Sarah have said."

I shook my head, feeling quite dejected, until my mind was somewhat buoyed by a realization, clinging, perhaps foolishly, to one last shred of hope.

"Perhaps you could serve as a witness," I ventured, eagerly grasping Mrs. Keep's hands in my own. "You know my character, Mrs. Keep. I have been a quiet lodger here for these three years, and could truly benefit from your defense."

Mrs. Keep sighed and looked at me regretfully. "Mary, I cannot involve myself on either side of this," she said. "I must try my best to remain impartial in this case. Sarah and Gemma are my lodgers as well as you, and it pains me to know that they are even now suffering and trying to heal from this strange illness that has befallen them, regardless of its source. It pains me even more to know that you girls had taken to drink without my knowledge. And so no, I cannot testify in any case, for it seems there was much I did not know about the happenings in this house."

"I see," came my terse reply, as I struggled to accept Mrs. Keep's words.

"I will be away from the home this evening," Mrs. Keep said, moving back toward the door. "There will be a vigil tonight at the town square, an opportunity for prayer, for Sarah and Gemma, that they might make a full and speedy recovery and return to the boarding home soon. We expect most of the townspeople to attend. I understand that Attorney Langston has counseled you to remain here at the boarding house, well away from the broader townsfolk, and so you should, for your own personal safety." Mrs. Keep sighed before continuing. "I want you to know, though, that I will say a prayer on your behalf, Mary, just as I pray for your roommates."

I thanked Mrs. Keep for her generosity, and just as she left my room, a thought occurred to me that I could not shake. It appeared to me that I must approach Ronan, if all other hopes for my own defense had failed. I could find him at that vigil, as he must surely attend to offer up his own condolences, his own prayers, for his intended. I could tell him of my situation, and counsel him not to reveal the true nature of our relationship, to say only as much in my defense as might absolve me of the heinous charges my roommates had brought against me. Surely Ronan would consent to this plan. Surely he would be eager to help me, if he so loved me, as he had professed. Though it would mean potential exposure to danger, I knew that I had to go to the vigil straightaway. I dressed quickly and left the Keep house, heading swiftly for the town square.

A large crowd gathered at the town square for the vigil, forming a circle around a makeshift podium, each person with his or her head bowed in somber meditation, holding a candle that illuminated each face under the night sky. I lurked just beyond the gathering, my face shrouded by a dark shawl, not daring to light my face with a candle of my own. Mrs. Keep's husband, the Reverend Keep, approached the center of the crowd, then began to address the congregants.

"As we gather here to pray for the recovery of Sarah Miles and Gemma Ennes, two young ladies who lie weakened and ill, let us not allow this tragedy to wrench us yet further apart," he said, his words falling onto the somber crowd. "This country is already divided by much hatred and animosity. Let our town be an example of what can happen when forgiveness, for whatever atrocities *might* have occurred, prevails."

Mrs. Keep, standing toward the front of the crowd with her face downturned, nodded at this. She stepped forward and began to lead the crowd into song, a somber hymn with deep, wafting chords that haunted the dark night sky. I listened as the notes floated into the night air, observing each face convened there. I saw Ronan near the edge of the gathering, and I allowed the sound of the music to obscure my footsteps as I moved closer to him, as I grabbed his arm.

Ronan turned and looked down at me, startled by my sudden touch. He took me by the arms and pulled me far away from the crowd and toward the woods as Reverend Keep asked those gathered to close their eyes and bow their heads in prayer, affording Ronan and I the opportunity for a private conference.

"You shouldn't be here," Ronan whispered, leaning close to my face and still firmly grasping my arms. "It isn't safe for you here."

"I needed to see you," I began, but Ronan only shook his head, frustrated that I seemed not to grasp his import.

"People are calling for your arrest," he insisted. "They're all enraged that you maintain your liberty. Surely, they'll take you into custody if you're seen here."

"That's precisely why I've come to speak with you," I said. "I need you to defend me. You can be a character witness, Ronan, if you so choose. You can speak to the sort of person that I am, say I would never hurt those girls no matter how they might have mistreated me."

His reply, when it came, was terser than I'd expected. "I can't be involved, Mary. You know that."

"But you are involved," I returned. "Your letter, Ronan. The things you wrote to me. You are as much a part of this case as I am," I declared, not revealing that I'd burned his letter, and all evidence of his affection for me.

"If I were to testify on your behalf," he said, "it would mean the effective end of my courtship with Gemma."

I recoiled at this, shocked to hear that betrothal to Gemma remained his intention. "And so, you still mean to marry her? To make a life with someone who is attempting to ruin my own?"

"What other choice do I have?" he asked. "We have spoken of this."

"You have the choice to do what is right," I replied. "You wrote that you wanted her removed from your life, and now you shun the opportunity to do so."

He shook his head. "I'm sorry, Mary," he said, taking my hands into his to underscore his regret.

I wrenched my hands from his grasp and began to walk away, not wanting him to see the tears that threatened to fall from my eyes.

"Mary," he said, running to stop me as I moved closer to the woodlands, pulling me by the arm to slow my step. "You can't walk home alone at this time of night. Someone might see you and apprehend you."

"And now you care about my welfare?" I returned, snatching my arm from him. "I'll be fine without you," I said, ignoring his protestations, his calling after me as I fled.

I walked swiftly toward North Main Street, wiping away my tears and pulling my shawl ever tighter around my head, bracing against the winter chill. The wind clawed at me as I walked, howling in my ears, confusing my senses. I decided to take the shorter way home, through a clearing in the woods, to a field just behind the Keep boarding house, so as not to prolong my exposure to the elements, and to anyone who might mean me harm.

When I was but a few miles away from the Keep home, I heard footsteps approaching behind me, and a sudden, heavy blow landed on the back of my head, knocking me to my knees. As I tried to regain my footing, a hand gripped at my hair and pulled me by it, my body scraping against the cold ground.

"We'll take care of this if the police won't," a man said, a voice unfamiliar and low.

Before I could scream for help, before I could even comprehend what was happening to me, several men came running toward me, their faces obscured behind scarves. They grabbed me and dragged me deeper into the woods, then began leveling blow after blow against me, a series of kicks against my stomach, several sharp strikes against my skull. Blood began to flow from my head, obscuring my vision, filling my mouth. I heard the crack of my bones, the ripping of my dress from my body, leaving me fully exposed upon the cold ground. I began to lose sight and consciousness as my eyes swelled shut from the blows and the pain overtook me. The last image I saw as the night grew still darker around me, just before I succumbed to unconsciousness, was Ronan yelling and running toward me, causing my attackers to scatter and flee into the woods.

"Mary, you must wake up," spoke a voice, insistent and distraught in my ear.

I shifted in bed, a sharp pain radiating through my collarbone as I did so. I tried to sit up but could not, finding my arms could not support my weight.

"Mrs. Keep," I said, as the speaker's image resolved before my eyes.

"Take this now," she said, pulling a tincture from her apron. "Laudanum, for the pain."

I did as instructed, opening my mouth and allowing the medicine to flow down my throat, grateful for the immediate relief that began to wash over me.

"The police are on their way here. We cannot hold them off any longer," Mrs. Keep said, speaking quickly and helping to sit me up as the laudanum obscured the pain. "I've sent a messenger to notify Attorney Langston."

"The police?" I repeated, struggling in my weakness to utter the words.

"You will be safer in jail than you are here," Mrs. Keep continued, moving quickly now to get me properly dressed. "Those men who attacked you have promised to find you here if you are not arrested. They would have killed you there in the woods,

Mary, had Ronan not come to your aid, had he not brought you here." She stopped for a moment in her efforts to button my dress, staring at me gravely as she spoke. "We have done all we can to protect you. This must go to the court of law now, Mary."

Mrs. Keep paused as the clatter of horses' hooves sounded in the front yard beyond. We heard heavy footsteps, the clank of chains and manacles, and the sound of the police entering the home and ascending the stairs. As two officers entered the bedroom, Mrs. Keep stood in front of me, almost involuntarily, it seemed, not yet able to fully relinquish her role as protector.

"Step aside now, Mrs. Keep," the first officer said. "Let's not make this more difficult than it needs to be."

Mrs. Keep complied, and the officer grabbed me by the arms, standing me up.

"Mary Lewis," the officer said. "You are hereby placed under arrest for the poisoning of Miss Sarah Evangeline Miles and Miss Gemma Abigail Ennes."

The second officer pulled my arms behind my back, placing manacles about my wrists, then fetters about my ankles, causing me to writhe in pain as he did so, my body still mangled and sore from the attack.

"You must not handle her so roughly," Mrs. Keep yelled, taking another step toward the officers. "Can't you see that she's incapacitated? She is not, she *cannot*, resist her arrest."

"Mrs. Keep," the first officer said, impatiently. "You must just stand back now. You will be able to see her when the hearing is called. Until that time, she will remain in our custody. We will determine what is best for her until then."

Mrs. Keep ignored this instruction and further wedged herself between me and the officers.

"Mrs. Keep, if you do not obey, we'll have to take you into custody, too, for obstructing an arrest," the officer yelled. "Please, do not let it come to that."

At this, Mrs. Keep stepped aside, allowing the officers to carry me forcibly out of her home. Several townspeople had gathered outside to gape at the scene, some of them cheering at my arrest, hurling insults and epithets at me as the officers secured me in the back of their wagon.

The officers transported me across rough roads that jostled me, that exacerbated my injuries, to the county jail, where I languished in a cold and solitary cell for much time, where my wounded and broken body bonded itself back together as best as it could under the unforgiving circumstances, and without much nourishment to aid in that purpose. Attorney Langston was himself still convalescing after his own injuries, and so he had no means to meet with me while I sat in that county jail. After what seemed to be an eternity imprisoned there with no one to consult, with no comfort or help, the day arrived when I was led in chains to the courthouse, where I would receive my final judgment.

# Chapter 12

THE COURTHOUSE WAS OVERCROWDED WITH TOWNSPEOPLE CURIOUS to see how my case would proceed, to get a glimpse of me, the monster who had lived among them for all that time. I scanned the crowd and saw Ronan, and Sarah's own beau, Daniel, seated amongst the spectators. Up high in the rafters, in that section designated for people of my own race, I saw Josephine and Cade seated together, sharing intermittent whispers between them, both looking grave, perhaps in disbelief that my life had come to such a wretched state. I saw my brother, Samuel, as well, seated there in the colored section, looking down at me with such concern that it reinforced my own fears of what might happen that day. Samuel had arrived, Attorney Langston whispered, only that morning, having endured difficult travels from California to be with me in my time of need. I only hoped that Samuel might have been there for me sooner, might have never sent me away to Oberlin College to be an example, when what I truly needed was his protection, and to have never left my home in New York.

I looked away from the crowd then, too nervous to continue meeting their eyes. I felt small and insignificant before them all within the capacious depths of the courthouse, feeling like the edifice could have easily consumed me, ingesting me whole. I found myself wishing that it would, as I sat at the wooden table next to Attorney Langston and Benjamin Stewart, mere feet from the prosecution, from the presiding Judge Rutherford who was elevated before us all, seated at his bench. The prosecuting attorney and his team were all seated and staring in my direction, with Sarah Miles sitting nervously among them. Attorney Langston leaned in close to me, beginning to tell me what I could expect from the hearing.

"No matter what they say of you," Attorney Langston whispered, "no matter what lies and abuses they hurl against your name, you must sit in silence," he said.

I nodded my understanding and leaned in to make a reply, but was suddenly interrupted as the judge began to read my charges aloud, two counts of attempted poisoning with a deadly substance.

"In the case of *Ohio v. Mary Lewis*, how does the defense plead?" Judge Rutherford called, disinterestedly beginning the hearing.

"Not guilty," Attorney Langston declared, standing and speaking for me.

The judge looked up over his glasses at me then, fixing me with a stare so disdainful I thought he might convict me in that moment, without delay.

"I now call the prosecution forward to present opening arguments," Judge Rutherford said, and the prosecutor stood to take his place before the bench.

The prosecutor, Attorney Elmer Woodford, glanced briefly at the notes he held in his hand, then tucked them into his pocket, seeming to believe he would fare better without relying on them.

"Oberlin was once a safe town," he began, looking first at Judge Rutherford, and then out at the townspeople seated in the gallery. "Students could attend Oberlin College without fear of violence, could learn and socialize without any threats of physical harm. But then it seemed that this safety, this certainty, was insufficient for that class of people called abolitionists, called progressives. They would not be happy, would not rest, until they had upended our system, and brought the Negro into our town."

The townspeople all murmured together at this, each seeming to have a strong opinion on this point that needed immediate venting, until finally, Judge Rutherford brought them back to silence.

"At first, it was believed, in the naïveté of the abolitionists, that these colored people would be grateful for such largesse, would assimilate, would work hard and keep quiet in this new circumstance. Mr. Jacob Ennes certainly believed as much, and even agreed to allow his daughter, Miss Gemma Ennes, to live with just such a colored girl who moved into this town. You might notice now, Judge Rutherford, that Gemma Ennes is not present with us, and that is because she is ill, Your Honor, too gravely ill by act of poisoning to be here today."

Attorney Woodford took a breath, then continued on. "Today, Your Honor, you are going to hear about a friendship between three young ladies, born in the first blush of youth, that has gone terribly awry. You will hear about the deep jealousy harbored by the defendant, Mary Lewis, and the way this jealousy manifested in a most malicious and wicked act, the very act of attempted murder by the poisoning of my two clients, Sarah Miles and Gemma Ennes, two innocent doves who never expected such an action from their supposed friend. This is the story of a stranger in our midst, of an untrustworthy young woman who managed to fool and blind all of those around her to her true intentions. This girl," he said, then pointing directly at me, "has come here and disrupted our way of life, our community, our safety. With your wise and able mind, Judge Rutherford, you will decide the appropriate fate for a woman of such questionable standing."

Had Attorney Langston not counseled me to do otherwise, I might have spoken out and defended my own name right away, so incensed was I at Attorney Woodford's characterization of me and my actions. In a moment, Attorney Woodford returned to his seat, and Judge Rutherford called for our own opening statement. Attorney Langston stood up without looking at me, appearing to be quite nervous, seeming not to know where to place his hands. His voice shook as he began to speak, and he cleared his throat several times before commencing his opening argument.

"Honorable Judge Rutherford," Attorney Langston intoned, finally meeting the judge's eyes, "I stand before you as a man who has been tasked with the great job of defending this young woman seated just behind me, Miss Mary Lewis. The power will ultimately lie in your hands as to whether you exonerate her of the heinous charge of attempted poisoning, or whether you will believe the story of Miss Lewis's supposed jealousy and betrayal of Miss Miles and Miss Ennes. I see in you, however, a certain discernment, a refinement of the senses, and I believe that you will ascertain which story is true, and which party is innocent, and will see that this case need not escalate beyond this hearing, that it is not necessary to go to trial."

Attorney Langston took a deep and steadying breath, then continued on. "My client, Miss Lewis, has lived a life of unusual circumstances, yes, being born free, orphaned and raised in part by Ojibwe aunts at Niagara Falls, then attending an abolitionists' school in McGrawville, New York, and now living under the ever-loving hands of the Reverend and Mrs. Keep, those cornerstones of Oberlin society with whom you are, in your own way, familiar."

Attorney Langston paused for a moment and looked to where the Keeps sat out in the gallery before continuing. "In all of those years, Miss Lewis has never had a charge like this brought against her. In all of those years, she has been an upstanding member of her society. Should a young lady like this not have the opportunity to gain an education, to make friends, to forge a family like any other? Must such odious and contemptible charges stop what is sure to be a long, successful, and happy life? We are all, those born free in this country, guaranteed life, liberty, and the pursuit of happiness, and it is that liberty today that I bid you preserve. I ask that you do not ultimately decide to punish a young woman for an act that she did not commit. I thank you for your time as you listen to the arguments today, and for your wisdom."

With that, Attorney Langston returned to his seat beside me, seeming to physically deflate after completing such an arduous task. His hands, I noticed, were shaking nearly as much as my own.

"Excellent work," Benjamin Stewart said, leaning close to Attorney Langston. Attorney Langston nodded his head and looked down at his papers, shuffling through them, still seeming unsteady, and unable to fully agree with Benjamin Stewart's assessment of his work.

Judge Rutherford called for the prosecution to present their primary witness, Sarah Miles, for her testimony, and cross-examination. It had been decided by the prosecution, apparently, that Gemma would not speak before the court, as she was still, supposedly, too unwell for such exertions, as Attorney Langston explained to me. I watched as Sarah made her way to the stand, walking slowly and deliberately with the help of one of the assistant prosecutors. This appeared to me an act of absolute theater, as her cheeks were full of color, her blue eyes still bright, and her auburn hair just as thick, curly, and shiny as if she had missed not one meal, not one nutrient, in the past few weeks. She was sworn in on a leatherbound Bible, took a deep breath, and faced the court as the prosecution began her interrogation, pelting her with small questions, quite simple, and handily answered. I hoped that Attorney Langston would not let her off so easily.

"Please," Attorney Woodford said, "state your name for the jury."

"Sarah Evangeline Miles," Sarah said, speaking much softer than I'd ever heard, an affectation, I thought, given her usual mischief, her loud joking and laughter, the crass language she'd often employ when we were alone in our room.

Attorney Woodford nodded. "And are you currently a student at Oberlin College, Miss Miles?"

"Yes, sir, I am," she answered.

"If you please, tell the court about your admission to that school," Attorney Woodford said, stepping aside so that Sarah could more easily be seen by all those gathered in the gallery.

"Well, I was admitted four years ago, in 1858. This is my senior year, you understand, and I was looking forward to completing my studies this year, though my circumstances over the past few weeks have caused me to take an unfortunate leave of absence." Sarah paused, looking off wistfully, another move that appeared to be rehearsed. "I was to be the first lady in my family to receive a college degree. It's such a shame that there should be any delay in that goal."

Attorney Woodford hesitated, seeming to allow this last remark to resonate with the courtroom. "And have you maintained high marks since your time at Oberlin?" he asked, after a moment.

"Oh yes, sir, I have," she answered. "Straight As since I've matriculated."

"Straight As, quite impressive. And have you maintained a social life in addition to your studies, Miss Miles?" he asked.

"Yes, I have many friends, Mr. Woodford. There is hardly a young lady at Oberlin that I could not count among them."

I nearly scoffed at this lie, thinking of all the girls my roommates had teased and tormented in the years that I had known them. Attorney Woodford continued his examination.

"What sorts of activities would you engage in with your friends?"

"Oh, all sorts of activities," Sarah said, seeming wistful, giving a slight smile and looking off into the distance. "We loved to go to the state fair, and to parades. We loved to dance, and to go for long walks together, and go for sleigh rides," she said. She paused for a moment, seeming to summon, to forcefully will, a pair of tears to fall from her eyes.

Attorney Woodford passed Sarah a handkerchief, and Judge Rutherford shifted in his seat, furrowing his eyebrows in deep care, before Attorney Woodford went on.

"And you did, at one time, consider Miss Mary Lewis to be one of those copious friends?"

"Yes, sir, I did at one time," Sarah said, keeping her eyes trained on Attorney Woodford, though I thought she might look toward me in that moment.

"Miss Miles, now, if you please, tell us about the day you first met Miss Mary Lewis."

Sarah sighed, hesitated, then began to speak. "I first met Mary Lewis on an autumn day in 1859. She had just arrived in Oberlin, and had moved into the Keep boarding home, where I live during the academic year. I thought at that time we might become close friends."

"Was there any sign then that Miss Lewis was jealous of you?" Attorney Woodford pursued.

"Objection," Attorney Langston interjected, so loudly that I shifted in my seat. "Leading the witness."

The judge peered at Attorney Langston contemptuously for a moment before he confirmed, "Objection sustained."

Attorney Woodford smiled, ever briefly, seemingly amused by Attorney Langston's efforts. He took a moment to collect himself, then asked, "What was Miss Lewis's behavior toward you in those early days of your acquaintance?"

"She was quite complimentary toward me in those early days, always telling me that she loved my hair, coveted my dresses, marveled at the freedom with which I moved through Oberlin society."

I sat in disbelief at how easily she lied, at how she rattled off this catalogue of words I had never spoken as her testimony continued.

"She asked me to show her around, and to teach her how to be a lady in this society, in the way that I was."

Attorney Woodford nodded and folded his arms behind his back. "And did you trust Miss Lewis?"

"Yes, wholeheartedly," Sarah assented. "In those early days, I did trust her."

"Was there any point when that trust began to shift?" Attorney Woodford questioned.

Sarah resituated herself in her seat. "There were times when I grew suspicious of Miss Lewis's behavior. She had a drinking habit, for instance, something I think she might have picked up back in New York. She always desired to have wine, or whiskey, and would often ask me and Gemma Ennes to help her procure it. I always told her no, and reminded her that alcohol was strictly forbidden in the Keep home. She would grow quite angry with me, so angry that I began to feel afraid."

My breath grew shallow as I listened to this lie, as I remembered the many days that it was Sarah herself who pressured me to join her in drinking.

"And she would exhibit strange behaviors, quite strange, Attorney Woodford," Sarah continued, unprompted. "I would catch her sometimes staring at me, or at Gemma, and sketching our likenesses down into her notebook. One evening, I perused one such notebook when Mary was asleep, and I found horrid images within, depictions of me and of Gemma in terrible situations. I couldn't sleep for some time after I saw those pictures, so fearful I was for my own safety. I began to feel that Mary Lewis was a bad person, a dangerous person, and I believe she was taught to be so, while at her previous school, learning such radical ideas from the likes of Henry Highland Garnet, and others like him. I read about that institution one day, and was horrified at what I saw, at what Mary Lewis had been taught there."

Attorney Woodford gave another moment for Judge Rutherford and the gallery to take this in, then pressed on. "Tell me about the events of January 27th of this year."

"Well," Sarah began, sniffling and dabbing at her nose with a white lace handkerchief. "It was quite an exciting morning. Gemma and I were going on a trip to Lorain, where we were planning to go on a sleigh ride with our beaus, Ronan and Daniel. Mary hadn't been invited, as she didn't have a beau to accompany her, and she had been quite incensed about this for some days. On the morning we were set to leave, however, she seemed cheerful, and invited Gemma and I to have a warming beverage before we departed."

"And did Miss Lewis give you this warming beverage, Miss Miles?" Attorney Woodford pursued.

"She did, indeed," Sarah said. "We thought she might offer us tea, or a mug of coffee, but it was a substance much harder than either Gemma or I expected. Mary gave us mulled wine, and she guaranteed that it would keep us warm on our sleigh ride. She directed us to drink, and so we did. We drank the mulled wine that she made us, and not a moment has gone by since then that I do not regret my actions." At this, Sarah began to cry, and she allowed the tears to remain on her face, not taking the time to wipe them away.

"Did Miss Lewis drink any of this mulled wine herself?" Attorney Woodford asked.

"No, she didn't," Sarah said, between sobs. "Gemma and I both found that quite strange at the time, but Mary insisted that she had too much coursework to complete to drink any wine herself."

Some of the townspeople shifted in their gallery seats, the creaking of the wood beneath them filling the courtroom.

"And what happened after you drank this wine, Miss Miles?" Attorney Woodford continued.

"We left for our sleigh ride. Our beaus came to meet us, and we got into a carriage with them, and we set off toward Lorain. Sometime after we departed, both Gemma and I began to feel sick. Ronan stopped the carriage, and Gemma and I began to retch. This lasted for at least ten minutes, and we grew so weak that it became clear we would not be able to engage in any of our planned activities."

Attorney Woodford stopped as Sarah's crying grew still more insistent.

"Are you able to go on?" he asked.

"Yes, sir, I think so," Sarah responded, before dabbing at her eyes.

Attorney Woodford continued. "What did you all decide to do next?"

"Ronan and Daniel made the decision to continue on toward Lorain, to Gemma's hometown, believing it would be best for us to convalesce at home. We rode to Gemma's parents' house, and there, our illness grew far worse. Gemma's father called for their physician, who asked what we had eaten that day, for fear of food poisoning. We told him that the only thing we had consumed that day was the mulled wine that Mary made for us."

Attorney Woodford looked indignant at this point. "And what did the physician say about that?"

Sarah took a deep breath, then said, "He told us that our symptoms were consistent with cantharides poisoning, and there was a very high likelihood Mary Lewis had placed that substance, better known as Spanish fly, into our wine."

Attorney Woodford stopped and placed his hand upon the witness stand, as if needing to steady himself after this last point.

"And I must ask you one more question, Miss Miles, and thank you, as you have been very brave thus far," he said. "How long were you sick after ingesting Miss Lewis's mulled wine?"

Sarah sniffled and tilted her head. "We were sick for several weeks, Mr. Woodford. We couldn't eat a thing. We came quite close to death, in fact, as we lost so much fluid that both Gemma and I reached a state of extreme dehydration. I grew disoriented. I could hardly even recognize my parents. Gemma is still on the mend, you see, or else she would be here to seek justice, even now. It is only by the grace of God that I sit before you today."

Attorney Woodford tapped the stand, nodded his head definitively, and said, "No further questions."

At this, Judge Rutherford called Attorney Langston forward for cross-examination.

Attorney Langston approached the stand, cleared his throat, and straightened his suit jacket.

"Miss Miles," Attorney Langston began, still appearing quite nervous, "you have stated before the court that Miss Lewis had a drinking habit. Had you ever tasted any alcoholic beverage before meeting Miss Lewis?"

Sarah paused and looked toward Attorney Woodford, who only shut his eyes briefly for a moment, then gave Sarah a curt nod.

"I had tasted wine before, of course," she averred, then quickly added, "but only in the act of Communion."

"And had you ever tasted whiskey before, Miss Miles?" Attorney Langston pressed.

"Objection," Attorney Woodford said. "Asked and answered. Miss Miles stated that she had only tasted one alcoholic beverage before, that being wine."

Judge Rutherford nodded his head. "Objection sustained."

"Let me ask a different question, then, if I may," Attorney Langston persisted. "Had you ever observed any other of your friends, or perhaps your beaus, imbibing alcoholic beverages before?"

"Well, yes," Sarah said, haltingly, "at dances, sure. But only those who were of legal drinking age, and only men. None of the ladies I knew ever drank any alcohol. No lady, that is, except Mary, if she can be called such."

Attorney Langston looked down, folded his hands behind his back, and paced for a moment before posing his next question. "Why, then, did you so readily agree to drink the mulled wine you say Miss Lewis offered you on January 27th?"

Sarah shook her head profusely. "I did not readily accept that wine. She pushed it on me, she practically forced it down our throats," Sarah said, looking toward me. "She said that it would warm us, that it would make our sleigh ride more fun. She said that we would—" With this, Sarah dissolved into tears, blubbering through the rest of her sentence. Judge Rutherford scowled at Attorney Langston over his spectacles, as if daring him to ask another question to further distress this helpless young woman.

Attorney Langston felt this shift in the room among both the judge and the townspeople gathered in the gallery behind him. He sighed, stopped his pacing, and said, "No further questions."

I came to feel, with this unpropitious start to our hearing, that it was all theater, an absolute spectacle, and that my fate had already been decided long before I set foot in that courtroom. This feeling only grew stronger with each subsequent witness that the prosecution called forward, from Mr. and Mrs. Miles, to other friends of the Miles family, and finally, to Sarah and Gemma's physician, Dr. Knoxley. Each cross-examination came to the same end; the townspeople seemed to grow incensed by the very presence of Attorney Langston before the witness stand, abhorring the sight of this colored man who dared to question the words spoken by these white witnesses. But Attorney Langston pressed on through that long day of witnesses the prosecution presented, indefatigable, undaunted, resolved.

When finally the time came for the defense to present our own witnesses, to begin our rebuttal of the charges brought against me, I watched as Attorney Langston leaned in close to Benjamin Stewart, whispering a few words to him. These two deliberated for some moments, and then, to my surprise, Attorney Langston ripped in half the sheets of paper on the desk before him, then approached the judge with no notes, no safeguard. Attorney Langston then spoke words that shocked me to my core.

"There is no need for me to present any rebuttal, nor any such witnesses, Your Honor, for there is no justification to hold my client any longer within this courtroom. Through all of the prosecution's testimony over the preceding several hours, there has been no presentation of the necessary evidence, required by law, for this trial to continue, and that is the evidence of poison in the stool or stomach samples from the plaintiffs. The corpus delicti has not been proved. With no such evidence having been preserved nor presented, it is thereby unlawful to hold my client any longer for questioning or trial."

Members of the public gallery erupted into noise, and began to shout out at Attorney Langston, calling him a snake, a cheat, and a liar, and many other epithets. Attorney Langston only stood solemnly before the judge, awaiting his comment.

"Order," Judge Rutherford called, the sound of his banging gavel reverberating throughout the room. "I will have order in my courtroom," he said again, raising his voice, though the whisperings and surprise continued to ripple through the courtroom.

Judge Rutherford took off his spectacles and leaned his head against the back of his hand for a moment, seeming utterly exasperated by Attorney Langston's words. Finally, after a delay of several moments, he said, "I will now take some time to consider both sides of this case, as presented to me. The court will stand at recess for one hour. We will reconvene at three o' clock. Will the prosecution and the defense convene with me in my chambers?"

With that request, Attorney Langston, Benjamin Stewart, Attorney Woodford, and his fleet of clerks all followed Judge Rutherford into his office, while I was escorted by the bailiff into a holding room, where I was to sit in solitude as the deliberations went on without me.

How long that one hour lasted, an interval that in happier times might have seemed but a mere second. I had never heard of corpus delicti, and had no idea that Attorney Langston was going to make such a brazen statement in my defense. Indeed, I did not even know that the legitimacy of a hearing could be questioned in such a way, and while I sat in that empty holding room with only the bailiff's stern gaze upon me, I meditated over the words that Attorney Langston had spoken, and prayed that my trial would, in fact, be dismissed due to this total lack of evidence of the charges brought against me.

At the end of the hour, I was escorted out of the holding room, and we all returned to our seats. I tried my best to ignore the murmuring crowds behind me, to focus only on the judge and what verdict he would read.

Judge Rutherford looked down at his papers for several moments, shuffling them, seeming conflicted and reluctant to speak his next words. After some time, he began to speak, slowly, but with much force.

"It is the opinion of this court, based on the lack of evidence presented by the State, and failure by the Prosecution to present the burden of proof, that the case of *Ohio v. Mary Lewis* is hereby dismissed."

A collective gasp overtook the courtroom, a sudden flurry of voices, of protestations began to fill the vast space.

Judge Rutherford banged his gavel against a wooden block, trying vainly to quiet the courtroom. "The defendant may exit the court," he said, standing up at his bench, relinquishing the effort to quiet the room.

I watched as Attorney Langston sat up straighter in his seat, his eyes wide in evident surprise. I leaned in closer to him, looking to confirm that I understood the judge's import.

"So, this means that I'm—" I began, but Attorney Langston finished my sentence.

"Free, Mary. You're free. Your case has been dismissed."

I couldn't control the emotion that sprang up at this revelation. I embraced Attorney Langston, who seemed surprised at first by the gesture, but then began to accept it, and embraced me, as well. As he did, I looked over his shoulder, seeing the undisguised anger on the faces of the townspeople there gathered, the pointing and clear plotting beginning to take place. I looked up toward the rafters, and saw my brother rise from his seat, beginning to push through crowds to come and meet me. I looked, then, to where Josephine and Cade had been seated, but saw that they were gone, and in their wake were only several others from the southern part of town, looking just as incensed at Judge Rutherford's determination as the white members of the courtroom, as they all seemed to feel that I had somehow gotten away with a heinous act. Attorney Langston seemed to notice this anger as well, as he broke from my embrace, and urgently turned to his clerk.

"We must leave, now," Attorney Langston said, speaking quickly. "Benjamin, we'll go to your home. Mary, your brother can join us at that location. No one else will know to look for us there. Prepare your wagon," he told Benjamin, and as soon as an officer removed the fetters from my wrists and ankles, Attorney Langston hurried me out to the awaiting transportation.

# Chapter 13

We gathered around Benjamin Stewart's kitchen table as his wife, Violet, brought us food to help sustain us after such a long day. I could not bring myself to touch anything, though I had eaten but very little since my time in custody, and was beginning to appear, I knew, emaciated and weak.

"You must have something, Mary," Violet pleaded, passing me a bowl of soup and a mug of tea. "You are still quite unwell. You need something to steady you."

I took a small sip of tea to appease her, and she, seeming pleased with the effort, returned to the kitchen where she continued cooking for us.

Samuel stared at me for a moment, a look of concern upon his face. He hadn't stopped staring at me since we'd been reunited there in Benjamin Stewart's home, almost as if he didn't recognize me in my weakened state. Finally, Samuel took my hand.

"I'll never forgive myself for what has happened to you here," he began. "I should have known better than to send you away. I only wanted you to have all of the advantages I never had, that our people can so rarely expect in this country. I could see how smart you always were, how special, and I didn't want that to go to waste. I didn't want that knowledge of squandered potential to fester within you, to corrode your spirit, as my own lost potential has so often corroded mine." He took a breath, then continued. "But that day at the train station in New York, before you left to come here to Ohio," he paused, not wanting to revisit the memory, but endured, "I should have listened to you. I should have kept you safe, and by my side. I should have called it all off then."

"There is no need to dwell on such matters now," I replied, pushing soup around in my bowl, without making a move to consume any. "We cannot change the past. The worst is behind me at this point, I do believe."

Attorney Langston turned to me then, wanting to disabuse me of this notion. "It won't be safe for you to stay here in Ohio now, Mary," he said. "The townspeople are still convinced of your guilt. They'll be furious that you've gotten by on what they consider a mere technicality, and we've already seen what their vigilante justice entails."

"Next time, they won't let you get away alive," Benjamin added, in case I hadn't understood Attorney Langston's full meaning.

I looked down at my cup of tea and shook my head, hopeless at this idea. "Where could I go?" I asked. "I haven't completed my studies, and there's no other school that will allow me to enroll. I won't be able to finish what I've started anywhere else, and I don't want the work I've done so far, and all that I've endured to get it done, to be for naught." I shook my head, hardly able to stand the idea that I would have to leave my studies, but more importantly, my art, if I needed to flee from Ohio.

"Your safety is more important than your degree," Samuel remarked.

"And just where in this country can I expect to be safe?" I asked, my tone sharp, though my voice was still weak. "I'll only be safe if I pretend to be subordinate, uneducated. Wherever I go I'll be treated as a servant, if not a slave. Without my degree, I'll only be able to find work as a housekeeper, if even that, and I know too much now, I've experienced too much of life to ever be happy in that sort of role."

Samuel sighed, seeming to understand this, and took a moment to think. "We could send you back to northern New York, to Niagara Falls. Though your aunts have relocated, you still know the terrain and the expectations of that area."

I shook my head. "That would be a step backward."

Samuel appeared to grow exasperated, though he tried not to show it. "It would be a step toward your safety, Mary," he said. "You can find work there. You can go back to selling your wares and souvenirs to tourists by the Falls. There are still many people there whom we know, and can help to get you reestablished."

I persisted. "That isn't the sort of work I want to do any longer."

"Then what do you suggest?" Samuel asked, growing impassioned. "What sort of work do you think you can do?"

I hesitated a moment, nervous to make the suggestion. "I can make a living as an artist."

Samuel scoffed and pushed back from the table, the legs of his chair scratching terribly against the floor. He stood up and walked away, as if the suggestion were too ludicrous to even merit a response. I continued speaking quickly, afraid of completely losing my audience, as even Attorney Langston and Benjamin Stewart seemed skeptical at the idea.

"Other women have done it before me," I asserted.

"But have any colored women ever made a living that way?" Samuel asked. "You truly seem to have forgotten your station in this country. Perhaps I have done you a disservice by sending you to live and learn among the white race. You seem to delude yourself, to think yourself one of them. How can I ever expect to keep you safe now if you choose to—"

"Wait, Samuel," Attorney Langston interjected. "Let's consider this for a moment. The abolitionist circle back east is always looking for new representatives. They have colored writers, orators, debaters, even those who work solely as agitators, but they don't, as yet, have any artists. I know many abolitionists in Boston, for instance, who would readily welcome a new face."

Benjamin shifted in his seat, then clasped his hands before

his face, seeming to descend into a deep rumination. "But will they accept her as a representative?" he finally asked.

My brother and Attorney Langston both turned toward Benjamin, seeming surprised by the question, though I expected it, and understood immediately the implication.

"The abolitionists back east will want someone pristine to represent their cause," Benjamin continued. "We've got to earnestly understand that. Regardless of the acquittal, Mary's reputation is tarnished by this case—"

"Her reputation *here* might be tarnished," Attorney Langston said. "Her reputation as Mary Lewis of Ohio."

We listened intently as Attorney Langston went on, clarifying his case.

"What if she became someone different, someone pristine?" he asked. "What if she created work so magnificent that it eclipsed all other details of her life? What if she served as such an integral part of the abolitionist cause that this work became the only news story that papers want to carry pertaining to her?"

"And if it's safety that I'm after, I'm sure these townspeople would be unable to pursue me all the way to Boston," I added, feeling increasingly confident in the idea.

Samuel took a moment to consider the proposal. "How would we get her there?" he asked. "I've exhausted my own funds on her tuition, and her stay at the Keep house was being subsidized. I wouldn't be able to afford a move that far, to a new city, a new abode, on my own."

"I'll send a letter of introduction to Garrison in Boston. He runs *The Liberator* newspaper there," Attorney Langston said. "He is known for providing help and shelter to all sorts of people in need. We can tell him that Mary is looking for work as an artist in town, after leaving New York Central College. He is familiar with the school, and will know that it has shut down. He will be happy to help any of its former attendees. We needn't tell him of the past few years you've spent here in Ohio."

I nodded, thinking it an irony that my deficient former school would serve such a critical purpose in my new life.

"In the meantime," Attorney Langston continued, "Mary must remain here, at the Stewarts' home, where she can live and continue to convalesce in safety. Violet can go to the Keep house and pack up her things. We'll send Mary forth to Boston as soon as we hear back from Garrison. We mustn't delay."

I struggled to sit up straighter in my chair and began to speak, almost involuntarily. I thought of Ronan, I thought of Cade, I thought of Josephine, all of these people with whom I had relationships that, though fraught, I was not yet ready to leave.

"That doesn't give me any time to bid farewell to—" I caught myself before speaking any more, before revealing any information that might lead to a long line of questioning. "Anyone here."

Samuel looked at me curiously, evidently wondering what friend or acquaintance I might have remaining here after the scandal of the case.

Attorney Langston seemed not to notice the small exchange, as he had already procured a sheet of paper and pen. He began writing his letter to Garrison, working quickly, furiously without a moment to waste. He stopped writing, suddenly, as a thought seemed to occur to him, and he turned to address me.

"What name should I use for your introduction to Garrison?" he asked. "It won't do to have you easily identifiable as Mary Lewis, if anyone discovers you have moved there from Oberlin."

I considered this for a moment, understanding this to be a critical decision, but knowing that I had not much time to make it. I considered selecting an Ojibwe name, in homage to the mother I never knew, to the aunts I had lived with for so much of my childhood. I wondered if a return to Wildfire might be appropriate, the name I'd been forced to part with all those years ago, but felt I was so far from that previous version of myself that it would no longer suit me, and would not fit with the sort of identity I wanted to reflect while in Boston. I then thought of a name that might honor my father, and my brother, perhaps Samantha or some other feminized version of their names. My middle name had always held some meaning for me since those

Baptist ministers had bestowed it upon me, and I felt like it might belong to a woman who was strong, who was independent and uncompromising, and so it was this name that I finally spoke to Attorney Langston, after ruminating over the question for a pause.

"Edmonia," I told Attorney Langston, with a certainty that surprised even myself. "Tell Mr. Garrison that my name is Edmonia Lewis, of New York."

# Part II

# The Stranger

## 1863–1865

# Chapter 14

I thought I might feel revived by the commotion of Boston's streets, that some measure of calm might be mine within its shroud of anonymity. Instead, my fears seemed to be compounded by the bustle of the city, as I expected each passing pedestrian to place a rough hand upon my shoulder, to arrest me, accuse me, assault me yet again, and this time finish the job, leaving me bloodied and breathless on the cobblestones. No enjoyment could I find in the vistas of my new home; the beauty of the Charles River, the height and majesty of the city's buildings were as bitter herbs to me, as mere breadcrumbs thrust at a starving beggar who would need far more to survive. With some effort, I made my way to *The Liberator* office on Cornhill Street, and knocking upon its door with a trembling hand, was ushered inside by a woman who introduced herself as Maria Weston Chapman, whom I perceived, through the fog of my anxiety, to be a personage both kind and industrious.

"Mr. Garrison will see you in his study," she said, leading me down a long corridor of separated offices, each room with an occupant immersed in some act of reading or writing or declamation. I envied their sustained focus, the singular purpose for which each seemed perfectly suited, and hoped that here in Boston, I might find a similar cause with my art.

Upon entering Mr. Garrison's study, I found him consumed by some letter, turning its pages and examining it closely. He seemed not to notice me initially as I stood before him, so engrossed was he by this letter, mumbling aloud to himself as he perused its pages. It took some time for me to realize that he was reading a letter pertaining to me, until I noticed that I formed the subject of the words he read aloud.

"'You will find, as I have, that Miss Lewis is possessed of a great latent ability, and that with some instruction, some honing and refining of her instinctive talents, she will be an asset to the abolitionist cause, and a tool for the liberation of her people.'" He set the letter down on his desk, and finally fixed his eyes upon me. "So it is that you come with high praise, if John Langston's letter is to be believed."

I demurred, not knowing how to acknowledge such commendation. "I fear that Mr. Langston has set your expectations far too high."

"Shyness won't do at this establishment, Miss Lewis. Timidity might be considered a recommendation in high society, but it is a hindrance here, at *The Liberator* offices. If nature has bestowed upon you a gift, you must use it, without apology."

"Yes, sir," I replied, taking the seat he then pulled out for me.

"Mr. Langston says that he knows you from your days at New York Central College. That institution has closed down some years ago. How have you occupied yourself in the intervening period?" he asked.

I took a moment before responding, mentally rehearsing what I should say. "I returned to my aunts by Niagara Falls," I said, hoping the lie was not legible on my face. "They are of the Ojibwe, a wandering people, and so I was never in one place for long."

This answer seemed sufficient for Mr. Garrison, and he continued on. "Life here in the city will be quite different for you, then," he said. "We live and work in close quarters, without the wilderness or broad space to which you might be accustomed. Will that be a problem for you?"

"Not at all," I replied, and then added, in truth, "I have been desperate for a change."

He nodded, pleased by this response. "That is good to hear," he said, "as you must have a certain level of endurance to live in this city and do this kind of work, the difficult labor of abolitionism. You must have an iron resolve that cannot be broken. Do you have that, Miss Lewis?"

"I do," I averred, thinking of all I had endured in Oberlin.

"And if your very life is threatened for doing this work, as mine and so many of *The Liberator*'s editors have been, will you remain committed to this cause?"

"Fully," I answered, without delay, as my very life had already been threatened for far less.

"Many say that I am a radical, Miss Lewis, that I am a violent person," he declared.

*Many say the same of me*, I thought, but dared not speak, as a vision of the Oberlin townspeople and their hatred toward me flashed through my mind. Mr. Garrison went on.

"Association with me and my paper might alienate you from some of the less progressive members of this cause. Are you prepared to handle that?"

"I am prepared to devote myself entirely to the abolitionist cause, come what may," I said, definitively. "I am not afraid of alienation, as I am not afraid of the threat of death, and indeed, have been to death's shores before, and found only relief and tranquility there."

"Then you will be in good company here indeed," Mr. Garrison said. "But not all will be bad or difficult here, Miss Lewis, I should say. Many have found some measure of fame and distinction through *The Liberator*'s pages. We might not claim a circulation as broad as some other periodicals, but we do quite well in disseminating our message. Frederick Douglass and many others, though they might forget it now, got their start right here with my paper, and are handsomely remunerated now for their efforts. The same sort of pay might come to you, if you'll stay the course. Now, your art—"

Before Mr. Garrison could complete the thought, someone

knocked on the frame of his open door and entered before receiving a response.

"William, my apologies. I didn't know you were with company," a woman, tall and dignified, seeming sure of her station and her right to intrude, said, as she walked still farther into the room.

"Mrs. Child, please, come in," Mr. Garrison responded. "No apology is necessary, as I'm glad for you to meet this new arrival to Boston. Miss Lewis, please meet Mrs. Lydia Maria Child," he said, as I stood to greet her. "Edmonia here is a former student of New York Central College, and a friend of John Mercer Langston, whom she met during her time there."

Mrs. Child shook my hand. "So, Mr. Garrison here has recruited another young lady to the cause. He's known for being a true friend to women as well as the colored race. I was just coming by to deliver some new literature for the women's rights movement, as it happens," Mrs. Child said, placing several pamphlets upon Mr. Garrison's desk, then continued speaking to me. "Will you be joining *The Liberator* as an editor?" she asked. "These pamphlets could use a keen eye before publication."

"She'll be joining us as an artist, Lydia," Mr. Garrison said. "John Langston says that she has quite the latent ability."

"Does she indeed?" Mrs. Child replied, giving me a kind glance. "And what is her medium?"

"No less than stone, if she is up to it," Mr. Garrison returned. "She needs only an instructor to help hone her talents."

"Then I know just the person," Mrs. Child said. "A Mr. Edward Brackett of Winchester, though he keeps his art studio here in Boston. An eccentric character, to be sure, but I know him to be of great skill."

Mr. Garrison nodded his head in familiarity with Brackett's name, and seemed to approve of the suggestion. "Brackett has sculpted all the great men of the abolitionist cause," he said. "His bust of John Brown is quite impressive. He went down to Virginia to meet with Brown before his execution. Sat with him in his jail cell to get his countenance correct. Risked his own life, just for his art. Brackett is the genuine article, alright," he said, jotting his address on a sheet of paper and handing it to me. "A wonderful recommendation, Lydia."

I felt thrilled at the possibility of learning from such a man, and began to feel, then, that perhaps my fortunes might truly turn here in Boston, a city where a colored girl might dare to remake herself, to advance her station, to shake off the fetters of her past.

# Chapter 15

Edward Brackett's studio was on Tremont Street in Scollay Square, where many other artists found their quarters, and a certain feeling of creative potential pervaded the air. For the first time in weeks, I felt my spirits begin to revive, buoyed by the prospect of a reunion with my beloved practice. I rapped upon Mr. Brackett's front door and heard some shuffling within, some clattering, some cursing, and finally, a heavy footstep approaching the spot where I stood.

Mr. Brackett opened the door abruptly, then looked down at me with some annoyance.

"I've already donated to the Freedmen's Fund," he groused, and shut the door.

His brusqueness not sufficient to extinguish my hope, I took a breath, rallied my spirits, and knocked again.

He opened the door again and pursued, with much exasperation. "I said that I've—"

"Mr. Brackett, my name is Edmonia Lewis," I began, before he could again shut me out. "I believe Mrs. Child sent word that I would be visiting you?"

Mr. Brackett stopped then, seeming to consider me fully for the first time, and said, somewhat dejectedly, "Oh yes, my new pupil."

He sighed and opened the door a bit wider for me to enter, though without uttering, I noted, an express invitation to do so.

"I'll have you know that I'm no teacher," he said, as he moved farther into his studio. "And I'm not exactly thrilled at the prospect of an interruption to my own practice. But I owe Mrs. Child more than a few favors, and it seems that you now rank among them. You may sit just there, and observe me, and take notes. I will brook no questions as I work, but might answer one or two at day's end, if I feel so inclined." He thrust toward me a notebook and pencil, then took his seat at a work in progress.

As I sat, I recognized across from me the bust of John Brown I'd heard Garrison mention, and I extended my fingers to feel that great work, to perhaps, by induction, gain the measure of skill to create something similar.

"You must not *touch* anything," Mr. Brackett snapped, turning to me. "I will send you home with what materials remain when my day's work is done, and you can practice creating your own sculpture, in your own space, but nothing so monumental as John Brown. You are not yet fit to sculpt the visage of a man so great. You will work on simply molding a bit of clay to begin with, perhaps fashioning it into a hand or a foot. In some weeks' time we will see if you are prepared to work with stone."

It was indeed a small lump of clay Mr. Brackett bestowed upon me at day's end, with instruction to return in the morning with the likeness of a foot, and nothing more. Far from being discouraged by so lowly an assignment, I felt thrilled to have some purpose, a reunion with my art, the first I'd had since my clandestine lessons with Ronan all that time ago, and since my work with Professor Westbrook was thwarted before it could commence.

I had taken as my lodging there in Boston a colored boarding house run by the Howard family, a friendly assemblage of fellow freeborn black people who were eager and delighted to welcome me into their space. It was there that I brought the spare clay and sculpting tools that Mr. Brackett gave me at day's end, and there that I planned to quietly complete my assignment, one that I believed would be quite simple, as clay was much easier to manipulate than stone.

In my room as I worked, my roommate, Addy Howard, watched me closely. Though she was a sweet girl, a bit younger than I, she bothered me quite as a smaller sibling would, as she was always too attentive to my doings, too curious about my interests.

"What is that?" Addy inquired, as I placed the spare clay and dull sculpting knives upon my desk.

"Art materials," was my terse reply, "for sculpting."

"What are you making?" she asked, coming yet closer to my workspace.

I bristled under such interrogation, and felt as if my roommate's gaze transformed into insects crawling upon me and burrowing into my skin. How I wished that she would leave me to my practice, and would find her own pastime to occupy her.

"A foot," I replied, as I sliced into the clay. "I am fashioning a foot."

She watched me for some time as I worked, leaning in close and blocking my lamplight.

"Perhaps you could shape a bit of bone just there," Addy said, leaving an impression in the clay as she pointed her finger into it. "See, here, look at my foot," she said, removing that member from a silk slipper and placing it upon my desk. She wiggled her toes before me and pointed, instructively. "Shaping something like that might make it look more realistic."

I stopped working for a moment and tried to calm myself before considering her. "Addy, I would appreciate some solitude as I complete my work," I said in a hushed tone, proud of the patience and restraint that I showed, when all I wanted to do was scream for her to leave me alone.

Addy threw her hands up in mock surrender. "Alright, understood," she said, retreating from me and going to her side of the room. "No need to yell," she added, despite the fact that my tone had been measured and quiet.

These interruptions from my roommate notwithstanding, I managed to complete Mr. Brackett's assignment, and proudly brought it to his studio first thing in the morning.

"What is this?" Mr. Brackett asked, as he unwrapped the clay sculpture I presented to him.

"A foot," I answered, confusedly. "The foot you told me to make."

"That is no foot," Mr. Brackett replied, in a low monotone. "At least nothing a human would claim. You must try again."

He gave me another hunk of leftover clay at the end of his day's work, sending me to my lodging yet again with the instruction to fashion another foot. I felt some small annoyance at this, as I knew that my work was not so bad as to be indecipherable; after all, I had worked in stone before, had been offered tutelage by an art professor, no less. I wanted to say as much to Mr. Brackett, to tell him of my previous accomplishments, but I knew that to do so would reveal too much of my past, and so I swallowed the retorts, and again completed the assignment he gave me.

"This is somewhat better," Mr. Brackett proclaimed the next morning, turning the newly fashioned clay foot over in his hands and observing it closely. "Perhaps passable enough that you are ready to sculpt a hand."

Yet again, Mr. Brackett produced a small block of leftover clay, this time somewhat bigger than what he had given me before. He gave me sharper sculpting tools, as well, and sent me home to begin the work. Several weeks and many attempts passed before he pronounced the sculpted hand acceptable, and gave me my next assignment, to sculpt a nose out of flint, a stone hardly more durable than clay itself. I did not voice my vexation at this, did not say that I could at the very least work in steatite, as I had done before. I only took the flint home, the small hammer and chisel he gave me, and worked at sculpting a nose, late into the night.

"That hammering noise is unbearable," Addy yelled from her bed as I worked. "How can you expect anyone to sleep?"

I ignored my roommate and continued my work, as even her incessant interruptions could not diminish my determination, nor sink my buoying hopes.

After some time, as I expected, Mr. Brackett pronounced the sculpted nose acceptable, and gave me a larger assignment, to sculpt two ears out of steatite, an endeavor that took many weeks of attempts before Mr. Brackett approved of the work.

Mr. Brackett and I began to have a certain rapport as the months progressed, a certain language comprehensible to only us two. I began to somewhat enjoy his crankiness, his curmudgeonly manner, and strangely understood his exasperation at my constant questions, my need to know more about our craft of sculpting. He simply wanted to be left alone with his art, knowing that no amount of time could be sufficient to produce the works that he envisioned. I experienced similar artistic sentiments, and Mr. Brackett and I came to bond over such feelings. He seemed better able to see the talent in my art as we grew closer, and trusted me with larger pieces, more detailed assignments. Mrs. Child visited us frequently in those days, seeming quite invested in my progress, hopeful that the teacher she had assigned me was helping as expected, and bringing with her Mrs. Anne Whitney, a fellow sculptress who would often comment upon my work and offer helpful advice.

"This work is quite good, Edmonia," Mrs. Whitney said, closely scrutinizing one of my latest pieces—a cameo profile of Abraham Lincoln—during one of her and Mrs. Child's frequent visits. "Even I struggle to fashion a profile so realistic."

"Thank you, Mrs. Whitney," I said. "That means quite a lot, coming from you. I find great inspiration from your own work, in fact," I added. "Your sculpture, *Ethiopia Shall Soon Stretch Out Her Hands to God*, is magnificent," I said, thinking of Mrs. Whitney's latest piece, a tribute to enslaved women. "I hope to one day make something quite like it."

"And so you shall," Mrs. Whitney replied. "If Brackett here ever allows you to sculpt the female form," she commented, observing our workspace. "It seems that those sorts of pieces do not have much of a place in this studio."

"If it is a thriving career that Edmonia wants, she must work to perfect the likeness of great men," Mr. Brackett said. "And so she has done with this medallion of Lincoln."

Mrs. Child nodded then, taking up the subject. "It is true that the general public seems to prefer sculptures of men," she said. "In fact, I believe I know of someone who would be interested in purchasing just such a piece," Mrs. Child added, taking the Lincoln cameo into her hands and turning it over.

Mr. Brackett nodded and leaned in close to me. "You should listen to Mrs. Child, Edmonia. She's quite connected in this city. She knows all of the folks in the market who purchase art."

Mrs. Child smiled at this assessment of her reputation. "I'd be happy to serve as an agent of sorts, for you," she said, looking at me, "as you begin to advance in your art."

Mr. Brackett laughed. "What she means to say is she could be a mother of sorts," he said. "She is always looking for a surrogate daughter, this one."

Mrs. Child did not laugh at this, only nodded, with some gravity. "I could be that to you, as well. I have no children of my own, and would be glad to provide you with the sort of maternal care that you might not have, and that I could not give to my own offspring."

Mr. Brackett continued to speak in a teasing tone, saying, "Only be aware that Lydia might expect total obedience to all of her orders, as any mother would. To go against any of her wishes would certainly be a catastrophic idea."

I took note of Mr. Brackett's advice, but still, I told Mrs. Child that I would quite appreciate her help, and would gladly sell my art to any patron willing to buy, to any customers she could procure.

Mrs. Child, evidently pleased by my response, left the studio then with Mrs. Whitney, and I continued my work with Mr. Brackett, and accepted another assignment from him, this one a depiction of the philosopher Voltaire, one that I was to complete in granite, the hardest stone he'd directed me to work in, thus far. He gave me much better and sharper sculpting tools to execute the task, and I began my work on this sculpture, straightaway, as soon as I returned to the Howard residence.

One morning, a few weeks later, as I brought back the bust of Voltaire in granite that Mr. Brackett had directed me to make, he took some time to study the work, then finally spoke the words I thought I might never hear him say.

"This face, Miss Lewis, is excellent," Mr. Brackett finally said. "Better than anything you have created before, even more skilled, I might say, than your cameo of Lincoln. I dare say that now, you are quite ready to work in marble."

And with these words, I entered into a new state of jubilance, and embarked upon a new phase of my artistic career.

# Chapter 16

Sleep evaded me for weeks after that triumphant day in Mr. Brackett's studio, as if fate sought retribution for the mere morsel of joy I dared to find. One night in particular brought terrible dreams, visions of a cloaked figure pursuing me, of the attack back in Oberlin that had left me but a shadow of my former self. When I awoke, pain radiated through my collarbone, almost as if it had been broken once again, and I tried to stifle the wail I emitted in the night.

"Bad dreams last night?" Addy asked the next morning, as we sat together at breakfast.

"Did you hear me?" I inquired.

"Dare say the whole house did," she returned. "What were they about? I'm a great interpreter of dreams."

I knew better than to reveal the true source of my troubles, and so I evaded the question, hoping my inquisitor might mercifully drop the subject.

"Well, we'd better set your mind on a different course today, in any case," she said, after some time spent eating her breakfast. She crunched into a piece of toast and smiled, her joviality as ever magnifying my woes. "Would you accompany me to the Fifty-Fourth Regiment parade through the town square this afternoon?"

I had heard of this regiment, the first of the war to allow colored soldiers to enlist, led by the son of the Shaws, a prominent

Boston family, but I had little interest in leaving my room and my art to see them, and relished the prospect of an afternoon alone to work.

"I will have to decline your invitation, Addy. My craft yet beckons. Mr. Brackett wants me to finish a new bust by Monday's lesson."

"Nonsense," Addy returned. "You've been cooped up in this house for weeks. Can't possibly be good for your health. This parade is sure to lift your spirits, and give you brighter images to reflect on in the night. You will come."

Not having the energy for a quarrel with my roommate after a night of such little rest, I assented, and we quickly finished our breakfast, dressed in our most festive attire, and departed for the parade.

The streets were festooned with American flags and pennants and banners, all waving merrily in the cool spring air. Confetti rained down from balconies and windows, creating a veritable storm of reds, whites, and blues among the crowds. A marching band played a triumphant tune, the sound of trumpets and drums bouncing off of the cobblestoned lanes, reverberating through my body. I had to admit that, indeed, I began to feel my spirits lift, and cheered for the regiment along with the other spectators, enthralled at seeing my own people appearing so distinguished, so purposeful. Colonel Robert Gould Shaw led the charge, riding upon a chestnut steed, his family calling down at him from a high balcony along the way. Colonel Shaw's men marched close behind him, all aligned in neat rows, their steps exact and united. I scanned each face, appreciating the pride upon their countenances, the confidence in their gaits.

And then, in an instant, all seemed to grow silent around me. The air itself seemed to still, time to halt. I saw, among the marchers, Cade Bronson, looking just as striking and determined as I remembered him in Oberlin. In an act so rapid I doubted its reality, Cade looked over at me once, then again, as if trying to confirm what he had seen, as well. Without thinking, acting entirely on impulse, I began to push through the crowds, elbowing spectators aside as I moved, trying to keep apace with Cade as he marched.

"Edmonia!" Addy called after me as I ran. "Edmonia! Where are you going?"

But I was already well on my way, and could offer Addy no reply. She caught up with me a few blocks later, and grabbed at my arm to stop me.

"Addy, where are they headed?" I asked, still distractedly staring at the regiment, not allowing Cade to leave my line of sight.

"To the seaport," Addy said, seeming confused by my question. "They're departing for battle in South Carolina at day's end."

Without waiting to hear another word, I parted once again from Addy, and ran toward the seaport, not stopping until I reached the spot where the regiment ended their march. The soldiers then congregated in a tavern overlooking the water, all men seeming relieved to have reached the end of that spectacle, and ready for a steadying beverage. I made my way inside the tavern, one of only a few women in that establishment, with most of the others serving as barkeeps, pouring drink after drink for the soldiers.

"Cade Bronson," I said, slowly, as I approached him, as if speaking his name might cause him to disappear, exposing him for the apparition I believed him to be. Cade, for his part, stared at me for some time before speaking, seeming to experience an equal shock at beholding me. As his figure became more real to me, I began to fear that he might still harbor much resentment against me from our time in Oberlin, from my refusal of his marriage proposal, and he might not want to speak to me, even after all of this time. When finally he did speak, however, after beholding me for some time, his words were kind, his voice and manner gentle.

"I never thought I would see you again," Cade said, leaning in close to my face. "Mary, you must take a seat," he said, producing the barstool beside him. "You must stay with me for some time, before my regiment leaves. You are the first familiar face I've seen in months. What'll you have?"

"A beer is just fine," I replied, taking my seat.

He ordered the drink for me, then took my hand in his reflexively.

"What are you doing here in Boston?" I asked, trying to deflate the tension, to return us to the present moment. "And in Union blues, no less?"

"I came all the way from Oberlin to volunteer for the military," Cade replied, still looking at me strangely, as if remaining in disbelief of my reality. "Many of us did. I told you I would fight in this war."

"And so you will," I responded, still speaking slowly as I struggled to process this reunion. "I want to say that I am glad you've enlisted, but I fear this would be a falsehood. This war has only grown bloodier, Cade, and more dangerous, especially for a colored soldier—"

"The Confederates have vowed to execute any Negro man they see in uniform," Cade interjected, finishing my thought. "But only after torturing him, first."

"A lowly, unmarked grave would be your final home," I said, to reinforce the point.

"But my spirit would rest well knowing my death was an honorable one." He considered me for a moment before again taking a sip of his own drink. "You'll forgive me for asking why you concern yourself so over my death. You are not my wife. You would be no widow."

"Am I not your friend?" I asked. "At least, was I not your friend at one time, long ago?"

"My friend only, and nothing more. Even our friendship I hold in question, for what sort of a friend would leave Oberlin without a goodbye, with no address where I could write to you?" he asked, scrutinizing me. "I worried myself sick thinking about you after your troubles there in Ohio. Josephine did, too. You've traversed half the nation, Mary, and it's only thanks to Fate that I've found you now."

I shook my head and looked deeper into Cade's eyes to ensure he understood me. "Boston was the only place I could find some modicum of safety after all that transpired," I said, lowering my voice upon breach of this subject. "I couldn't stay in Oberlin, not when the majority of that town wanted me dead. Even among our own people I could hardly find a supporter."

Cade raised his eyebrows and took a long drink of his beer, seeming reproved by that last note. I pressed on.

"I've found good people here in Boston, Cade, who want to help me. And on that point, I am Edmonia in this city. You mustn't call me Mary any longer."

Cade seemed to understand the gravity of my words. "Edmonia," he said. "Edmonia has risen from the torment of her past."

"You are much changed, as well," I said, a bit embarrassed by his tone, his great regard for me. "A greater self-possession is now yours it seems."

"I suppose I have the army to thank for that. Colonel Shaw suffers no fools. He has turned this mere fugitive into a warrior. We've had several months of training, time to grow accustomed to our arms, our power. Had I then, in Oberlin, the strength that I have now, had I then the weaponry that I have now . . ." He hesitated a moment and looked off before speaking again. "Those roommates of yours might not have run you out of town so easily."

I shook my head and looked down at my hands. "Let us not speak of those times, lest we be overheard," I said. "Those are matters which concern Mary, but to Edmonia, they hold no significance."

"Edmonia," he repeated then, dropping the sensitive subject, and seeming to grow more accustomed to my new name. "So, it seems your regard for me has changed along with your name. I might venture to repeat a certain question I asked you some years ago, to see if your answer to that has changed, as well."

I could hardly respond to this, as his candor, his rupture of the silence we seemed to maintain around that subject, subdued me.

"I claim a greater salary now, Edmonia, and though it might

be less than some soldiers receive, it's more than I ever dreamed I could call my own," he said, continuing on, his voice level and earnest. "I might be entitled to some benefits at the end of this war if the Union claims victory and I make it out alive. I could give you a real home, a proper one, with space even for your own studio in which to work. We could make our home here, in Boston, if that is what you want. You wouldn't need to choose between your family and your art. I could support it all."

Such earnestness Cade's eyes held as he spoke, such kindness was then in his face, that I nearly agreed to be his wife at that very moment, to forsake all delusions of a life without him. I hadn't realized how lonely I'd been in Boston, living as a relative stranger among the city folk, constantly afraid that someone would find out about my past, and would hate me for it. Yet here was someone who knew all about my past, and loved me all the more for it, understood me more deeply than anyone in Boston ever could. I sat there for a moment longer, feeling Cade's warmth, his genuine regard for my well-being, before he spoke yet again.

"Surely it is no coincidence that we have seen each other again, here, halfway across the country," Cade pursued. "Surely you would not ignore what Providence seems determined to make you see."

I held Cade's hands tightly in my own, looked deep into his eyes, and avowed to him that this vision of our potential life he presented was perfect in my mind.

"At the end of this war, we will become man and wife," I said, forgetting all aspirations toward my art, thinking only of the happiness I might find with Cade, a contentment I would not again lose. Cade nodded and smiled, placing his head against my own.

"You will be my wife, Edmonia Lewis," he said, again and again, as if repeating the words would make them feel more real in his mind, "as soon as this war is over."

We stayed in that tavern for quite a while after that, speaking only to one another, catching up on all that had transpired, all that had changed while we were apart. We spoke until Colonel Shaw announced that it was time for the regiment's departure, and Cade had no choice but to take his hand from mine, and obey his colonel's command. Cade told me, before he left, that he would come back to me. He promised he would return.

# Chapter 17

Cruel Sunday, that began so sweetly, meeting me fresh and expectant in the dawn, ignorant of what was to come. Some months had passed since the Fifty-Fourth Regiment had gone into battle, and yet I still clung fiercely to the reunion I'd had with Cade, to the promise of marriage we'd made each other, and had been cheered by the prospect each day since his departure. Had I known what horrors awaited me on that particular Sunday, however, I might have remained in bed. I might not have awoken with a song in my heart, might not have harbored such optimism for the day, might not have attended that usual church service with Addy, where we would gather with others to pray for our soldiers, to pray for our nation.

Addy and I stood together in our regular pew, hymn books open in our palms, though we had memorized the songs we sang, and hardly needed to glance down. Verses from the "Battle Hymn of the Republic" then filled the sanctuary, the organists' chords loud and decisive, as if by his very playing he might produce that desired Union victory. The organist struck his final, triumphant notes, the sound reverberating through the sacred space, mingling with the angelic sound of our voices as we proclaimed God's truth to be marching on, as we invested our trust in those simple lyrics. The church doors flew open then, and a young boy, no older than eleven or twelve, came running down the aisle, his arm raised with a note in his hand. He approached our pastor, then whispered into his ear, passing him the note. Pastor Hinton accepted it and read, his face growing pallid, an ashen gray, before he took his place at the pulpit.

"You may be seated," Pastor Hinton intoned, and we all complied, looking toward each other as if to confirm this sudden change in the pastor's demeanor. The pastor lingered there for a long moment, looking down at his podium, though not seeming to see what was before him, not appearing to read the words in his open Bible, but instead searching the air for the appropriate words to speak.

"Today's sermon was to be on David's victory over the Philistines, a triumphant story that I hoped would boost our own morale as the war rages on," he said, so quiet that we congregants all strained to hear him. "But it seems that such an address, such a message of victory, would be inappropriate for this service." Pastor Hinton took a moment to breathe, looking down at his hands tightly gripping the podium. "I've just received word that the Fifty-Fourth Massachusetts Regiment, led by our own beloved Robert Gould Shaw, has been defeated at Fort Wagner in South Carolina."

The congregants commenced to speak amongst themselves, and even Addy turned to the young lady beside her and exchanged a few sentences, but I only sat in silence, awaiting the pastor's next words.

"It seems, if the word I've received is correct, that more than half of that battalion has been killed in action," Pastor Hinton continued, "and many others are now missing, presumed dead. Colonel Shaw himself is among the deceased."

Pastor Hinton then further unfolded the paper that young man had handed him, and proceeded to read off a list of names of all those soldiers who were confirmed deceased or missing and presumed dead, and I felt my heart cease its beating as he read the name I dreaded to hear: Cade Bronson.

Addy turned to me then, but I continued to look forward, as if meeting her gaze would make the pastor's words real. She began to speak to me, but I felt as if someone had covered my ears, as if I were underwater, or buried beneath the earth, for her words sounded distant, obscured, illusory.

"Oh, Edmonia, I'm so sorry," Addy whispered, grabbing my hand. "You and Cade only just reunited. The plans you two had. The life you might have lived together."

There came a ringing in my head, a sharp and dissonant noise that I could not shake, as Pastor Hinton spoke again. "May we bow our heads in prayer for those fallen soldiers," he said, "and for the Shaw family, as they work to process and accept this news."

No comfort could I find in the days following that news. I sought guidance from Pastor Hinton, from Garrison, from Mrs. Child, and Mrs. Whitney, and the Howard family. I wrote to my brother without divulging too much of my personal connection to the news, only saying that the Fifty-Fourth Massachusetts Regiment, that historic battalion that meant so much to us all, had been decimated. Even Samuel's response could not help me, for he only said that death was guaranteed for us all, and that I should be glad these soldiers died in the service of emancipation. I tried to convince myself that somehow, Cade might still be alive, though he was presumed to be dead, that somehow, Pastor Hinton's list of names was incorrect, but even this was no comfort, as I could not harbor such a delusion, such a denial, for long. I soon realized that my only recourse would be my art, and so I went to Mr. Brackett's studio with a revived passion, a singularity of purpose. We crafted bust after bust, copies of John Brown, of General Grant, of other heroes of the Union cause, but none of these seemed to assuage the pain I felt.

"I'd like to make a sculpture of Colonel Shaw," I finally said one day, after much deliberation.

Mr. Brackett paused and looked at me. "Colonel Shaw?" he asked. "That would be . . ." He hesitated, considering the best word to help me understand. "Inadvisable."

"No other subject will do," I replied. "I see him constantly. He visits me in my dreams. He is haunting me, tormenting me. He wants to be immortalized, and I do believe he wants me to do it.

Sculpting him, letting him live in stone, is the only way to rid myself of these terrible visions."

It was true that I'd been tormented by visions of Colonel Shaw, but more than him, of course, it was Cade's own visage that appeared before me each night. I knew, however, that Mr. Brackett would never allow me to sculpt a man unknown to him, a colored man, in a material as expensive as marble, and so I did not even broach the topic. I felt that if I could simply sculpt Colonel Shaw, I would release some of the anguish that I could not otherwise seem to shake.

Mr. Brackett sighed and looked down at the table before which he then stood. "Colonel Shaw has only just deceased, Edmonia. His family is still grieving. It won't do to worsen their pain by crafting an image of their son, without their blessing."

I persisted, shaking my head, and speaking more quickly. "I must create this sculpture, Mr. Brackett. You can't imagine what the Fifty-Fourth Regiment meant to me, to all of my people. You cannot deny me this project."

Mr. Brackett sighed. "You must speak with Lydia Child about it, then," he said. "She is quite close to Colonel Shaw's mother, Sarah Shaw, and can speak with her about this potential project. If both Sarah and Lydia approve of the idea, I will help you to sculpt Colonel Shaw. But if either of them disapproves, Edmonia, then we must close the subject."

Knowing that I could not delay this work, lest I be driven mad by my nightly terrors, I broached the subject with Mrs. Child that very day, rushing to her home and proposing my idea to her with a rapidity that communicated its urgency. I explained all that I had told Mr. Brackett, and told Mrs. Child that I believed I could create a worthy sculptural tribute to Colonel Shaw, one that communicated the importance he held for my people.

"Absolutely not," Mrs. Child said, definitively, hardly moving from the spot where she sat in her study. "I will not even bother the Shaw family with such a preposterous idea. You have but an unpracticed hand. Colonel Shaw deserves immortalization by an artist with much more skill than you can yet claim."

I pressed on, undeterred. "Perhaps if I could just speak with his mother, Mrs. Sarah Shaw, about it myself, she would—"

"You will do no such thing," Mrs. Child interjected. "Sarah Shaw is yet mourning, and I will not have you interfering with her, or her family. You are but a stranger, a nonentity to them, and you will not disturb such a distinguished family."

I stepped closer to Mrs. Child, to the fire she sat beside, warming herself in her study. "Mrs. Child, Colonel Shaw means quite a lot to me, more than you can imagine. He volunteered for the Union cause when he need not have done it. He had his wealth, his Harvard education, his powerful family. And yet he sacrificed himself for the cause of my people."

"Surely you don't think you are alone in those feelings, Edmonia. He means as much to this whole city, as does his family," Mrs. Child said. "They will want, and do deserve, quite a monument to their son. We will all await such a work by a true artist, and in the meantime, you will speak no further of the idea. You will allow the Shaw family, and this city, to mourn a man so great, and in due time, someone prominent will cast his likeness into stone, will create that worthy monument."

But despite Mrs. Child's commands, despite the fact that she expected me to obey her, to treat her with the deference that I should a mother, I could not await this monument to Colonel Shaw, nor could I drop the idea that I would be the first artist to immortalize him in stone.

I went to Mr. Brackett's studio first thing in the morning, my determination having only grown by Mrs. Child's rejection.

"Mrs. Child had given you permission to create this sculpture?" Mr. Brackett asked in disbelief, as I dressed in my apron and took up my sculpting tools.

"Not in so many words," I admitted, still preparing for my work.

"And yet you defy her," Mr. Brackett said, watching me in disbelief as I sat before a block of marble.

"I can do nothing else," I said. "Mr. Brackett, you understand an artist's need, an artist's very compulsion, to give life to those visions which plague us."

Mr. Brackett took a step toward me and held his hands behind his back, breathing for a moment, as if for strength. The bond we had forged over our many months working together helped him to understand me and my artistic yearnings, and it was from this understanding that he next spoke. "Then you will create this sculpture of Colonel Shaw," he said. "But you are to speak no word of it to anyone as you work, least of all Lydia Child. She will be quite upset with me if she knows that I've facilitated such a work, without her permission, and I don't want to risk my own place in Boston society. You will work diligently on this sculpture each day, and upon its completion, if we deem it a worthy piece, we might allow it to be seen. If the sculpture is strong enough, Lydia Child, and indeed, Sarah Shaw herself, will see why you needed to create it, and will approve of your efforts."

I commenced to work on this sculpture of Colonel Shaw, to pay tribute to this great man, and transitorily to honor my beloved Cade, who had labored under Colonel Shaw's command. After the space of some months, I had produced a bust that, while falling short of my unreachable goal of sheer perfection, was still, I deemed, quite impressive.

Mr. Brackett seemed to agree with my assessment of this piece. "If Lydia Child could see this, she would understand why you needed to make it."

"I want her to see it," I replied. "And Mrs. Anne Whitney, too, since she is a sculptress, herself. She has encouraged my art over these many months, and may be proud to see how far I've come." I hesitated a moment, then spoke again. "I want Mrs. Sarah Shaw to see it, as well."

Mr. Brackett nodded, but sighed, seeming reluctant. "You know that Lydia won't be pleased to see that you've disobeyed her," he said. "No matter how good this sculpture might be, she will scold you. It may be that she'll do much worse to me for allowing this transgression."

"I understand that," I said. "But it's a risk we must take, for this work cannot just be hidden away. I am proud of what I've done, here, and believe that Colonel Shaw would be, as well."

Mr. Brackett finally relented, seeming to understand that I would not abandon the idea, and in a week's time, he welcomed Mrs. Child, Mrs. Whitney, and Mrs. Shaw into his studio, with the express purpose of viewing my sculpture of Colonel Shaw.

The day to reveal my sculpture finally arrived, and my heart raced as I heard the ladies' footsteps at Mr. Brackett's doorway. Mr. Brackett welcomed, first, Mrs. Child and Mrs. Whitney, who each embraced me in turn, eager to see what sort of work was so urgent as to require a formal invitation to Mr. Brackett's studio. Mrs. Sarah Shaw entered next, a beautiful and elegant woman, her societal stature evident in her fine dress and gentle manners. I introduced myself to her, quietly, nervously, and thanked her for taking the time to view my latest work. Finally, when no more stalling could be permitted, Mr. Brackett revealed my Colonel Shaw sculpture from beneath its shroud, and we all stood silent for quite some time, until finally those three ladies began to walk closer to the sculpture, circling it, scrutinizing its every feature and facet.

"So, this is what was so necessary to create that Edmonia needed to disregard my words," Mrs. Child finally said. "She shouldn't even be working in marble yet, Brackett. You can see that as well as I. She is not good enough to be working with material so expensive, and depicting a man so great. You should know, Sarah," Mrs. Child added, turning to Mrs. Shaw, "That I expressly advised against Miss Lewis creating such a sculpture."

"Lydia, I believe it is quite good," Mrs. Whitney interjected, as Mrs. Shaw still silently observed the sculpture. "Can't you see the spark in his eye, just here, as Robert Shaw always had, and the care Edmonia has taken with his expression? Take it from me, that is no easy feat to accomplish, when working in stone."

Mrs. Shaw continued walking around the bust, completing a full revolution, then placing a cheerful hand upon it before speaking. "Miss Lewis has captured his soul, indeed. That is my boy, my own son," she said, and stopped speaking as her voice broke on the last words.

Mrs. Shaw's emotion seemed to quell, at least for the moment,

Mrs. Child's anger at my insubordination, and we remained in Mr. Brackett's studio for some time after that, well after the sun had set, as Mrs. Shaw shared memories of her son, and recited lines verbatim from the many letters he had sent her during his time in combat. Finally, seeming to have exhausted the subject, or at least herself, Mrs. Shaw said that it was time for her to depart, and Mrs. Whitney said the same.

"You will come to speak to me, at my home, in the morning," Mrs. Child said, in a low and stern voice, pulling me away from the others as they said their goodbyes at the doorway. "At nine o'clock, just after the breakfast hour. Do not be late."

I went to Mrs. Child's home the next morning as directed, walking swiftly, feeling nervous and unmoored all the while. I found her in her library, quietly reading a novel, not looking up from that book as I knocked on her open doorway.

"Sit," she said, upon my entry, without so much as a hello.

I complied, taking the overstuffed seat at the fireplace across from her. She was silent for some time, still reading, or pretending to do so, slowly turning the pages of her book. Finally, I could take the silence no longer.

"You might have found a kind word to say about my Colonel Shaw sculpture, Mrs. Child," I said. "Something encouraging about the work I've done."

"I saw nothing in that work to encourage," Mrs. Child retorted, shutting her book closed with some force. "I warned you not to embark upon such a momentous task, but you did it anyway. You've wasted your time, and Brackett's marble, besides. I suppose you won't be happy until you've offended every Brahmin family here in Boston."

"Mrs. Whitney approves of it," I said. "And as she herself is a sculptress, surely her approval holds much merit. Mrs. Shaw approves of the sculpture as well, and it is a depiction of her own late son. Why can't you approve of my work, if they can?"

Mrs. Child sighed in clear annoyance. "Because it is not worthy of approval," she said, raising her voice, losing all pretense of composure. "Sarah Shaw was being polite, Edmonia, do you not understand that? You have put her into an impossible position by creating that sculpture of her son. She won't be able to find anyone else to complete a better memorial to him, now." Mrs. Child looked down at me curiously, and somewhat cruelly, as she added, "I don't know what you were taught at your previous school, in your previous life there in New York, but your behavior as of late has been quite cruel, and impudent. I will not readily stand by and allow you to act this way."

"It seems that nothing I do is ever good enough for you," I said, growing quite agitated myself. "And why is that?" I pursued. "You claim to be a friend of my people, you claimed that you would be a friend to me, and yet all you ever give me is condescension."

Mrs. Child bristled at this, and stood up from her seat, then moved to the door. "I believe we have said all that is necessary, Miss Lewis, and now, I must ask that you leave my home."

I followed her to the door, then turned to face her, wanting to apologize for my insolence, to better explain myself, to ask for forgiveness, but all I saw in Mrs. Child's countenance was coldness. I left without a goodbye.

The following week, when I came for my usual art lesson with Mr. Brackett, I found his door locked, the curtains of all his windows closed. I knocked upon his door, calling out for him, quite embarrassed to be making such a scene there at his doorstep, on the street and in view of all the bustling pedestrians. After some time, Mr. Brackett opened his door, and looked down at me with much regret.

"You must leave now, Edmonia," he said hastily. "You cannot be my student any longer."

I recoiled my head at these words. "And whyever not?" I asked, as Mr. Brackett moved to close the door upon me. I wedged my foot into the doorway, then pushed against it with my shoulder. "Mr. Brackett," I pursued, entering his studio despite his protestations. "We have worked together for some time now. I should think you owe me an explanation, before terminating our lessons so abruptly."

Mr. Brackett seemed nervous, looking behind me and out onto the street. "I've been told that I cannot teach you any longer," he said, by way of explanation.

"Told by whom?" I asked. Mr. Brackett was silent, and so I repeated myself, more forcefully this time. "Told by whom, Mr. Brackett?"

He sighed. "I think you know very well."

"You have been told by Mrs. Child that you must terminate our lessons," I said, speaking the words in disbelief. "And are you her ward, are you her son, that you must obey all that she says to you?"

"You needn't have been so impudent to her, Edmonia," Brackett replied. "She told me of what you said in her study. It will not serve you to speak harshly to those who have helped you so, especially to someone as prominent and powerful as Mrs. Child. It will only get you into trouble."

I scoffed at this. "And if I am quiet and well behaved, if I do all I am told, I will be truly accepted here in Boston?" I asked. "It is an easy life I will then find, if I do all that Mrs. Child tells me?"

Mr. Brackett did not dispute me, and only gave me a regretful glance. "You are still too young to truly understand the workings of Boston society, the forces to which we all, including myself, are beholden. You must leave now, Edmonia," was Mr. Brackett's quiet reply. "There is nothing for you here any longer."

I did as I was told. I fled from that place, and I never entered Mr. Brackett's studio again.

# Chapter 18

WHAT CHANGES TWO YEARS CAN BRING, WHAT UPHEAVALS THAT stretch of time can contain. It seemed that I was but a child when I received word of Cade's death, but the shock of his loss, the pain of the disagreements I then had with Mrs. Child, the loss of the only teacher I had left in Mr. Edward Brackett, disabused me of all infantile notions, and indeed nearly wrenched from me any optimism or hope I might have had remaining within me. Compounding this despair was President Lincoln's assassination, the sad irony of this attack occurring on Good Friday, with him being shot in his seat as an audience watched a scene in a play. Even the war's end was insufficient to buoy me, for I could no longer believe that the Union victory would make much difference in a country that seemed determined to ignore its newly freed men and women.

Addy noticed my melancholia, and for once, I found myself grateful for her perseverance, her untiring attempts to lift me from my doldrums. One day she approached me as I languished on my bed, finding neither the strength nor resolve to work on any art since having no teacher to direct me. She thrust a newspaper clipping toward me and, though she bid me to read it, she recited it nearly verbatim before I could do so.

"The Freedmen's Bureau is seeking volunteers to help with recovery efforts in the South," she said, with much exigence. "They especially want young women to serve as teachers to the emancipated children."

I accepted the newspaper and read the indicated advertisement.

"We're going," she said, without waiting to hear my thoughts. "You haven't been working on your art, so that's no excuse. It'll be summertime soon, so I'll have no classes to attend. It'll be just the thing we need to get out of this house, to make ourselves useful."

For once, I did not debate Addy's point. I agreed that going South to volunteer with the Freedmen's Bureau would give me a purpose and knew, though I did not say, that my years in Mrs. Dascomb's Young Ladies' Course, back in Oberlin, would make me a suitable teacher. We wrote to the Freedmen's Bureau for an assignment, and received a reply that we were to go to Richmond, in Virginia. We purchased our train tickets in a month's time, and headed South in the heat of the summer, the air heavier and more stifling than anything I'd felt before.

It was shocking, the degradation, the poverty that we saw in the South. I had read of the disarray, the chaos left in the war's wake, but could not truly imagine it until our arrival in Richmond. Addy and I traveled to the schoolhouse where we were to teach for the next few weeks, a small and dilapidated structure, with children ranging from toddlers to adolescents filling its small hallways and classrooms.

"Surprised a child can learn anything here, in such squalor," Addy said, looking around at the room where we were to teach, unable to disguise her disdain for the wretched state in which these children had been left.

The headmistress, Mrs. Farlow, seemed not to hear her, or at least had the sense not to engage her, or encourage her indelicateness, for she only said, "This is your classroom, ages six to twelve. Addy, you will teach the younger children, and, Edmonia, you'll work with the older children, the ten- to twelve-year-olds, given your age. Not even the oldest among them can read, and they've got no parents, no family to speak of, so it shouldn't be expected that they'll receive any help from home. Grammar and composition are the most critical subjects for them to receive, but any time you have left may be devoted to math, biology, and history."

I nodded and told Headmistress Farlow that I could do this, though I soon learned I should not have given such hasty assurance, as the students were all quite distracted from my lessons, and understandably so. They had seen horrors even I could not imagine, had been torn from their parents, their siblings, and even in emancipation, had no hope for any possible reunion with these loved ones. I wanted to adopt them all if I had the means, to pull them all close to my bosom and guarantee that somehow, I would make everything alright, but the most I could offer them was an education, and I passionately pursued that goal. It was thrilling and satisfying to see the progress my students began to make over those summer days, however slowly, and I found myself ever grateful for the studies I had completed, and finally felt there was a true purpose for all of the academic work I had done. All of the children were deeply grateful for the work that Addy and I did, for each of the lessons we taught, and though I had told myself I would show no partiality toward any of the students, in my quieter moments, I had to admit that Winnie was my favorite among them, a girl of ten years old, though she was not much bigger than someone half her age.

She was a bright student, preternaturally so, able to quickly grasp difficult concepts that the other students labored over for days. She was always the first to arrive to class, as neat as she could manage to be without a mother's help, placing her freshly sharpened pencils in an exact row on her desk, pulling her books from her small bag and opening them to the day's required page, quietly and eagerly awaiting my instruction. The slight teasing she endured from other students did not dampen her acquisitiveness, her passion to learn and gratitude for the opportunity the Freedmen's Bureau had given her, and so I was quite surprised to see that she missed our classes one day, after a record of perfect attendance.

"Where is Winnie?" I inquired, looking around the classroom and noting her empty seat.

"She's ill, miss," her older neighbor, Julius, said. "She's been in bed all weekend."

"Well," I replied, trying not to show my dismay at this news. "We can't let her fall behind. I'll visit her directly after class, and bring along her schoolwork."

Winnie's home was some miles away from the schoolhouse, so I was unable to reach it until much later that day. A girl not much older than me let me inside, and introduced herself as Delilah, Winnie's guardian of some years, since she found her abandoned in the woods at the start of the war.

"She's just here in the bedroom," Delilah said, and then, noting my heavy bags filled with books, added, "There won't be much space to work in there, I should warn you. Not sure Winnie would be up to it, in any case."

I assured Delilah that this was fine, that we'd find a way to endure under the circumstances, but upon entering Winnie's bedroom, I understood that Delilah was correct, and that Winnie was in no state to complete any schoolwork.

"Hi there, little one," I began, speaking quietly and sitting on the edge of Winnie's small bed. She turned to me, weakly, and tried to give one of her familiar smiles, but seemed unable to summon the energy. The smell of illness was within the room, of camphor and vinegar, and beads of sweat were upon Winnie's forehead, though she shivered all the while despite the late-summer heat.

"What does she have?" I asked Delilah, who stood observing us quietly from the doorway.

"No diagnosis as of yet, ma'am," she said. "No doctor has been to see her."

"In this condition?" I asked, incredulously. "Why hasn't a doctor visited yet?"

"Closest colored doctor is many miles off," Delilah answered. "Would take a trip of several days. We've sent word to the apothecary here for some sort of palliative, but all of his laudanum is going toward the wounded soldiers."

I shook my head. "And where is the closest white doctor?" I asked.

Delilah looked at me as if I were insane. "Not sure why that would matter, ma'am. Of course he wouldn't provide his services to us."

"I will speak to him personally," I assured her. "I'm accustomed to such conversations, with such people."

Delilah shrugged, resignedly. "You might do as you please," she said. "His office is just north of here, on Victoria Street."

I went to the doctor's office straightaway, knowing that with each moment, Winnie's condition was deteriorating. A nurse, seeing me standing outside the office, closed the shutters with a loud bang, then hung a sign saying "Closed" on the front door, though I saw her welcome in a white patron not a minute afterward. I left the doctor's office and returned to the room I shared with Addy, though I did not sleep at all that night, and only wished that the illness ravaging Winnie might visit me instead.

Winnie's condition worsened over the following days, and though I enlisted Addy's help in finding some sort of medicine, anything that could provide, if not healing, at least palliation, we learned there was no such help to be found, even with my offers to pay all the money that I could then call my own. After quite some time, I gave up the effort, understanding that I could not make medicine appear where it did not exist.

Delilah came to the schoolhouse the next week, alarming me by her presence. I knew that she would not have come all that way to visit me with good news.

"You'd better come and see Winnie today if you want to say goodbye," Delilah said, an air of quiet acceptance, of resignation in her tone. "She won't be here much longer, Miss Lewis. Don't know if she's quite aware of all that's going on, but it might bring her some comfort to have you near, one last time."

I went to Winnie's home directly after the day's classes were done, and let the tears flow freely as I held her small hand while she labored to breathe, barely able to open her eyes and see me sitting there with her.

"Stay strong, sweet Winnie," I said, though I could tell that she was fading, that mere words would be insufficient to revive her. "You've got to endure."

Winnie did endure for a few more moments, until with a final apoplectic thrust, and that infamous rattle of death, she succumbed to her illness, and parted from this world.

Addy found me in our room that night, sitting in shock and disbelief upon my bed. She sat beside me, and for once, she seemed speechless, and remained completely silent for some time, before abiding the silence no longer. "I don't know what to say," she began, quietly. "Winnie was only a child, a little girl. She deserved so much more than what this world dealt her."

I remained silent for several moments, unable to find the words to speak, with any utterance feeling like it would be an unfit tribute to that innocent soul so lately lost.

"I can't stay here any longer," I told Addy, when finally I found the strength to speak. "I must go."

"I feel the same way," she returned, taking my hand and holding it gently in her own. "The South is so constricting, so backward. It's almost as if I can feel the ghosts of the enslaved walking amongst us. We'll be out of Richmond soon enough."

"No, Addy," I replied, shaking my head slowly, mechanically, still in a daze. "It isn't just Richmond. It isn't just the South. It's this country."

Addy looked up from my hand and viewed me curiously.

"I will never find peace as long as I remain here. I can't stand to see the way that our people are treated here. This country will kill me if I stay here much longer," I averred, taking my hand from Addy's and standing up from the bed.

Addy looked at me incredulously. "You shouldn't speak that way," she said, quietly. "Not with all the advantages you've had here. You've gone to school, as have I, you've had many opportunities for achievement. You've been warmly welcomed by all of the abolitionists in Boston, and have only found small troubles when you've overstepped the boundaries of your station.

You ought to be thankful for all that you've been given, Edmonia, and yes, all that this country has given you, too."

I shook my head, and had to still my tongue in quite an effort not to respond harshly, for Addy knew nothing of what I'd seen, what I'd endured while in Oberlin. I took some time before again speaking to her, pacing back and forth in our small room.

"I could never be thankful for the treatment I've received in this country," I finally told Addy, the last words I found necessary to speak to her until our departure from Richmond.

Immediately upon my return to Boston, I began my preparations to move away. No time could I waste in this effort, as I felt that one more moment in this country of my birth might cause me to lose my faculties, what little self-possession that remained. I began to organize an exhibition, a way to sell what art I had created to finance a trip to I knew not yet where. I decided that I would let the money I earned from the exhibition dictate how far I would go.

Word of my exhibition spread quickly, as I had expected it might, and as I posted many flyers and advertisements toward that effort. Many people appeared at the Howard boarding house on the night of my exhibition, going to the small attic space the Howards allowed me to use as a studio, most of them Bostonians I had never met, but who wanted to see me, the oddity, the curiosity, the colored girl who believed herself to be an artist. The attic space was crowded with all of the works I'd completed since moving to Boston, with many copies of my Lincoln cameos, as well as the Voltaire bust, and of course, copies of my Colonel Shaw sculpture among them. Though Mr. Brackett did not appear that night, as I'd hoped he might see on display the many pieces I'd completed under his tutelage, Mrs. Anne Whitney did attend, as did Mr. Garrison, and the Howards, and what few acquaintances I had made while living in Boston. It was one voice in particular, however, that I heard from behind me, late in the evening, that jolted me, and took all my attention away from the other attendees then in the exhibition space.

"To sculpt Robert Shaw's likeness without permission is one thing, but to sell it is quite another," Mrs. Child said, standing beside one of the many copies of the Colonel Shaw bust I'd created, hoping that they would sell better than any of my other pieces in the room.

"And yet, it is the best-selling piece of the evening, thus far," I told Mrs. Child, regaining my composure, and meeting her with an even gaze. I had not expected that I would ever see her again, so incensed she was with me during our last meeting, but I was determined not to show her how unsettling, how intimidating I found her presence.

Mrs. Child waited a moment, then placed a hand upon another sculpture close to her side. "I am not here to view your art, but to speak with you on matters that I have found quite strange, Edmonia," she began. "I have found your conduct so disrespectful, so baffling, that I had no choice but to take a closer look at you, this stranger we've accepted into Boston society."

I took a breath to steady myself. Mrs. Child went on. "You should know that I've inquired about you from your old schoolmasters back in New York. It was quite difficult to attain much information, initially, as New York Central College has not maintained many of its records since closing. But I persevered, and finally heard from a Miss Keziah King, who worked there some years back."

I took a step back from Mrs. Child at the mention of my old teacher's name. She continued her story, her voice calm, even, and measured.

"She said that she did not know any Edmonia Lewis, but then, upon closer inspection of her old records, she found information about a Mary Edmonia Lewis, someone she hadn't thought about for quite some time. Well, Miss King confirmed to me that you hadn't lived there in McGrawville in many years, and the last she had heard, you were headed off to Oberlin to attend the college there. It seems that you were supposed to be living with the Keep family there in Ohio until your graduation."

I felt the blood rise to my face, my heart rate quicken, as Mrs.

Child continued to speak. "I am familiar with the Keeps, and many of the abolitionist families there in Oberlin. And so, I wrote to Mrs. Keep to ask about you, to see if you had earned your degree from that institution, as I found it quite strange that you had not mentioned Oberlin at all since your arrival in Boston. Mrs. Keep said that you had not, in fact, graduated from Oberlin College, and had left that school after a peculiar incident, though she said she was not at liberty to discuss any of the details of your case."

I grew incensed then, finding it difficult to quell my increasing anger with each word that Mrs. Child spoke. How dare she pry into my past, correspond with those people even I had not the nerve to contact any longer?

"What case is she speaking about?" Mrs. Child asked. "What peculiar incident, Edmonia? What happened there in Oberlin? These are details you should have disclosed to Garrison, to me, to this community, when you moved here."

"There is nothing about my past that I need to disclose to you," I seethed, speaking sharply but quietly, determined not to let anyone else in the room hear our conversation. "Not when I know you to be so far from the sort of protector I might have hoped you would be." I shook my head as I pressed on. "You said that you would be a mother to me, Mrs. Child," I said, my emotions beginning to overtake me.

Mrs. Child furrowed her eyebrows in a performance of confusion and innocence. "I have only been giving correction to you as a mother would—"

"I was a fool to ever believe you," I interjected. "I should have known better than to expect protection from someone who believes herself above me."

Mrs. Child continued, undaunted, accusatory in tone. "You want too much, Edmonia. You expect too much, too quickly—"

"I expect only what is due me, as the talent that I am," I said, knowing not where I found the gall to speak in such a way. "I am a great artist, Mrs. Child, and I will be even greater when I am rid of you."

Mrs. Child turned and stormed away from me then, leaving nothing but my anger in her wake. Mrs. Anne Whitney, who must have been quietly observing my conversation with Mrs. Child, approached me quickly after Mrs. Child departed.

"Edmonia, whatever is the matter?" Mrs. Whitney asked. "What have you said to Lydia?"

I knew better than to reply truthfully to her question, and only said in response, "I must leave this place, Mrs. Whitney. There is nothing for me here. Mrs. Child has thwarted all of my connections here in Boston, so I have nothing, and no one left. It's why I've been compelled to hold this exhibition, to sell all of the art I have created, even the pieces that I hold dear. I must raise the funds to relocate myself."

"But where will you go?" Mrs. Whitney asked, seeming genuinely concerned for my welfare.

I dropped my shoulders, knowing that I had not answered this question, even for myself. "To Canada, if I can find a way," I replied. "I have family there, distant relations on my maternal side. Perhaps I can find some means to reunite with them, and be useful to them in some way."

"And what of your art?" Mrs. Whitney pressed, gesturing around at all of the work then exhibited in the studio.

I shook my head. "I will have to leave it behind, as well," I said. "The peripatetic lifestyle of my aunts up in Canada will not support the trade of sculpture."

Mrs. Whitney sighed and looked back at the door where Mrs. Child had just departed, clearly nervous that she might return, and overhear her. It was clear to me then that even a sculptress as prominent as Mrs. Anne Whitney must still be careful not to upset those high in Boston society.

"You will go abroad," Mrs. Whitney said, quickly. "To Rome. A woman artist might work freely there."

"To Rome?" I repeated. "I could never afford that, even if I sold every piece in this room, and—"

"I will help you," Mrs. Whitney interrupted, knowing we had not much time for the conversation. "I couldn't well call myself a friend to you if I allowed this sort of talent," she said, gesturing around the room, "to simply die away."

"But I would hate to be so indebted to you," I said. "You've already shown me such kindness since I've been here in Boston, I couldn't readily accept much more from you, and certainly not as much as a move to Rome would cost."

Mrs. Whitney waved her hand at this. "You will make it up to me," she said. "If you continue to create work like this, you'll be well remunerated for your efforts, and you can repay me in due time."

"But will I be welcome there, in Rome?" I asked. Though I had learned much of its ancient society, I hardly knew what I could expect were I to live there in present times.

"Quite welcome, Edmonia," Mrs. Whitney insisted. "Harriet Hosmer works there, along with Emma Stebbins, Louisa Lander, and Vinnie Ream, all accomplished sculptresses in their own right. Even actresses, like Charlotte Cushman, have found a way there."

I took a moment to consider this, knowing that even though Mrs. Whitney had named many women, she had not named any artists of color that I might find there.

"Harriet Hosmer, especially, would not shun you," Mrs. Whitney said, seeming to sense my continued reluctance. "She knows what it means to be maltreated in this country, based simply on one's difference. I can write to her directly, and arrange for you to have a studio space in the building where she works."

I nodded my head and looked down, not knowing how to respond, or whether I should agree to go. I did not want to accept such generosity, such magnanimity, but I could not readily refuse the prospect of a situation in Rome, of the space and the funds to freely work, at least until the time came to repay my debts. I stood for such a long time, ruminating over the benefits and negatives of accepting Mrs. Whitney's offer, that finally, she had to call out to me again to bring me back to the present moment.

"Shall I write to Miss Hosmer, Edmonia?" Mrs. Whitney pressed. "If I give you the necessary funds, could you find the nerve to go to Rome?"

"I can do it," came my final reply, as I looked around the room, at all of the art I had created thus far, and imagined how much more I could create in Europe. "I can make my way as an artist in Rome."

# Part III

# The Sculptress
## 1866–1896

# Chapter 19

It seemed that I released much anguish with each mile traversed across the Atlantic, with each wave and swell that rocked my great steamship. By the time I arrived in Rome, I felt revived, and renewed, believing that the terrors that chased me in America could not easily find me there. My studio overlooked the Piazza Barberini, and was located just beneath that of Harriet Hosmer, as Mrs. Whitney had arranged. I stood in that new space, looking out of the broad windows that I threw open wide, breathing in the brisk air, looking out at the Basilica and the Trevi Fountain, the Pantheon and the Colosseum far in the distance.

"It'll never get old, that view," came a voice from behind me, husky and warm. "You'll never tire of it. At least, I haven't, in all these years."

I turned to see a woman whom I understood, by the description Mrs. Whitney had given me, to be Harriet Hosmer. She smiled at me and came closer, extending a callused hand, strong with the evidence of her assiduous sculptural work.

"A pleasure to meet you, Miss Hosmer," I said.

"Do I appear to be that old?" she asked, seeming somewhat amused by my deference. "Harriet is just fine. We're colleagues here, after all. Anne Whitney says that you are quite talented, and so I see that it is so," she said, placing a hand upon a copy of my Colonel Shaw sculpture. "What are you working on now?"

I went to the center of my studio and removed a sheet from a small marble block there, revealing an unfinished bust of President Lincoln, based on the cameo I'd completed while in Boston, under Mr. Brackett's tutelage. Harriet stared at it for a moment in silence, and so I began to speak quickly, nervous that she disapproved of this work.

"I want to create something that pays tribute to our late president," I said. "Perhaps his features are a bit disproportionate, just now, but I will even them out, as I work."

"It's excellent," Harriet pronounced, after a stretch of silent contemplation. "You'll want to get his eyes right, of course, which might take a bit more time. There was a certain melancholy in them, a kind of shadow, as if he always knew what his fate would be. But, and this is the important part, you've captured something of his essence here, and that is no easy feat to accomplish."

"Some will think it's too soon for me to make such a sculpture," I said, thinking of Mrs. Child and her admonishments about my Colonel Shaw sculpture, our contentious final parting. "But I won't be able to sleep unless I get this right."

"I understand completely," Harriet responded. "I'm working on my own Lincoln memorial, as is Vinnie Ream. She sat with him, you know, before he was killed. Perhaps she can tell you what that experience was like, when you meet her. I never had the honor of meeting President Lincoln, but I've closely studied his portraits and daguerreotypes."

"Perhaps I really shouldn't spend my time on such a sculpture then," I said, "if my work would be competing with yours and Vinnie Ream's, with the both of you being so much more established and well-known than I am."

"Oh, nonsense," Harriet said. "There is room for all of us to work, to produce our own tributes. I don't think President Lincoln will turn in his grave, believing himself to be too revered."

She clapped her hands together then, seeming to have an epiphany. "Come up to my studio," she said. "I'll show you what I have of my own Lincoln memorial, so far."

Harriet led me up the stone staircase of that studio building, past door after door, telling me of the artists who occupied each space as we went, a catalogue of impressive names and accomplishments that made me feel inadequate by comparison, as if I didn't deserve to have a studio in the same space as these others.

"Here we are," Harriet said, leading me into her own studio and unveiling her work in progress. "My own memorial to the late President Lincoln."

I observed the sculpture closely, impressed by Harriet's vision, the height and majesty of this monument. She showed President Lincoln surrounded by the newly liberated, these men and women appearing not subordinate before the president, but triumphant, and proud. I had never seen my people rendered in this way, so strong, with such agency, so victorious, and felt thrilled at Harriet's vision, the possibility that this model could be constructed and perhaps, someday, displayed in America.

"Do you mind if I sketch this?" I asked, already pulling a notepad and pencil from my skirt pocket.

"Certainly not," Harriet said. "A little inspiration might be just what you need to complete your own memorial to the late president."

I sat down before Harriet's memorial model and began to sketch it into my notepad, careful to render each feature and angle as faithfully as I could.

"I take it as quite the compliment that you believe I've rendered your people correctly," she said, watching me as I sketched.

"You'll think it strange, perhaps," I said, pausing and looking up from my sketchpad, "but I've never had the opportunity to sculpt my people in such a way, as freedmen and freedwomen, as strong and victorious."

I thought of the fugitive slave sculpture I had begun back in Oberlin, the piece that almost led to my lessons with Professor Westbrook. I shook the thought from my mind, still, after all of those years, finding it weighted with far too much pain. "In your sculpture it almost seems as if the formerly enslaved had no need for President Lincoln. It almost seems as if they wrested that freedom for themselves."

"I've taken care to construct it that way," Harriet said.

I lightly touched the sculpture, then stepped back from it again and took a seat next to Harriet, quite enjoying our conversation, and her company, feeling that I might truly have found an artistic companion here in Rome, after all.

"I was never permitted to sculpt these sorts of figures while I was in Boston," I said. "I wasn't even permitted to sculpt any women. My teacher there thought it necessary for me to render the likenesses of prominent men if I hoped to gain any fame, make any money. Voltaire and John Brown, President Lincoln, and eventually, Colonel Shaw were all deemed appropriate subjects, but no one of my own race nor sex."

Harriet leaned in close to me, a conspirator in my cause. "I say to hell with that," she said. "You must sculpt whatever, and whomever, you please."

A man labored into the room then, heaving and carrying a huge block of marble upon his back.

"Just place it there, Domenico," Harriet said, as the man set the marble where directed, and then turning to me, she added, "my studio assistant, Domenico Costa. He works as a stone mason for most of the year, but he helps me when his own business is slow. Who are you employing as an assistant?"

"I haven't one," I replied, a bit self-consciously, not knowing an assistant was something I'd need, and not wanting to spend more of Mrs. Whitney's money to employ someone if it was not completely necessary.

"You can't possibly mean to move all of the marble around your own studio by yourself," Harriet said. "Domenico, please, come meet Miss Edmonia Lewis. She's new here to Rome. She could use your help around her studio, just downstairs."

Domenico's eyes moved up to mine and lingered there for a moment. He nodded at me. "I'd be glad to be of assistance."

"I'm not sure that it's quite within my budget," I replied, a bit sheepishly. "Or at least, I wouldn't want to ask my benefactress, Mrs. Whitney, to pay for any additional help."

"Then I shall have to help you for free," Domenico said, smiling at me. "And perhaps you can simply repay me with your time, a bit of conversation when the work is slow. I am sure that someone like you must have a few interesting stories to tell," he said, still observing me closely, and I found myself growing warm and self-conscious under his careful scrutiny.

Laughter wafted in from the hallway then, slicing through the tension of the moment. Two women appeared at Harriet's doorway, dressed for a social occasion, quite different from the working skirts and aprons that Harriet and I wore.

"Still working at this hour?" the first woman prodded, looking in at where Harriet and I stood. "Well, that simply won't do."

Harriet glanced at the grandfather clock in the corner of her studio. "The time got away from me, I must concede," she said, removing her apron. "Edmonia, will you join us for a drink at the taverna?" And then, before I replied, she added, "Domenico, you must come, as well. You've had a long day of it, and a drink might do you well."

I knew better than to miss this opportunity for fellowship and conviviality, this chance to learn more about my artistic peers there in Rome, and so I readily agreed to the invitation, eager to discover more about Domenico, as well.

I sat at the taverna table, slowly sipping a glass of chianti, careful not to over-imbibe, to drink too quickly, lest I grow too comfortable and reveal more to my new acquaintances than intended. I observed the room around me, the relative ease with which we women—Harriet, Charlotte, Louisa, Emma, Vinnie, and I—were able to sit with Domenico, and drink and talk and laugh. The sporadic stares that did come my way were not quite of disdain, as I might have expected in Oberlin, nor of appraisal, which I'd grown accustomed to within Boston's high society, but rather looks of benevolent interest and approval.

"Is it always like this, here in Rome?" I asked Harriet over the din of the room, the other drinkers. "So free, so accepting?"

Harriet smiled. "You're still accustomed to Boston society," she said. "Yes, you can relax here. You can be yourself. No one is going to remove you from this establishment." She playfully loosened the button at the top of my lace collar, then leaned in close to me. "Only Boston Brahmins wear their collars high in that way. You shouldn't be so prim and proper."

"And Harriet here would know," Louisa said, eavesdropping on our conversation. "Her family is most prominent among that high society."

"You oughtn't believe that because she comes from money, she hasn't had her own struggles," Charlotte Cushman said, coming to Harriet's defense. "You aren't the only one who has had to traverse an ocean, just to be freely yourself."

"Enough about that," Harriet said, seeming uncomfortable, and desiring to change the subject. "We must speak of your art, Edmonia," she said. "It's why you're here, after all."

"Yes," Charlotte said, seemingly genuinely interested in me for the first time. "What sort of work do you make?"

"Great figures of the war mostly," I said. "Those brave men who defended the American Union."

Charlotte waved a dismissive hand. "That's been done quite enough, I say," she declared. "The war is over now. It's time for us all to move on."

"I think it's a worthy subject," I replied. "The war has only just been won, and there are still many struggles ahead, much work to do. Emancipation is not the same as egalitarianism, and my work can help to bring about such true equality."

Domenico turned to me then, taking a genuine interest in my response. "Perhaps you could create something similar, for the Italian Risorgimento," he said. "We, too, have our troubles here in Rome, and a vision like yours could give voice to the oppressed here, as in America."

"The Risorgimento?" I asked, embarrassed at my ignorance, my subpar pronunciation of the word.

Domenico paused for a moment, struggling for a way to explain it. "It means renewal in your language. A way of rising, once again." He looked at me closely to see if I understood him, and I felt myself yet again grow warm under his penetrating gaze. "Our own sort of civil war," he finally said, by way of easier explanation. "We are fighting to liberate Rome now, to shake it free from papal authority. We have been working for decades now to unify the country, to liberate it from foreign rule, but it has been no easy task with brother fighting against brother. I've seen much of the combat myself."

I could tell by Domenico's countenance, by the lowering of his voice, that he did not want many questions on the subject, that there were still raw feelings, an open wound extant within him. And so it was with a lowered voice of my own that I only answered him, simply, "I would love to create that sort of work, to aid with the Risorgimento, and perhaps you can help me to create sculptures worthy of such a cause."

And in his returned gaze, there was such trust, such earnestness, that I resolved then to do all that I could to help Domenico and his cause, come what may.

# Chapter 20

Time took on a different quality there in Rome as I began my career in earnest. I worked tirelessly each day, sculpting figure after figure, often working without commission, and only in the hopes that if I continued my work, the customers would eventually come. Ever-present in my mind was Mrs. Whitney's largesse, her belief in me, the exorbitant fees she had paid to get me settled in Rome, to provide me with art supplies, and I was determined to find a way to eventually find some number of consumers for my work. Even without many paying customers, I still grew in popularity, and became something of a fixture, if not a celebrity, in Roman society.

"It's good to see that you're beginning to get the recognition you deserve," Harriet said, visiting me one day a few months after my arrival, and moving past several gawking patrons to step into my studio.

"It's starting to feel a bit overwhelming," I replied, though in truth, I quite enjoyed the attention, the constant praise, the children's shouts of *Inglesi! Inglesi!* whenever I passed them on the street. I could see, however, that despite her words, Harriet was not quite pleased with my growing fame, and perhaps resented that her own attention and praise was being diverted to me.

"I can send some of these folks up to your studio if you prefer," I said with a smile, hoping to soften her evident disdain.

"No, no," Harriet replied. "My work requires solitude, unbroken focus."

"Mine does, as well," I returned. "But I'm able to see past the observers. Nothing can break my focus from my art when the time is right to create."

Harriet raised an eyebrow. "I remember a time when my studio was bustling with visitors, as well. That was back when I was the newest one in town, and now, that would be you. They were mostly interested in me because I was a woman, a proper *sculptress.* You've got another attribute in your race to interest them, as well."

I paused and looked at Harriet, surprised she would make the insulting inference that the attention I was receiving was all due to my race. She took a breath and went on.

"I understand that Anne Whitney will be here in a month's time," Harriet said, trying to calm herself, to change the subject. "She'll be pleased to see what her largesse has brought about, I suppose."

"I do hope so," I replied. "She is still paying the rent on this studio, and for my meals, as well as my art materials and incidentals. I couldn't well rest if I weren't constantly working with the aim of making her proud."

"Where shall I place this, Miss Lewis?" Domenico asked then, hoisting a large marble block into my studio.

"Just before me, Domenico. I've got to get started on this piece right away," I said.

"I do admire your urgency," Harriet admitted, as I set immediately to work. "What piece must you begin? Surely this one must be for a large commission, if it is so pressing."

"It's a piece I've volunteered to create," I said.

"One that was arranged by me," Domenico added, as he moved other sculptures away from my workspace.

"By you?" Harriet repeated, looking from Domenico and back to me as if we were in jest. "I didn't realize you socialized with art patrons, Domenico," she said, clearly finding the idea to be ridiculous.

"It's a sculpture for one of the resistance groups," Domenico said, "For the Italian Legion, the Redshirts. Edmonia will complete a sculpture of Garibaldi, in fact. It will go on display in our meeting room."

"Garibaldi," Harriet repeated. She took a moment to quietly observe me as I worked, then said, "Domenico, I should be receiving a delivery shortly, a mass of granite just downstairs. Would you mind seeing if it has arrived, and carrying it up to my studio?"

Domenico nodded. "Of course, Miss Hosmer, right away."

As he left, Harriet turned to me, forgetting her apparent envy to fix me with a look of genuine concern. "Is that the sort of sculpture you should be creating?" she asked, gesturing toward my new work.

"Why wouldn't it be?" I asked.

"I don't think you should be getting involved with the Risorgimento," she returned. "Certainly, Anne Whitney wouldn't want you to in any case."

"Domenico wants me to," I said. "Surely I must be allowed to consider his opinion on the matter."

"And surely his opinion should not matter more to you than Anne's, who is funding your time here in Rome," Harriet argued.

"What matters most to me is my art, and anything that I feel passionate about creating," I said. "Garibaldi is a suitable figure, I'd say just now."

"But do you truly understand Garibaldi's cause? What sort of beliefs the Redshirts harbor?" she asked.

"Harriet, despite what you may think of me, I am no fool," I replied. "I understand quite well what they are fighting for, and that is the unification of Italy."

I had done much research into the Risorgimento since Domenico first mentioned it to me, and devoured the books and pamphlets he provided me to further educate me on the cause. I resented Harriet's inference that I might embark upon such a sculpture without a clear understanding of the man I depicted.

"And do you understand the methods by which they fight?" Harriet pressed. "Some of these men can grow quite violent," she said. "Domenico does not seem to be the most revolutionary among them, nor the most pugilistic, but for you to create a sculpture for this group, for many men who might be quite brutal in their tactics, indeed, could truly alienate you from certain parts of Roman society."

"I am not afraid of alienation, Harriet," I answered her. "I have been treated as alien, as stranger, as interloper, many times before."

Harriet had no choice but to accept my response, but I could see, in the raise of her eyebrows, in the tension of her face, that she remained quite concerned about my involvement with this revolutionary cause, and I did, in truth, worry that Mrs. Whitney would be concerned, as well.

I hardly had any time to fret over Harriet's admonishment, for I was soon joining her for one of Charlotte Cushman's vaunted performances, a staging of Shakespeare's *Romeo and Juliet*, in which she was playing Romeo. It was an interesting performance, indeed, and quite different to see a woman taking on that masculine role. I found myself enjoying it, but soon learned that Domenico, who had been invited as well, and who sat by my side, did not.

"It is quite a long play," Domenico said, leaning close and whispering in my ear. "Do you understand it all?"

"Much of it," I said, thinking of long school days spent studying the Bard. "I am quite familiar with Shakespeare's works."

"It is not for me," Domenico returned. "The Old English, the strange costumes. I would prefer to be somewhere that I can find some enjoyment."

"And where would that be?" I asked, whispering back to him.

He stood from his seat, taking care to remain low and as inconspicuous as he could be. With his head, he motioned for me to follow him out of my own seat. I complied, and as we moved out of the small aisle, I glanced behind me, and saw Harriet giving me a disapproving look.

Domenico and I ran out of the theater, laughing like children all the way, in disbelief that we were able to so easily escape the confines of the theater, of Rome's polite society. Domenico stopped suddenly in the street, then, grabbed my face, and kissed me. I pulled away, looking at him strangely, bringing a hand to my lips.

"Domenico, I cannot—" I began, but he interrupted me.

"You mustn't pretend to be like the other ladies," he said. "You are different. You will never conform to their society anyway. You are free to behave as you please."

He moved to kiss me again, and that time, I allowed him to, though I was unsure whether this was something I truly wanted. Cade's face appeared before mine as Domenico kissed me. I could not tell if my apprehension at returning Domenico's kiss stemmed from that guilt, from the memory of a love unfulfilled, or if I simply was nervous after Harriet's warning, at the thought of the revolutionary activity in which Domenico engaged. I felt too, that I should perhaps have been offended by Domenico taking this liberty with me, by his assumption that I should not behave as properly as other women would in a similar situation. And yet, I was so swept up in the passion of the moment, the genuine attraction Domenico seemed to have for me, that I swept aside all conflicting feelings, and allowed myself to enjoy Domenico's presence.

Domenico looked down at me approvingly, then took my hand. "Come, there are some people I want you to meet."

Domenico led me to a boarding house a few blocks away from the theater, then took me down to the cellar, where a small group of people had gathered in a dimly lit room. The windows were all covered and boarded, and a flag with the letters of the Italian Legion hung high above a doorway.

"Everyone, this is Edmonia Lewis, the sculptress I told you about," Domenico said, as we entered the room. "And, Edmonia, these are some of the fighters of the Risorgimento, the Redshirts, followers of Garibaldi, volunteers for his army."

"And so it is you who will be creating the Garibaldi sculpture for our cause?" a man asked.

"Indeed, I will," I replied. "I've been reading about him as I work, and he seems to be a quite worthy subject."

"Even your own President Lincoln thought so," another man added. "He invited him to command the Union Army, though Garibaldi did not accept the invitation."

I nodded. "It seems those two great men shared a mutual admiration and respect."

Domenico agreed. "I'd say few Italians were prouder when President Lincoln freed your people. I remember learning what Garibaldi wrote to Lincoln when he received word of emancipation. My father used to read it to me and my brothers, made us memorize it."

Domenico cleared his throat and affected a voice as he recited the words. "'If an entire race of human beings, subjugated into slavery by human egoism, has been restored to human dignity, to civilization and human love,'" Domenico quoted, "'this is by your doing and at the price of the most noble lives in America.'"

"It is good that Garibaldi recognized what monumental work Lincoln did," I said. "It was not easy, and certainly not popular for him to free the people of my race."

"And now it seems that you take up the mantle of President Lincoln's work," Domenico said, looking down at me fondly.

"A heavy task," another man said, looking at me earnestly.

"Indeed, it is," I said. "Since I was a little girl, I've been told that my achievements were all to be for the greater advancement of my people. I am proud to take on such an honorable duty, but sometimes, I must admit, it can be a daunting, not to say an impossible, expectation."

"But you are equipped for such high expectations," Domenico said. "You are the sort of person who realizes this critical truth, that when the world does not give you what you want, you must force it to. You must take it," Domenico said, leaning in close to me. "That is what we are doing here with our own work in the Italian Legion."

I nodded, and looked around the room, feeling ignited by the passion of all those gathered before me.

Domenico brought my attention back to him. "I see that same determination, that same revolutionary spirit of the Italian Legion, in you," he said. He placed a hand on my cheek before speaking his next words. "Never let anyone dampen it."

I couldn't help but remember Harriet's warning then, the idea that I should not involve myself with Domenico beyond his help in my studio, that I should shun association with his comrades, Garibaldi's supporters. But if these men of the Italian Legion, these Redshirts, were so dangerous, why did I feel such safety, such protection and care, there among them?

I soon received word that one of my dear aunts had passed away, and that my other aunt, perhaps in her grief, had died shortly thereafter. I could not handle the idea that those pillars of my early life, those maternal figures who had been such prominent presences in my youth, were no longer on this earth. Visions, as ever, began to plague me after my aunts' deaths, and the idea that I had not yet done enough for the Native peoples in America, my mother's people, would not let me rest. I embarked upon pieces that would, I hoped, elevate the status of the indigenous, and specifically of the Ojibwe, among whom I had, at one time, found a home.

I had been inspired by a recent rereading of Henry Wadsworth Longfellow's *The Song of Hiawatha*—that epic poem of the Ojibwe chief Hiawatha and the Dakota Minnehaha, and the love that blossomed between these two from warring nations—and I decided to sculpt various scenes from this literary masterpiece. Never had I seen a marble, idealized depiction of a native person, and I prided myself on the idea that I would be the first artist to create such sculptures. I began with a bust of Hiawatha, carefully sculpting his feathered headdress, his turquoise necklace, his buckskin covering, until each piece of his garb communicated his eminence. I then crafted an idyllic bust of Minnehaha, giving her the sort of innocent, angelic face I imagined would woo any chief, even one from an opposing tribe. Following this, I created a piece that I deemed *The Old Indian Arrowmaker and His Daughter*, showing a young Minnehaha in the care of her father, contentedly working alongside this patriarch to braid a mat as he sharpens arrowheads. At their feet lies a fawn, gifted to them by Hiawatha himself in his love for Minnehaha.

My next work, which I called *Indian Combat*, was a trinity of Native figures in the midst of a battle, an ambitious work that imbued each Indian with movement and grace and necessitated a careful attention from the viewer to fully appreciate the subtleties and stories that each angle of this sculpture told. It would take me a few years to truly execute this vision in a final copy of *Indian Combat*, by which point I satisfied myself that I had, indeed, come close to the mental visions I had of the sculpture. Finally, to complete what I came to think of as my *Native Series*, I sculpted *The Marriage of Hiawatha*, showing Hiawatha and Minnehaha joined in matrimony, bodies turned toward each other, and hands clasped, Hiawatha's countenance full of satisfaction, and Minnehaha's, full of possibility and expectation. In sculpting this, I remembered the lines from Longfellow's poem, as Hiawatha's grandmother first warned him against marrying Minnehaha, saying:

*"Bring not to my lodge a stranger*
*From the land of the Dacotahs!*
*Very fierce are the Dacotahs,*
*Often is there war between us,*
*There are feuds yet unforgotten,*
*Wounds that ache and still may open!"*

I remembered, too, Hiawatha's answer to this naysaying, as he laughingly told his grandmother:

*"For that reason, if no other,*
*Would I wed the fair Dacotah,*
*That our tribes might be united,*

*That old feuds might be forgotten,*
*And old wounds be healed forever!"*

But it was, to my chagrin, that I could find few customers for my Native sculptures. It seemed that art buyers had no interest in such scenes of indigenous life, even if they were based upon the work of a popular poet. I wrote to my brother, Samuel, for advice, sending daguerreotypes of the sculptures for him to see if any American art patrons might be more interested, as they lived more closely to Native American life, but yet and still, the response was in the negative, and even Samuel himself seemed to find but little interest in that particular set of works.

Henry Wadsworth Longfellow himself soon arrived for a grand tour of Rome, and I felt as if I'd summoned him, as if I'd conjured him there, after my repeated readings of his *The Song of Hiawatha.* I felt that if he could find success with his depictions of Native life, perhaps I could, too, if only I could find a way to speak with him, to ask for some advice, some knowledge of how to proceed with my works.

I began to trail Longfellow, to follow him on his travels, joining the crowds for his lectures, reserving tables at the restaurants where he dined. I became obsessed with the idea of meeting with him, consumed by the notion that he might give me some artistic fortitude, and I began to sketch him, compulsively, as I pursued him along his tour. One day, his brother, Samuel Longfellow, noticed me there at the back of one of Henry's lectures, as I sketched his brother's countenance upon a page of my notebook.

"That is quite good," Samuel said, pointing down at my sketchbook. "Quite more than the work of a mere amateur, I might say."

"I am no amateur," I assured him, "but a working artist, a sculptress, here in Rome."

"Are you indeed?" Samuel inquired, intrigued. "My brother is just now looking for a sculptor. He'd like to have a portrait bust completed before we depart from the Continent. He hasn't yet found an artist that he believes is up to the task. But you . . ." Samuel said, trailing off and looking up to where his brother continued his lecture. "You might be just the person."

That afternoon when Longfellow came to sit for me was transcendent, as we conversed for hours in my studio as I further sketched and sculpted his bust. As it happened, Longfellow himself had also received much criticism of, and insult toward, his own art, and comforted me when I told him of the difficulty I'd had in selling my Native sculptures.

"Though I have seen much success and celebration in my lifetime, I have also seen much hatred and vitriol directed not only at my poetry, but at my very person. I believe it has all made me stronger," he said, careful not to shift his countenance too dramatically as I sat before him, chiseling away at a block of marble.

"I find it so hard to believe that anyone could find fault with your work, or with you," I said, as I worked. "Such a kind and gentle soul I've found you to be this afternoon."

"Ah, yes," Longfellow said. "When you've worked for as long as I have, you will hear it all. I have been told that my work is lacking in emotional depth and force, that it is more suited for children than adults because of its simplicity, that poems over which I'd labored for *decades* amounted to nothing more than mere nursery rhyme. I've been told by men as great as Walt Whitman that I'm merely an imitator of European poets, and have had friends like Poe turn on me, and call me a mere plagiarist. But what I have learned, Miss Lewis, is that you must create with no mind for the naysayers, for the people who dismiss your efforts," he said, with some finality. "For every detractor and disparager, there are a dozen wonderful people like you, who adore my work, and therein find inspiration. You must focus on your admirers, and disregard the others. That is the only way."

I inscribed Longfellow's words that afternoon onto my heart, and his guidance would prove especially prescient to me as the months wore on, and as both my fame, and my critics, began to grow.

# Chapter 21

"Mr. Wreford, please, come just this way," I said. "I've been expecting you."

"Miss Lewis, it's an honor to meet you," the journalist, Mr. Henry Wreford, replied. "And evidently all of these people agree."

Mr. Wreford made his way into my studio, past groups of tourists and locals, for a scheduled interview for the *Athenaeum*, an art magazine with a large circulation in England. He had written to me specifically to request the interview, as he had heard of me after my Henry Wadsworth Longfellow bust gained much attention, both there in Rome, and abroad. It seemed that Mr. Brackett had been correct all those years ago when he told me that I must sculpt the likenesses of famous men in order to gain any attention, for I found that the Longfellow sculpture was the first of my works to sell quite well, and allow me to send a small but meaningful repayment back to Mrs. Whitney. While I found that my Native sculptures could not find many customers, they still attracted much attention, as evidenced by the hordes of people then gathered in my studio.

"How can you work with such mayhem around you?" Mr. Wreford asked, as we pushed our way through my studio visitors, past gawks and points and stares.

"I've grown accustomed to it, I suppose. Please," I said, gesturing toward a chair at the back of my studio where we could find a modicum of more quietude, "take a seat."

Mr. Wreford complied.

"Can I get you anything?" I inquired. "Coffee? Tea?"

"I would think I should be asking you such a question," he said. "You are the star, the genius sculptress. I am but a lowly journalist, an observer if you will, here to report on your doings."

"Well, it is favorable coverage, I seek," I laughed. "And so, you must let me serve you before we begin."

I poured an espresso for Mr. Wreford, then sat beside him, ready to be interviewed, dissected, examined.

Mr. Wreford accepted the coffee and took a sip, then took out a pen and notebook. "I had heard tell of you for some time in the art circles I frequent, but when I heard that Longfellow made it a point to stop by your studio, well, I felt that I must do the same."

I smiled at this. "I'm glad that you've done so," I replied.

"Your background is quite unique, Miss Lewis, if you don't mind me deeming it so," Mr. Wreford said. "It seems to have inspired these marvelous works, such as I have never seen," he said, gesturing toward a copy of my *Hiawatha* sculpture.

"If only I could find more customers for such works," I replied, with an effort at a laugh. "Copies of my *Longfellow* bust have found some purchasers, but none for my Native series."

"Well, we shall see if my coverage of you will change those fortunes," he said, opening his notepad and beginning to write, as I regaled him with tales of my youth spent in the wilds of northern New York, with my Ojibwe relatives.

It was interesting how easily I could create this character, how quickly I could slip into that exaggerated, that dramatized version of my early life. I had already gained much skill in such fabrications when I fled from Oberlin to Boston, but this embellishment of my life was much more enjoyable to create. I could see that Mr. Wreford enjoyed it as well, as he wrote ever more quickly as I spoke, laughing when appropriate, asking thoughtful questions to encourage my speech, as I embellished those tales of my early life with the Native population.

Harriet Hosmer soon appeared in my studio, and made her way to the back where Mr. Wreford and I conversed.

"Henry," Harriet said, seeming surprised, if not a bit wounded, and clearly quite familiar with Mr. Wreford. "I didn't know you were coming to our studio building today."

"It was an impromptu visit," Mr. Wreford replied, sounding caught, cornered.

"Well, you might have called on me first, as the old friend of mine that you are," she said. "You used to cover my art quite frequently, some years ago."

"I haven't much time to be here, you understand," Mr. Wreford said, in effort at explanation. "And I desired to interview a new subject, Miss Lewis here. Her fresh perspectives are something I think the readers of the *Athenaeum* might quite appreciate."

I might have asked Mr. Wreford to end his explanation, to stop speaking altogether, lest he wound Harriet's feelings even more than he evidently had. Harriet fixed me then with a look of much disdain and condescension before finally saying, "I see. Then I suppose I will leave you to it."

With that, she quitted my studio, taking with her any of the joy I might have felt at the Wreford interview, and leaving me with only the strangest sensation of anxiety, and of dread.

Mrs. Anne Whitney soon arrived in Rome, and came directly to my studio to visit me, to see how her largesse was paying off.

"You have grown quite prolific since I've seen you last," she said, approvingly looking around at the myriad sculptures in my studio. She placed a hand upon one, my *Hiawatha* depiction. "And do you find many customers, for such figures?"

"I've been creating many of these without commission," I said. "While my Longfellow sculpture sold some copies, my Native figures have not, as of yet. I do believe, however, that they will find a proper home when the time is right."

Mrs. Whitney sighed, and looked concerned. "You are devoting your time, and the financial resources I've been sending you, to create uncommissioned works?" She shook her head in disbelief. "In the mere hope that they will sell?"

I nodded and took a step toward her. "It is only a matter of time, Mrs. Whitney. You should see the sort of attention, the sort of admiration I get here. The Roman people are enthralled by my art. They come by to watch me sculpt, to see my mind at work."

"Attention is not remuneration, Edmonia," Mrs. Whitney said. "You must remember that, as well. Is there nothing here aside from the Longfellow copies that could be sold for some small fee?"

"The only types of sculptures people seem interested in purchasing these days are small and frivolous, as these are," I said, gesturing toward a few pieces I had recently completed, *Asleep*, *Awake*, and *Love Ensnared*, depicting Cupid with his arm in a trap. "*Putti*, they call them here."

These were silly pieces, I thought, created solely for the American tourists who visited my studio, but absent of any real merit or meaning.

"I see," Mrs. Whitney said, seeming to understand my disdain for those pieces. "And those do not fit with the sort of work you'd personally like to create. Certainly, those are not anything that would gain traction among the higher society back in America, especially in Boston. Is there anything else you have here that might be suitable for a more refined audience?"

I hesitated, thinking and looking about the room.

"Domenico, will you bring out my emancipation sculpture?" I asked. "*Forever Free.* I'd like to show it to Mrs. Whitney."

Domenico quickly complied, and I unveiled the sculpture. Mrs. Whitney fell silent, staring for an extended time at the sculpture. I was nervous that she disapproved of it, that she would tell me I'd wasted my time in crafting such a figure. Domenico seemed to notice my nervousness, and stood close by my side as Mrs. Whitney observed my sculpture.

"This," she said, bringing her clasped hands up to her face. "This is exactly the sort of work you should be making." She nodded and walked around the sculpture. "This quite reminds me of the piece I created some years ago, *Ethiopia Shall Soon Stretch Out Her Hands to* God. Your vision here, Edmonia, is superb. The emancipated man, free from his chains, triumphant, his face toward heaven. The young woman, subordinate to the man, perhaps, but equally grateful to God. This is excellent work, Edmonia."

Domenico grabbed my waist and pulled me close, smiling down at me in an equal measure of glee. He remembered himself, then, and quickly released me. "I must go to the quarry now," he said. "I will be back later should you need anything else."

Mrs. Whitney watched Domenico as he left my studio, his familiarity and intimacy with me sufficient to distract her from my emancipation sculpture.

"You are not involved with that young man?" Mrs. Whitney asked me, slowly, as if she were afraid of the answer.

I did not answer her, but only coyly looked down at my clasped hands.

"Edmonia, I am not funding your stay here for you to gallivant with someone of his—" she stopped herself, considered, then tried again, "Someone of his ilk. He is a stone mason, a studio assistant, and indeed, a troublemaker, from what I have been told. You are to remain focused on your art. Do you understand me?"

I shook my head. "But, Mrs. Whitney, you do not know him. Domenico is a good man, committed to an important cause, much like the cause to which you have devoted your own life, and—"

"I know all about his cause, Edmonia," Mrs. Whitney said. "And while the idea of Italian Unification might be noble, the methods by which he is trying to bring it about are not."

I stepped closer to Mrs. Whitney, ready to further argue my case, but she interrupted me yet again.

"You have something here. Something special, with your art," she said. "It is why I have taken this financial chance on you. We cannot let your talent go to waste. You must end whatever relationship you've had with that young man, before it leads to any trouble. Do you understand me?"

I told Mrs. Whitney that I did, and indeed, I did not want to run this risk of losing her financial support for the sake of a romantic entanglement.

I watched then as Mrs. Whitney placed a hand upon my emancipation sculpture. "I am going to write to a Mr. John Forney," she said. "He is currently soliciting work for the upcoming American Centennial celebration. This might be just the sort of piece that he desires. If you can get a place there at the Centennial Exposition, you will certainly begin to get the sort of remuneration you deserve, and will be able to pay me back fully, in due time."

I smiled wide, in disbelief at the idea of showing my own work at the American Centennial, and shouted out in excitement. Harriet must have heard my cheers, for she soon arrived at my door, and entered with a quick knock upon the frame.

"May I join in on the celebration?" Harriet asked.

I stood in front of my emancipation sculpture, obscuring it from Harriet's view.

"Of course you may," Mrs. Whitney said, much to my dismay. "Edmonia has completed the most marvelous piece. *Forever Free*, I believe you called it? We will submit it for consideration as a part of the American Centennial celebration, to be held in Philadelphia. I will see, too, if it can be put on permanent display after the Centennial, as a memorial in the District of Columbia. Come and take a look, Harriet."

Harriet neared the sculpture and viewed it with an odd expression.

"It is—" she began.

"Magnificent, is it not?" Mrs. Whitney interjected.

"Familiar," Harriet said.

"Familiar?" Mrs. Whitney repeated. "In what sense?"

"In the sense that I've created the very same piece," she said, turning to me, her tone accusatory. "And created it first."

Mrs. Whitney looked at me to confirm whether Harriet's words were true.

"Would you dispute this, Edmonia?" Harriet asked. "Did you not sketch, in your own notepad, these very figures, copied from my own memorial to President Lincoln, to the emancipation of the enslaved? I believe it should be my own work that is submitted to the Centennial," she said, "and not yours."

"I might have gotten some inspiration from your work, Harriet," I conceded, "as any artist would, as you yourself have gotten inspiration from the sculptors who came before you. Our work is an iterative process, you know as well as I."

"This appears to be more an act of outright thievery than inspiration," Harriet spat, "of plagiarism than any creative process."

I shook my head, then turned to Mrs. Whitney. "The same sort of accusations have been made against my people for centuries," I declared. "People throughout the years have said that the colored race is only capable of imitation, and not true creativity, nor invention. Well, I take umbrage at that idea. This work is the product of my own mind, my own hand, and to say otherwise is to lie, to deceive."

Harriet made a move toward me as if to strike me. I stood my ground and continued to speak.

"Who are you, Harriet, to say how my people should be depicted? Why should you even have the right to make an emancipation sculpture? You have known nothing of bondage, of enslavement."

"And neither do you," she said. "You were born free, as was your brother, and your parents before you."

"I will serve as the voice of my people," I pursued, unshaken by Harriet's words. "It is my work that should be used in memorial of our freedom."

Harriet scoffed, then stormed out of my studio, slamming the door behind her as she went. Mrs. Whitney placed a hand upon my shoulder and spoke quietly, comfortingly to me.

"Stay the course, Edmonia," she said, showing herself to be on my side in that argument with Harriet Hosmer. "You do not need Miss Hosmer's approval. Your work will pay off in due time."

"It is late, Miss Lewis," Domenico said, approaching me one evening when all was quiet and dark in my studio, "and yet still, you work."

I looked up at him over the flicker of a candle, the light and shadows of flames from the fireplace dancing upon the walls. "I cannot sleep," came my hushed reply.

"Nor can I," he said, taking a seat next to me and near the sculpture over which I then labored. "What troubles your mind?"

"It is only this sculpture," I said, "*Hagar in the Wilderness.* I want to capture the fear, the agony Hagar must have felt after fleeing from her home, but it seems that I cannot do it justice."

"Perhaps a change of scenery can help," Domenico said. "I must go to an Italian Legion meeting tonight. You could join me again. You will always be welcome there, after the work you did on the Garibaldi sculpture."

I shook my head. "I must remain here, with my work, until I get this right."

Domenico sat still closer to me. "Then I must remain with you."

I gave him an appeasing smile, but still, I insisted, "You should go."

"Should I?" he asked, taking my hand, then pulling me close. He kissed me, then looked into my eyes to gauge the result. "Should I still?" And again, he kissed me, then moved to lower me onto the floor. "And now, must I still go?"

I sat up and pushed him away, feeling unsettled at the liberties he was taking. "Yes, you must."

Domenico looked at me in confusion. "Has there been a change in your feelings for me?" he asked. "Was I wrong to believe that we both felt some mutual affection for one another?"

"You were not wrong to think so," I said. "But it is that I now find greater expectations have been placed upon me, more eyes observing my every move. Since the Henry Wreford interview, and a potential chance that I will have to show my work at the American Centennial, I have been told, by my benefactress, Mrs. Whitney, that I must behave in a different, more careful manner."

Domenico looked surprised. "I thought you were a free woman, someone who might behave as she pleased."

"I am a free woman, Domenico," I replied. "How else could I be here, living and working in Rome, as I do?"

Domenico went on undeterred by my tone. "But it is not so different from being enslaved, if these people of a higher class can dictate your every move."

I bristled at this, released my arm from Domenico's grasp, and moved away from him.

"You know nothing of which you speak," I said. "Simply abiding by the counsel of a benefactress is nothing like the plight of those who were once enslaved. You shouldn't talk of such subjects when you have no true understanding of them."

Domenico pursued the point. "But I know of oppression, Edmonia. After all, we here in Rome who have existed under the Pope's authority all—"

"I speak still of a greater oppression," I said, growing quite agitated at the subject.

Domenico took a breath, not wanting to further escalate my emotions.

"I am only saying that you must choose whether you will simply obey this benefactress, this Mrs. Whitney, or whether you are free to make your own decisions."

I stopped and stared at Domenico then. "I am quite free to make my own decisions, to do as I want."

"And what do you want, Edmonia?" he asked, though it was clear from his countenance that he believed he knew the answer. I surprised him, then, with my response.

"I want to pursue my work, tonight, Domenico, without your interruption."

Domenico hesitated at this, looking a bit wounded, but finally, after another moment, he accepted my response, and left the studio, allowing me to continue my *Hagar in the Wilderness* sculpture, in relative peace.

John Forney arrived at my studio in a few weeks' time, after having traveled through Florence and Rome in search of artists to display their work at the upcoming American Centennial. I handed him a flute of Prosecco upon his entrance, hoping that this drink might help to bathe my sculptures in a positive, golden light as he assessed them.

"You must be quite tired after all of the visits you've made to different artists," I said, as I led him into my studio.

Mr. Forney raised his eyebrows and sighed, seeming exhausted. "Yours is the final studio I must visit. You are a newer sculptress here than the others, but Mrs. Whitney assured me the visit would be worth my time."

I hastened to unveil *Forever Free* then, not wanting to waste Mr. Forney's time, and I stood back from the sculpture, allowing Mr. Forney the space to view it on his own, without my intervention.

He gave the sculpture a cursory glance before speaking again. "It won't be easy for me to convince the board to allow a colored artist to exhibit her work at the Centennial," he said. "Especially work with such a frank depiction of the Negro race."

I drew back my head. My breath seemed to stop.

"This Exposition is to celebrate the hundredth anniversary of American independence," he said, "and a work like this might feel accusatory, like an indictment of America's past, rather than a celebration of it."

Mr. Forney continued to stare at the sculpture, then went beyond the first superficial glance to examine its contours and each of its angles. "Still, it is quite impressive, quite unique. It would be a shame to not have anything of yours on display at the Centennial." He turned to me. "Have you got anything else I could consider for the Centennial?"

"I have my Native sculptures, *Hiawatha, Minnehaha, Old Arrow-*

*maker,*" I said. "Longfellow himself visited my studio and pronounced them to be masterpieces."

Mr. Forney seemed unenthused, so I continued on. "I have *Hagar in the Wilderness*, if it's a Biblical depiction you're after. I have my Longfellow bust, and a Lincoln bust, and Voltaire, and Colonel Shaw, as well," I added, desperate to name something that might impress this powerful man.

Mr. Forney shook his head. "If I am going to convince the board to allow you entry to the American Centennial, it would have to be for something grand, something spectators have never seen before, and I understand that all of the other pieces you mention are ones that might already be familiar to many people," he said. "Whatever sculpture you exhibit would have to be worthy of the Centennial. It seems that sort of piece isn't here in your studio, Miss Lewis, though I thank you for your time."

Mr. Forney placed his hat upon his head, then moved toward the door.

"Wait," I said, stopping him before he could depart. "What if I guarantee you that I can create something like that?" I asked, speaking the words before I had quite considered their import.

"You guarantee it?" Mr. Forney repeated, seeming interested.

"Yes," I replied. "I've been wanting to sculpt something grand, just as you've described," I said, going to my desk and rummaging through its myriad papers. I produced a sketch I'd been laboring over for weeks, a depiction of Cleopatra in the moments just after her death, her head thrown back, eyes closed, the poison asp still coiling around her wrist. I envisioned it as a massive sculpture, much taller than myself, even than Mr. Forney, and a work much more dramatic and arresting than anything I'd created before. I had hidden the sketch away for some time, nervous that creating such a frank depiction of a poisoning might resurface the rumors of my youth, concerned that portraying a woman in the midst of such a shocking act might be too difficult for the public to face, but as Mr. Forney stood there in my studio, wanting to see a more impressive work, I knew that I must show him, despite the risks.

Mr. Forney accepted the paper from me, then studying it, said, "You should take care to soften her features," he said. "Cleopatra was of Greek, not African blood, despite what some in your circle may claim. But yes, with the right execution, this is just the sort of work the rest of the Centennial Commission will want to see. It is different, quite different than anything the spectators will have seen before, and will surely satisfy the public's current craze for Egyptology. I will send word to the Commission to reserve a space for this piece. And can you have this completed by May of the Centennial year?"

"Nothing could stop me from doing so," I said, without fully considering all the time, money, and resources that this would require from me.

"Wonderful, Miss Lewis."

With a final shake of my hand, Mr. Forney departed. I turned to Domenico and squealed with glee, leaping up and jumping into his arms, in total disbelief that I had secured my place at the Centennial Exposition. Domenico spun me around then, and after placing me back upon the ground, continued to hold me close.

"People from all over the globe are going to that Centennial fair," he said. "You will be world famous, just as you deserve to be."

I demurred, shaking my head and waving a dismissive hand. "It is not me, but my work, that should be famous."

Domenico continued to hold me close. "You will need an escort back to America," Domenico said. "I will apply for my passport so that it is ready in time."

I broke away from him then, slowly, carefully. "I won't be in need of an escort," I said. "It's a journey I must make on my own."

"Then we will have a proper celebration before you depart," Domenico pressed. "You must allow me to tell my friends. We will organize a party for you, or a dinner if you prefer."

I shook my head, wishing he would pick up on my meaning, that he wouldn't force me to speak the words that should have been clear.

"Domenico, Mrs. Whitney has arranged this all for me. She

has been quite generous in helping to pay for this studio, for my art materials, for my meals," I said. "I've already told you that she views our relationship as a distraction, if not a detriment to my career, and I have to obey her wishes. If you were to accompany me to America, it would be a direct dismissal of all that Mrs. Whitney has told me, of all that she has done for me."

While it hurt me to reject Domenico in such a way, I knew that I could not afford another broken relationship, another benefactress who shunned me in the way that Mrs. Child now did, since I went against her wishes, back in Boston. I was determined to make Mrs. Whitney proud, to show that her belief in me, her financial support of me, was not going to waste.

Domenico grew quiet, pensive. He turned away from me and toward the window, looking out at the view and the crowds beyond. "You should take care not to lose yourself in pursuit of your dreams," he said, his voice barely audible. "I'll be here waiting for you, when you return. I'll always be here for you, Edmonia."

I thanked Domenico for his words, for his support, for his affection, but I couldn't help but feel that there was a flash of anger in his eyes as he spoke those last words.

Hardly could I celebrate my acceptance to the American Centennial before the letters began to arrive. They were slow enough, initially one or two strange notes buried within the myriad others that the postman delivered, short missives, all written in an unknown hand. Then, the letters increased in frequency, bombarding me, crowding both my studio and my mind, their words echoing in my head until they became a sort of incantation, a sort of curse.

*A return to America will bring about your death.*

*I know the truth of who you are, and will reveal all at the Centennial.*

*As you tried to take their lives in Oberlin, so I will take yours.*

I ripped the letters to shreds, I threw them into the fire, and still they came, still they tormented me. In the night, I would stare out of my studio window for as long as I could, afraid that I might catch a glimpse of the person who sent these anonymous letters, that if this person knew my studio location, this stranger could surely make it to Rome, could come and harm me as I slept. And yet, I could never see anyone stalking me, no enemy in the night, though I would keep my watch until I finally fell into a fitful sleep. I wracked my brain to think of who might be sending these notes, cataloging all of the people who might have meant me harm over the years, who felt incensed by my very being. I thought of Sarah Miles and Gemma Ennes, of course, but I thought, too, of Mrs. Child, and of Harriet Hosmer, so lately upset by my emancipation sculpture, and even Domenico, who might greatly resent me for ending our short-lived affair. These letters might have been coming from anyone else in America, too, one of the myriad townspeople in Oberlin, one of my attackers from all those years ago, or simply someone who saw the news of my exhibition and felt incensed that a colored girl could have a place at such an august exposition.

I grew unfocused because of these letters, unbalanced, and many of my peers began to notice this, commenting upon my clear and constant distraction.

"Are you sure you're alright?" Louisa Lander asked, while visiting my studio one day, hoping to catch a glimpse of my work in progress for the Centennial. I was pacing back and forth, muttering to myself, and glancing out of my window every few moments, afraid that someone was coming to enact all of the threats outlined in the letters.

"Quite alright," I said, though it was clear she could see otherwise. I feared that word of my mental malady would spread, that Mr. Forney, and Mrs. Whitney, would hear of my anguish, would remove me from the Centennial roster. And so, it was with this fear in my mind that I sought out help, the relief that only medicine could provide, and I made an appointment with a doctor, straightaway.

"I just need something to help me sleep," I told the doctor, as I sat uncomfortable in his cold office. "I've been having terrible dreams. I feel like I'm being pursued, hunted," I said, growing tearful as I made the admission. "And it has begun to inhibit my work."

The doctor stared at me for a moment, as if trying to discern whether he should believe me, take me seriously. Finally, he scribbled a prescription upon a notepad, ripped out the sheet of paper, and handed it to me.

"Take it only as needed," he said, viewing me sternly. "It's a powerful dosage."

I promised to be careful, to practice moderation with the opium he'd prescribed, though I was unsure if moderation was ever my true intent.

# Chapter 22

Advertisements soon plastered the city, announcing my upcoming exhibition at the American World's Fair. This increased the city's interest in me, and it appeared that every Roman citizen desired to visit me, to watch me work in my studio, to say they saw this great artist before she was an international star with work at the spectacular World's Fair. I could no longer find even a modicum of enjoyment in the attention, for it only further distracted me from the work I was supposed to be completing. Each day and each night, I would sit before the massive marble that I was meant to transform into Cleopatra, and felt that I could hardly complete one stroke of hammer against chisel, one movement of the file against that great stone, so tormented was I by the threatening letters I still received, those notes which told me I must not return to America. While the opium prescription allowed me to sleep, I began, at times, to sleep too much, to lose some of the motivation to even force myself from the bed. I barely ate during that time, which was just as well, as I could hardly afford bread and butter, a slice of cheese or olives at the market. All of the money Mrs. Whitney sent me would go to the rent for my studio, as I could not work on any new or commissioned piece, as what little energy I could summon had to go to completing *Death of Cleopatra.*

I began to hold many exhibitions in my studio to sell the work I'd previously completed, this in an effort to raise money for completion of the Cleopatra piece, and to save further funds for my fare and stay in Philadelphia, where the Centennial would be held. I felt that I was often sleepwalking through these studio exhibitions, needing an extra dose of opium just to take away the pain of being watched, to calm the fears that the sender of those threatening letters would be among the viewers in my studio.

I was holding just such an exhibition, entertaining and speaking with the various visitors through the fog of my opium, granting brief interviews to journalists of Italian periodicals and magazines. I stood speaking with one visitor, a young woman who said that she, too, desired to become an artist. I told her of the work it had taken to receive an invitation to the Centennial, and she listened, quite enthralled, hanging on to my every word. I felt like an automaton during this conversation, making the herculean effort to break through the fog of my medicine in order to perform every part the artist, the exhibition hostess. After a few moments spent in this conversation, I saw my studio door open, and watched a man enter, looking nervous and uncertain.

He removed his hat and held it against his person, looking at me in disbelief for quite some time, until he finally gave me a nervous smile.

"Excuse me one moment," I managed to say to the young woman, though I felt that all language might abandon me. I made my way to the visitor at the door.

"Ronan," I said, when I finally found the strength to speak. "What are you doing here? How long have you been in Rome?"

Ronan embraced me, and then held me at arm's length to better observe me. "I only arrived here yesterday. I settled into my hotel and came straight here. I knew that I had to see you."

"But how did you know that I was here? That this was my studio, that I had a studio at all?" I asked.

"I read about you in the papers, and I couldn't believe it," he said. "The article listed your studio as being located here. You've made it, Mary. I always knew you would."

"In the papers?" I repeated, unable to disguise the fear I felt at hearing this. "In Oberlin?"

"Indeed," he said, excitedly. "There was a story about you in the *Oberlin Lorain County News.* It seems that they reprinted it from a British paper, the *Athenaeum,* I believe it was."

I nodded, remembering the interview with Henry Wreford, how excited I was, how naïve then, and how ignorant to think that such a story would never make its way to Ohio. I felt that this must have been, at least in some part, the cause of the threatening notes I'd been receiving. Someone from my past now knew where I was, knew how to find me in Rome, knew exactly when I would be returning to America, and where I would be staying.

Domenico, who was helping to move a marble block at the side of my studio, must have noticed my fallen countenance, the nerves with which I absorbed Ronan's news, his unexpected presence. Domenico walked over to me as I stood with Ronan, standing at his full height, which was somewhat taller than Ronan's.

"Is everything alright?" Domenico inquired, unsmiling.

"Yes, Domenico," I attested. "Quite alright. This is Ronan Clarke, someone I knew in America."

"How do you do?" Domenico said, disinterestedly, with no move to extend a hand in Ronan's direction. Ronan seemed to notice Domenico's impertinence, but did not comment upon it.

I took a breath and shook my head, not wanting my fear of the letters to ruin this moment, and holding Ronan's hands ever tighter. "I hardly know what to say to you," I said. "I can hardly believe that you're real, and not a hallucination."

"You must allow me to take you to dinner," Ronan replied. "A celebratory reunion, between friends. You'll see that I'm no hallucination, but quite real."

I hesitated, looking back at the guests then in my studio, all of those people I had not the strength to entertain.

"A dinner, yes, alright," I said, my voice wavering in my nervousness, my excitement. "Just let me finish up here, and then we'll depart."

* * *

I stared at Ronan's face across the candlelight of the dinner table, trying to discern which of his features had changed, matured, improved, or even deteriorated with time. Ronan summoned the waiter for more wine as I stared, but I demurred, wanting to keep my wits about me for our meal.

"No thank you," I said. "No more for me."

Ronan furrowed his eyebrows. "But you must, Mary," he said. "We're celebrating. We haven't seen each other in years."

I considered this for a moment, eyeing Ronan above my wine glass. "Alright," I consented, "just a bit more. And you must remember, Ronan, that I am known as Edmonia, now, and not Mary."

Ronan stared at me then as the waiter refilled my glass. When the waiter finally moved away, Ronan resumed our conversation. "So, you've managed to find a friend here," he teased with a sly smile. "Domenico was his name?"

"Does that bother you?" I asked, not disabusing him of the idea that Domenico and I were in a relationship.

"Not me," Ronan said with a shrug, setting his wine back upon the table. "It was you who said that such a relationship was impossible."

"In America it would be," I answered him.

"So, if I relocated here to Rome," Ronan began, "could you and I have the relationship that we couldn't have back in Oberlin?"

I shifted in my seat and looked down at the table, pushing the veal osso buco around my plate. "The only relationship I can now have is with my work," I said. "I've got to complete my Cleopatra piece before the Centennial."

Ronan raised his eyebrows and took a sip of his wine, seeming to find this a suitable answer. "And how is the work on that going?"

"It isn't, really, if I'm being honest," I said. "I've had a sort of creative block, I suppose, though I know that I must overcome it, as the Centennial date grows near."

Ronan nodded, seeming to understand this. "Can I see what you have so far?"

I hesitated. "This piece is quite different than anything I've created before," I said. "I don't know if I should reveal it to anyone before it's completed.

"Perhaps I can help you overcome the creative block," Ronan offered, "Quite as I did when we were younger."

I was silent for a moment, taking a large sip from my own drink. "Perhaps you can," I finally said, grateful as always for the steadying effect of my drink. I decided that I could trust Ronan to see my work in progress, and could perhaps summon from him some piece of advice that would help me to complete that sculpture.

It was strange bringing Ronan into my studio at that time of night, sharing my sacred space with this man I'd been separated from for so many years. Ronan walked through the darkened space and observed each sculpture, placing his hand upon some, lingering even longer at others. Finally, we came to *Death of Cleopatra.* I was quite nervous to show Ronan this piece, and felt a strange sort of protectiveness over that Egyptian queen, as if I might be exposing some portion of myself by showing Ronan this piece. Ronan observed the sculpture for quite some time before speaking.

"A fine start," Ronan said, looking mildly impressed with the work I'd completed thus far. "Though I'd say she looks rather more like the Queen of England, than the Queen of the Nile." He took a breath, as if fortifying himself, and went on. "She doesn't look much like the sort of figure you said you wanted to sculpt back when we were younger, back in Oberlin. You said you wanted to craft your own people, to set their likenesses into stone, to show the world your humanity. I don't see very much of that in this piece, and this is what you'll be showing during your grand return to America. This is the sort of work you do now?" he asked, turning to me and looking genuinely curious.

I bristled at the implication. "It's the work that sells," I answered him curtly. "It's the work that has gotten me a spot at the Centennial."

Ronan raised his eyebrows. "I remember a time when you were less concerned with what would sell than what would mean something to you, and to your people."

I scoffed, not appreciating this lecture from someone who had no idea what it truly took to make it as an artist. "Well, everything was theoretical before I left Oberlin. I had no real responsibilities beyond making my brother proud. I didn't have my own studio to maintain, my own debts to repay. Works depicting my own people, whether the African or the Ojibwe, simply do not sell as well, and would never have been accepted for the Centennial Exposition."

"So, it's a mercenary existence you have now," Ronan said. "The young Mary Lewis would shudder at the thought."

"I'm not Mary Lewis anymore, Ronan," I said, growing incensed. "I've told you that, and yet you insist on giving me my old name. Mary Lewis was a powerless young girl. She was weak, and immature, and in the end, she was friendless. Edmonia is nothing like that girl."

Ronan stared at me. "I only wish you wouldn't speak of her so. Mary Lewis is the girl I fell in love with, after all," he said, moving closer to me. "And I only wish that she could see how special, how perfect I always found her."

I rounded on him then, allowing a release of my true feelings. "Do you suppose that matters to me? What you think of me? That you loved me? That you found me *special*?" I scoffed. "I don't have to care about your opinion any longer. I have found more success in my life than you could even imagine. You, who were too afraid to try and make a living with your own art, who just accepted his station in life. In America, my people have been treated as less than animals, and yet even I managed to find a way to make a name for myself, despite it all. So, no. I will not allow you to come here and question the methods by which I have found my success—"

Ronan stepped forward and grabbed my face, kissing me and stopping me from speaking. I pushed him away and wiped my mouth with the back of my hand, then thrust a finger into his face.

"Don't," I scolded. "Don't you dare try this now." I turned away from him for a moment, gathering myself, trying and failing to steady my breath. "You weren't there for me, Ronan," I finally said. "When I needed you the most, when I was at my lowest, you weren't there for me. You chose *her* over me. I am haunted by those events every day of my life, by the accusations that your own Gemma Ennes made against me, and now you return to me, bringing with you all of those memories from Oberlin, forcing me to confront the ghosts of my past."

Ronan walked toward me, not allowing me to flee from him. "I'm haunted by it all, too," he said. "I ended my relationship with Gemma shortly after your acquittal. I realized then, and I understand now, that I should have defended you. I should have testified on your behalf. Had I done that, you might not have had to flee from Oberlin. You could have finished your education there. I should have said that I knew—" Ronan stopped himself then, seeming to terminate his thought.

"That you knew what?" I asked, slowly, quietly, afraid of what he might reveal, but knowing that I had to find out, for my own sanity.

Ronan hesitated, seeming to grasp for the words, almost as if he wanted to save himself from whatever admission he had almost made. "That I knew what kind of person Gemma was. What she was capable of."

I felt enraged by these words, this seeming omission of what Ronan truly knew about the poisoning case, about the hell that Gemma and Sarah caused me to endure. I stormed to my writing desk, unlocked the drawer, and began to pull from its entrails the evidence of my torment, letter after letter after letter, all written in the same unfamiliar hand, all absent of any return address, any identifying information. I threw them at Ronan, one at a time, until he was forced to approach me, to grab my hands, to stop me from assaulting him any further.

"I can't escape that Oberlin past, not even here in Rome," I said. "I've never been able to escape it, and it seems I never will."

Ronan picked up one of the letters and began to read it, his countenance falling, his eyes showing disbelief that such abuse, such horrid words could be sent to me.

"The threats have been increasing in severity," I finally managed to say, though my voice was unsteady. "Someone is determined to stop me from going to the American Centennial, and it must be someone who knew me back in Ohio. If you know of something, anything, that can truly absolve me from all that happened in Oberlin, you must say it now, Ronan."

"All I know is that you should stay here, in Rome," Ronan said, reading another letter, then letting it drop to the floor. "Someone is saying that you will be killed if you go to the Centennial, if you dare show your art and your face there."

He took a moment to look at me before speaking, to ensure that I truly understood the severity of my situation. "These threats might be credible, Edmonia. By returning to America, you could be putting yourself into serious danger," he said.

"You're suggesting that I quit the Centennial?" I asked incredulously.

"I'm suggesting you do what is best for your safety, yes," he replied.

"For my safety, I should remain here, but for my art, for my career—" I shook my head. "I didn't allow threats, nor even physical harm to stop me back then at Oberlin, and I won't allow them to stop me now."

"Stay," Ronan said, looking at me, unsmiling. "Stay here, in Rome. Stay with me," he repeated, taking my hands and pulling me closer to him. "I can extend my time here in Rome. We can take the time we need to be together. We can rediscover each other. You won't even remember that the Centennial is happening, and you will still have your art career here, even if you don't have the broader exposure that the Centennial could provide."

Ronan's face was so kind, so earnest, that I did genuinely consider his proposition. Of course, I desired safety and protection, and I entertained the thought that Ronan could be the sort of person to provide that for me. But then, just as persistent, just as gnawing, was the thought that Ronan would be a hindrance to my art, would send me back to the girl I once was, and so it was then that I asked him, in no uncertain terms, to leave my studio, to leave me to my work.

Ronan did leave me there, alone in my studio, and I found that this decision, and my determination, did help to lift my spirits in the coming days. My spirits were so buoyed, my resolve so strengthened, that I found I was no longer fearful of the threatening letters I received. I was able to quit the opium I'd been prescribed, and I finished the Centennial sculpture, crafting an image of Cleopatra so majestic that even I felt in awe of her power. And even on the day of Ronan's departure from Rome, when he once again sought me out, when he asked me, and even begged me, to stay away from America, to not allow myself to be exposed and vulnerable at the Centennial, I knew that still, I must return to America, come what may.

# Chapter 23

I RETURNED TO AMERICA AFTER A SPACE OF MANY YEARS, A WOMAN much changed from who I'd been upon departing. No longer did I feel the insecurity of my youth, the idea that I was not good enough for high society, that I would not be able to carve out a space for myself among the educated and moneyed class. I hoped that my brother might not dislike the change in me, as he had taken a temporary lodging in Philadelphia for my Centennial debut, and we had arranged to meet there upon my arrival stateside, a few days before that World's Fair was to commence.

Samuel greeted me with a broad smile and warm embrace. I found him to be much changed as well, the hard work he'd completed over the years showing in his aged face, yes, but also in his fine clothing.

"How is Melissa?" I asked, inquiring after his wife, "and how are the children?"

"All is well back in Montana," Samuel said, speaking of the new home he'd made in that state. "The barber shop is finally taking off. Melissa is minding it, and the children, while I'm here. My household erupted into quite a commotion when I set off to come here without them," he said. "The children all wanted to come and meet their famous aunt. You have allowed them to be quite popular around the neighborhood, you see," he said. "I promised to bring back your autograph."

"You can bring them back more than that," I said, producing

a few of the medallions and cameos I'd brought along for just such a purpose, as a gift to the nieces and nephews I had not yet met. "Tell the children that their aunt anticipates the day when she can meet them as well, but in the meantime, such trinkets must suffice."

Samuel accepted the gifts. "Even mere trinkets from a famous artist will be as treasures to them," Samuel said. "And do you think you'll really be able to make such a trip one day, to Montana, to meet my family?" he asked. It was then I could see that the distance, the ocean between us, had similarly affected Samuel as it had me.

"Of course," I said. "Nothing could stop me from coming to your home, from meeting your family."

"That would be wonderful," Samuel replied. "You'll forgive me if I show you off around town when you visit. No one believes me, you know, when I tell them that you're my sister. I've been showing this article off so much that the townsfolk must be quite sickened of it. I've nearly got it memorized," he said, pulling the tattered page from his coat pocket, a small advertisement announcing my attendance at the American Centennial. "And now I am here in Philadelphia where I can see what art, what magnificence, all your sacrifices have produced."

"It took your sacrifices, as well," I said.

Samuel dismissed this. "Well, it was all nothing," he said. "And it's paying off for me, here in Philadelphia, with all the excitement about the Centennial going on. I've been telling every pub owner that I'm your brother, and it's gotten me plenty of free beer," he laughed. "Which reminds me, you must take this now, lest I forget," Samuel said, removing from his pocket a small note with an address. "A gentleman at the pub overheard me talking about you some days ago. He said that he was an old friend of yours. Said he saw an advertisement that you'd be exhibiting your work at the Centennial, and that he's been trying to get in contact with you ever since. He said he'd traveled all the way to Philadelphia in the mere hopes of seeing you again. I promised I'd pass along his information."

I accepted the note from my brother's hand and unfolded it, reading upon that paper a name I thought I would never see again, a name that made my breath catch in my throat.

"Cade Bronson?" I said aloud, speaking the name as much to Samuel as to Providence, the deity that must have brought that man back from the grave.

"Yes, that was the gentleman's name," Samuel said. "He seemed quite eager to meet with you. How do you know him? Is he someone you met in Boston?"

I shook my head in silent bewilderment. My brother seemed to sense the depths of my emotions, and allowed me some moments to read the note again and again.

"He will only be here for a few days, he said, to see the opening of the Centennial," Samuel told me. "He'll have to leave shortly after that to return to his work. You should go to him now, Edmonia, if he holds such importance to you. I'll still be here when you return."

I nodded, thankful for my brother's understanding, and quickly left Samuel's hotel room, nervous at the thought of a reunion with Cade.

It was in a stupor that I walked to Cade's hotel, barely noticing the people in the streets around me, the ongoing preparations I passed for the Centennial in Fairmount Park and its pathways. I nearly jumped when Cade opened his hotel room door, once again experiencing the uncanny sense that I was encountering an apparition, a preternatural being. He appeared to me even more striking, even more handsome than he had been before, the years giving him a greater confidence, a more distinguished stature than what he'd previously possessed. I noticed some scars upon his face and hands, evidence of his war service, of the unspoken horrors he'd experienced in battle.

"Cade," I whispered, touching a hand to my face, then reaching for his. "I thought that you—" I stopped myself, as if saying the word *died* would suddenly make it true, would make him vanish before my eyes. "I heard that the Fifty-Fourth Regiment was decimated. I was told you were among those missing, presumed dead. After so many years without hearing from you, I forced myself to accept that this was true, that you were gone from me, forever."

"Indeed, the regiment was decimated," Cade averred. "And yes, I was among the missing presumed to be dead. I wandered for some time in the South Carolina wilds, foraging, living off of whatever I could find. I thought about returning to the battlegrounds to try and find those soldiers who were left of my regiment, to continue fighting, if I could, but I'm ashamed to say that I hid, Edmonia," he said. "I was afraid. The Confederate threats against us were too intense, too horrible to consider. I thought that my life had been spared by some divine intervention, and that to reenlist, to rejoin the fighting would be to spit in the very face of Providence. That is why I was believed to be dead, as no one, not even my aunt Grace, heard from me for many years."

I nodded my head, trying my best to be supportive, an understanding ear for Cade, though the words he then spoke were quite surprising to me. I had never known him to be the sort of person who would submit to fear in such a way.

"When the war ended, I used some of the money I'd saved to buy a train ticket North. I came back to Boston. I came back for you," Cade said, "just like I said I would."

"Though perhaps a bit later than you said you would," I added, to a conciliatory look from Cade.

"I sought out Garrison's office when I got to Boston, remembering that he was one of the abolitionists who welcomed you there," he went on, "but I saw that *The Liberator* had been disbanded. I tried my best to find Addy in the hopes that she could contact you, but the Howards had moved, I learned, when I looked for their boarding house"

"The end of the war brought with it many changes," I said.

Cade nodded. "Indeed, it seems that it did. But then I remembered you mentioning Mrs. Lydia Maria Child, so I sought her out at last, though she told me she had no idea of your whereabouts. She sent me away from her home with the instruction not to return there, and not to go around inquiring about you any longer. And so I went back to Oberlin, to be with my aunt Grace, to be back on land that was familiar to me, where I felt somewhat welcomed."

I shook my head in disbelief. "Mrs. Child knew that I had gone on to Rome. She could have told you. You might have found me there," I said. "You could have written to me there, had she told you. I would have come back to America for you, if you couldn't find a way to get to Europe."

"I could have made the trip," Cade said. "I had enough to purchase passage on a steamship. I had my savings from the war, and other money from a few odd jobs, since I could work as a truly free man." Cade looked down, growing misty at the thought of a lost opportunity. "We might have begun a life there in Rome. We might have been together."

"But we are together now," I said. I took a step toward him and lifted his head. "We are yet young, young enough to marry, to start the family you always wanted."

Cade shook his head, still looking dejected. I hurried on.

"We could begin now, Cade. We can return to Rome together after the Centennial."

He stopped me. "I have my work here, Edmonia—"

"Does Rome not have employment?" I interrupted. "You might command a greater salary there than anything you could expect to find here with the Reconstruction."

Cade hesitated again, looking down again so as not to meet my gaze, refusing to speak what was truly on his mind.

At that moment, I heard voices in the hallway beyond, and the hotel room door flung open. Three children ran in, their eager cries of "Father! Father!" filling the room. As absurd as it seemed, it took me several moments to understand that these children were speaking to Cade, were calling *him* father, were then climbing onto his lap with the familiarity that could only speak to such a relationship. I stared at these children, openly scrutinizing each of their faces in turn, until one noticed me and asked, "Who is she?"

That child's face was so familiar to me, though it was not only Cade's likeness that I saw there, but another as well, a face I had not thought about in several years. And then, entering the room a few moments after the children, breathless and holding several grocery bags, was Josephine Campbell, whom I now understood was Josephine Bronson, Cade's wife, and the mother of his children.

Josephine stopped short in the doorway as she saw me, nearly dropping the heavy bags in her hands.

"Mary," Josephine said, her voice barely above a whisper. "Though I suppose it is Edmonia, now."

Cade took a breath, then stood up from his chair and helped Josephine with the grocery bags. "Edmonia, you remember Josephine," Cade said, and then, hesitatingly, he added, "my wife. And here are our children, Gracie, Charlotte, and Cade, Junior."

The children ran around the small hotel room, jumping onto and off of the bed, running behind the long window curtains, laughing and jostling each other around.

"You said you would take us to the park," Gracie said, pulling on her father's arm.

"So, I did. We'll go there now, so that your mother can speak with her friend here," Cade said. "It was a privilege to see you again, Edmonia," he said, and then placing a hand on Josephine's back, showing a united front with her, his wife, added, "Josephine and I are both so proud of all that you've done."

Cade left the room then, swiftly, clearly grateful for the opportunity of escape. His children were all in tow, yelling and jumping behind him. The door closed, leaving Josephine and me in utter silence, so total and awkward that I wished for my own chance of escape. I took a moment to observe Josephine, seeing in her all of the stresses that the years had brought her, yes, but seeing still, a certain grace, a certain beauty and charm quite familiar to what she'd had, all those years ago in Oberlin.

"You never did let anything stop you," Josephine began, looking at me with curiosity, but also with pride. "I've always admired you for that attribute. Perhaps I've always envied it, your courage. Not even the letters, the threats of death could stop you from coming back to America, for the Centennial."

Time seemed to stop as Josephine spoke these words. I stared at her for a moment, mouth agape.

"You know of the letters?" I finally managed to ask.

"I know of them, Edmonia," she said, then slowly added, "I sent them. Twenty-three in total, all mailed in unmarked envelopes. I went without food just to afford the postage," she whispered.

I shook my head in disbelief, feeling as if I'd received a physical blow. I lowered myself into a chair and took several breaths before speaking again.

"Josephine, what would possess you to commit such a heinous act?"

She looked sheepish, embarrassed, and made no move to explain herself.

"I've lost weeks of sleep. I've barely eaten. I was almost unable to finish my Centennial sculpture," I said, my voice growing loud. "I truly considered not coming here, so heavy was my fear. You nearly ended my career, Josephine," I said, and then thinking of my heavy opium usage, added, "you nearly ended my life."

Josephine took a moment before speaking, allowing me to vent my frustrations in full.

"Cade and I both saw your name in the papers announcing your attendance at the Centennial," Josephine said. "I had already known for some time that you'd been working in Rome. I'd seen the article in the *Oberlin Lorain County News* some years ago, but Cade had no idea, at first. Once news of the World's Fair began to spread around town, there was no longer any way to keep the word away from him. I felt a physical pain when I saw how excited Cade was to read your name there in the papers, to see the advertisements for your sculpture. He was still in love, that much was clear. I dare say he still is to this very day."

Josephine shook her head and looked down at her hands. "He was so taken by the thought of you, the artist, the great success, that I truly felt he would leave me, would even leave the children should you two be reunited, should you decide that you returned his feelings. You, the woman with the incredible mind, the incredible career, and me, the housewife, the maid. There was simply no comparison, there would be no way for me to compete."

I shifted in my seat, growing uncomfortable now to hear the ways that Josephine viewed herself. She went on.

"Cade became obsessed, determined that we would come here to Philadelphia to see you. We hadn't the money for it in truth. Three growing children, a household to upkeep. His work as a farmhand, mine as a housemaid, are hardly enough to live on, much less to take a trip halfway across the country. But then he told the children we'd go, that they'd see the Liberty Bell, and the room where the Constitution was written. They were so excited at the prospect. What kind of a mother would I be to let them down?"

I shook my head, still silent as Josephine continued.

"My only choice was to ensure that you would not come here, Edmonia. And so, I began sending letters to that studio in Rome I saw advertised in the papers. I felt sick over the first one I sent, I really did. But then, with each letter, the work became easier, my task became clearer, more urgent. I had to stop you from coming here, you see, in order to preserve, to protect my own family, to keep my husband."

Josephine finally met my eye once again, and said, slowly, uncertain as to what my response would be, "And so it is that I owe you an apology, Edmonia. I'm sorry that I allowed my jealousy, my insecurity to overcome me. I'm sorry that I did my best to frighten you, to keep you away from this important—this monumental—work."

I took a moment to allow Josephine's words to sink in. When I finally did speak, it was not to admonish her, nor yell, nor vent any more of the emotions I then felt. It was only to make my own apology, one I realized then was long overdue.

"I'm sorry, as well," I said. Josephine looked at me in surprise.

"I wasn't a true friend to you back in Oberlin. When my roommates showed their disdain for you, when they told me I wasn't to spend time with you, I simply obeyed them as if they were my masters. I was afraid, I suppose, that they would make my life hell, more of a hell than they'd already created for me. But that is no excuse. I should have been there for you. I should have understood back then that you were my only true friend."

Josephine looked quite surprised, as if she had been expecting a scolding, or a physical assault, instead of the apology I offered her.

I went on. "You always told me that Cade would make a wonderful husband. It seems that he is," I said.

Josephine laughed, seeming relieved. "Sometimes I forget it, always running behind the children, never having any time for him," she said.

"It's a beautiful life you've created for yourself," I told her, and I meant the words that I spoke. I could see that she was, despite her criticisms of herself, contented by her domestic life, the happy familial demands of her children and her husband, that she was fulfilled by this work in a way that I never could have been. This was why she felt so fiercely protective of that life, and of Cade. I knew that Cade had found a wonderful wife in Josephine, the sort of wife I never could have been.

"I should say the same to you, Edmonia," she said. "And tomorrow, the whole world will see what a life you've created."

I nodded and smiled at Josephine, then swept her into a warm and genuine embrace. In that moment, I truly did forgive her for all transgressions, and felt absolved of those I myself had committed. I knew that she was correct, that the world would soon see the life I had created, that all of those who said that artistry, that genius itself, was outside of the realm of the colored woman would be disabused of all such notions in the morning. The grand American Centennial yet beckoned, and I would answer its call, alone, and undaunted.

# Chapter 24

Crowds swelled outside of Philadelphia's Memorial Hall, a haze, a miasma of different people and races and languages, all clamoring for entrance into the Centennial art exhibition.

"Exhibitors step this way," a man yelled above the noise of the crowds. "Spectators, step aside. The doors aren't open to the general public just yet."

I stepped toward the indicated line for exhibitors when the man stopped me with a rough and heavy arm.

"I said exhibitors only," the man repeated, his voice rude and gruff. "The help must go through the back entrance."

"Sir," I said, somehow managing to maintain my patience. "I am an artist, Edmonia Lewis. My *Death of Cleopatra* is being put on display here."

I pulled the advertisement from my skirt pocket and thrust it toward the man, one with a small sketch of my face, hoping that this would help to prove my identity, but before he could review it, Mr. Forney burst out of the exhibition hall.

"Miss Lewis, please, hurry this way," Mr. Forney said. "I'll show you where we've placed your sculpture. You'll have a few moments to settle in, and then the crowds will enter, and the exhibition will begin."

I followed Mr. Forney into Memorial Hall, feeling the gruff man's disbelieving eyes upon my back as I did so. Mr. Forney led me deep into the building, past grand marble staircases and gleaming chandeliers. We came to Gallery K, and the rotunda, its glass ceiling glittering and magnificent above us. And there, just beneath the skylights, was my sculpture, *Death of Cleopatra,* with that Nile queen seated in all of her glory and beauty, even in those moments just after her suicide.

"These newspapermen won't let me hear the end of it," Mr. Forney told me. "They've been waiting for you all day. Everyone wants to see the genius, they say, the Negro sculptress."

I took a breath at his words, at the idea that I was being called a genius. Mr. Forney went on.

"I told them they could see your work along with everyone else once we open the doors. It seems that your sculpture is the one to see," he said, appearing pleased that he would receive a return on his investment in me, that my work was taken seriously by journalists, desired to be seen by all of the spectators. I took a moment to let Mr. Forney's words sink in, to imagine that first moment when I unveiled my sculpture, to see the looks of wonder and awe on the spectators' faces, to answer the journalists' thoughtful questions about my work, my process, my inspirations. I inhaled deeply, placed a hand upon the sculpture, then placed a violet shroud over it, and readied myself for all of the wonderment to come.

With that, the doors opened, and the crowds poured into Memorial Hall. I scanned the many faces entering the exhibition space, seeing, it seemed, representatives from all nations on earth, and I felt, once again, a sense of disbelief that so many varied people would be able to view my work.

"There she is," a woman said, looking up from her brochure and pointing toward me. "The great Negro sculptress." This announcement made several other groups of spectators turn toward me, and approach me and my shrouded sculpture.

"She is a Negro, indeed," a man answered her. "The rest is yet to be seen."

"Strange to see her standing there like that," said another man, moving closer to me. "She looks more like a common cook than an artist. I half expect to see a dinner spread underneath that veil, rather than a sculpture."

There were some snickers, some scattered agreement, and to my great shock, I saw the name tag on the man who made that disparaging comment, and surmised that he was one of the journalists, and a prominent art collector, a Mr. William Hayes Ackland, present there to interview me for the papers. While I was surprised by his demeaning words, expecting someone as distinguished as he to be a bit more careful in his speaking, I did not allow his thoughts to deflate my excitement, and I still smiled as more people gathered around my sculpture. Finally, the time came to reveal my work.

Mr. Forney stepped forward then and cleared his throat.

"Thank you, ladies and gentlemen, for coming here today," he began. I looked out at the crowds and saw Samuel, Cade and his family, and Mrs. Whitney toward the back, breathless, rushing in to see my sculpture's debut. I had expected to feel calmed by their presence before my sculpture, but I found that suddenly, it only made me more nervous, for I began to see that the spectators gathered before me might not be as kind and fawning as I had hoped, and I did not want my loved ones to see that.

"What you will see here today may surprise you, yes," Mr. Forney continued, turning toward the man, Mr. Ackland, who had made the snide comment, and seeming to address him in particular. "Even more so because it was created by colored hands."

Mr. Ackland rocked on his heels uncomfortably as Mr. Forney went on. "But as you view this work, *Death of Cleopatra* by Edmonia Lewis, may you see what sort of talent this country can breed, may you reflect on that, on this occasion of our country's Centennial, though Miss Lewis had to travel to Rome so that her talent could find ultimate expression. Miss Lewis," Mr. Forney said, turning then to me, "if you please."

I stepped forward onto the platform, took a deep breath, and removed the purple velvet shroud from my sculpture, from that work over which I'd labored, through fear, through illness, through threat of physical harm, for so much time. The crowd gasped as they viewed the sculpture, seeing Cleopatra there, her head thrown back, mouth agape, in the unrelenting throes of death.

"A shocking thing," a woman yelled.

"Vile," agreed another.

"She's barely clothed," said a man, seeming to find this abhorrent, though he did not look away.

"Miss Lewis's people are known for such vulgarity," another man said. "What else did you expect?"

A journalist tried to get a word in, shouting above the noise of the other spectators, "How long did it take you to complete this, Miss Lewis?"

Appreciating this attempt to take my work seriously, I answered him directly, and quickly.

"Several years," I replied. "Especially if you consider the time for its conception, its incubation, the sketching, the early plaster models, and—"

"Several years?" a woman repeated, looking to her companion beside her in disbelief. "This version of Cleopatra looks like a common wench—"

"I do believe I could create as much, in half the time," a man said with a short and incredulous laugh. "And this woman, this Edmonia Lewis, is said to be a genius?"

"Anyone can traffic in the erotic, in vulgarity," someone called from the depths of the crowd. "A true artist can convey a message with some subtlety, some nuance."

I tried to press on, raising my voice to be heard above the growing commotion. "I studied ancient medallions to get Cleopatra's countenance just right, and I—"

"Those medallions showed her in life, not after her death," a journalist yelled. "What you've crafted here is something quite different, something base. Why have you chosen to depict her so, to defile a queen, to show her in such a brutal moment?"

"She is a violent woman, that's why," a man declared, with much confidence. "She delights in death and destruction. As Cleopatra poisoned herself with the asp, Edmonia Lewis poisoned two young girls, her roommates, while she was at Oberlin College. Her weapon was not a snake, as Cleopatra's asp, but Spanish fly."

"I think I read of that case, as well," said another man. "Yes, it's coming back to me, now. She was known as Mary, then. Mary Lewis, of Ohio."

I swallowed hard and looked out toward the crowd, trying to discern the looks on the faces of Samuel, of Cade and Josephine, and of Mrs. Whitney. Even there, in that vaunted space at the American Centennial Exposition, I could not escape the demons of my past. Even there, the crowds were determined to remind me that I was nothing, that they deemed me unworthy of all I had achieved. How ridiculous of me to have expected anything else, to have imagined that I might find respect and awe here in America. My hands began to shake as I stood there before the crowds, as I began to feel as weak and unprotected as I had when I was but a child, sent into society for the very first time.

The people continued their chatter, pointing and scowling, some laughing at me quite openly. I saw Samuel, Cade and Josephine, and their children make their departure, not wanting to witness any more of the abuse to which I was being subjected. I felt more like a circus animal than an artist, then, as if all of those people had gathered to see what a beast could do, when trained, and desired only to jeer at me for daring to pretend I was human. It felt as if several months passed as I endured those insults, but it was only one day, and as evening fell, Mr. Forney approached the platform to finally give them leave.

"Ladies, gentlemen," Mr. Forney called out. "The Centennial grounds are closing for the day. Miss Lewis can answer more questions at a later time. Indeed, she'll be here with her work for a few more weeks before her return to Europe."

The crowds began to disperse at Mr. Forney's instruction, but one figure, I noticed, remained. It was Mrs. Anne Whitney, and she approached me and Mr. Forney slowly as we stood there at the platform.

"Mr. Forney," Mrs. Whitney said. "You'll oblige me if I take a few moments to speak with Miss Lewis?"

"But of course, Mrs. Whitney," Mr. Forney replied. "It's thanks to you we even knew to include Miss Lewis in our fair. She's had quite the effect, as you saw. She's selling tickets faster than we can stamp them, indeed, as everyone wants to see the controversial figure she's rendered, and the controversial figure she is, herself."

"Indeed," Mrs. Whitney said, giving Mr. Forney a tight smile, then turning to me as he departed.

"How do you feel?" Mrs. Whitney began. "Your Centennial debut, your return to America?" she asked. It seemed that she was asking these questions more out of politeness than genuine curiosity, but I answered her earnestly, all the same.

"It was strange," I replied. "Not what I'd expected, though perhaps I should have. I wanted the spectators to take my work seriously, to ask me questions about my work that were generous, earnest, and not merely insulting. Some criticism I can handle, and indeed, have endured throughout my career, but I find that I cannot countenance such purposefully malicious views of my work."

Mrs. Whitney looked at me for a moment, silent that I might continue on.

"These people were not here to engage with me, or my work, in any true way," I said, shaking my head, my voice quivering as I spoke. "I am not real to them. I am not worthy of their true attention as a human being might be. I am an animal to them, a beast in a circus, a counting horse, a talking dog."

Mrs. Whitney, though she seemed to feel some sense of the pain I then described, only gave a curt nod. I found her behavior so strange as we talked in that exhibition hall, as she met me with coldness where I expected warmth and understanding, shortness where I expected patience. Finally, she came to the question it seemed she'd wanted to ask all along, the point that seemed to bother her, from which she could not easily proceed without an answer. "What is this business about your time in Oberlin?" she asked.

"It is nothing," I told her, quickly, hoping to hastily dispense with the subject. "Some nonsense that occurred in my youth."

"Nonsense that was written about in the papers?" Mrs. Whitney pursued. "That has imprinted itself upon the minds of these spectators?"

I grew even more fatigued, felt even more powerless, as she continued on.

"You never told me that you spent time in Ohio. You never told me you attended any other institution than New York Central College," Mrs. Whitney said. When I did not respond, and only lowered my head in shame, she pressed on, growing ever more angry. "Edmonia, you must explain yourself to me, this instant."

I shook my head and opened my mouth to speak, though she interrupted me before I could begin to offer an explanation.

"Did you not think you should disclose such information to me, before I invested such time and money into your career?" she asked. "If I had known I was supporting a common criminal, I might have saved my money, I might not have risked my own reputation, I might have—"

"Mrs. Whitney, I am no criminal," I said, now growing emotional. "I was a woman accused, that is all."

"There is often some morsel of truth to even the wildest accusations," she said. "You must tell me the truth now. You owe me as much, after all of the funding and support I've given you."

I moved closer to Mrs. Whitney and spoke quickly, understanding the urgency of the moment. "I do not know the reality of what happened to those girls, my former roommates, Mrs. Whitney," I said. "They said that they were poisoned. I never knew the truth. I only know that I was always innocent of all charges."

Mrs. Whitney drew in her lips and raised her eyebrows. "Well, that closes the matter, I suppose, though it doesn't so much as explain it." She took a moment to gather her thoughts, then looked up at my sculpture, appearing even more massive now that the crowds had dispersed. "I've gotten you here, Edmonia, to the Centennial. I've supported your time in Rome. I'm not sure there's much more that I can offer you," she declared. "I cannot be tied to someone with . . ." She hesitated, searching for the right words. "With such a history."

She pulled her hat farther down on her head as she prepared to leave.

"Mrs. Whitney, please," I cried, grabbing her arm, which she promptly pulled away. "You cannot just leave me this way. You have gotten to know me over all of these years. You know my character, you know that I am—"

"You know my address," Mrs. Whitney hastened to say, interrupting my words. "You can send the last money you owe me there. The payment you receive for this exhibition should be enough to settle your debts with me, yes?"

Before I could respond, Mrs. Whitney turned away from me, then quickly moved toward the exhibition hall exit, and made her final departure from that space and from my life. It seemed that she could not risk one more second spent in my presence, could not allow, any longer, association with someone she believed to be a common criminal. Her reputation was too important to associate with someone like me, as was Mrs. Child's, as was Mr. Brackett's, as was the case with so many of the people who had abandoned me in the past.

I stood for several moments in complete silence, shocked at Mrs. Whitney's treatment of me, but relieved to finally be away from all of the people who had come to see me that day. I believed myself to be quite alone with Memorial Hall silent, the spectators all having moved out into the streets, the sound of their revelry, the festivities, lightly echoing in the halls. This solitude would allow me the opportunity to process all that had happened that day, to reflect on Mrs. Whitney's words, to determine a path forward, to devise a plan to make a living completely on my own, without Mrs. Whitney's support, once I returned to Rome. I leaned my head against my sculpture, taking a deep breath and trying, yet failing, to release all of the stress of the day. A sudden noise interrupted me, the sound of footsteps, a lady's heel echoing in the hall. I looked behind me and scanned the premises, but still, I saw no one, and tried yet again to believe that I was completely alone in Memorial Hall.

"Hello?" I called out, to no reply. I tried yet again, but even then, no one answered me, though I still sensed, even more than I heard, someone there. When I could finally stand it no longer, I turned from my statue, ready to flee from Memorial Hall, when a cloaked figure approached me from the shadows.

"I've waited for years now," the shrouded woman said, moving ever closer to me, her voice eerie and low. "Fourteen years now, to rid myself of this horrible secret."

The shrouded woman moved in front of me, blocking my exit as I turned to run, then removed her hood and smiled, a look absent of all mirth, and indeed, of all feeling. A chill ran through me as I realized that Gemma Ennes stood before me, aged much more than the time would suggest. I took a step back from her, and another, until my back met with my sculpture, and I found myself quite cornered, quite vulnerable before this madwoman.

"What do you want from me?" I demanded.

"I only want to talk to you," she replied, her voice even and calm. "I only want to explain to you what happened all those years ago."

I shook my head. "Gemma, I want nothing to do with this now. The case was dropped, and I just want to move on. I just want to leave all of that behind me." I looked her full in the face then, almost begging her to understand, seeing that her countenance was haggard and pale. "Please, just let me leave it all behind me now."

"I will after tonight," Gemma replied. "But first, only listen."

I looked around, hoping to see Mr. Forney or one of the Centennial commissioners still lingering in the exhibition hall, but there was no one present, no one to protect me, as had so often been the case in my life.

"I couldn't stand it when you moved in with us," Gemma said, speaking slowly, seemingly transported back to the day when we first met. "Your eloquence, your fine dresses. I felt that you were entitled, when you should have been grateful, you should have been kissing the ground we walked on for letting you live with us."

My breath grew shallow as she talked. I felt as if it were impossible for me to inhale the air I so desperately needed to handle all that Gemma was then telling me. She went on, seeming to speak to herself as much as she was speaking to me, seeming to have rehearsed these words many times before saying them to me, reciting them coldly, strangely, as an automaton might.

"And then, even Mrs. Dascomb's course wasn't enough for you. We girls were all just thankful to be allowed to learn, and you wanted more. You expected more out of life. When I found out you were pursuing art, that you were taking lessons with my intended . . ." She paused, clearly appearing to still harbor some feelings for Ronan, "I didn't know what to make of it all."

I stepped forward, finally regaining some of my composure, and hoping that I could reason with Gemma.

"Gemma, please, listen, I—"

"But still, that wasn't the biggest affront," she said, speaking over me, seeming not to even realize that I had uttered any words. "The biggest affront, the most maddening part of it all, was that your art was excellent. Ronan showed me some of what you were working on. I made him show me that night, after the Christmas dance. And what you were creating, your vision, your ideas—it was all so powerful that I knew if anyone could see your art, they would see your humanity. They would see that your people should be free. They would *ensure* your peoples' liberation."

Gemma shook her head, seeming to be physically transported back to that time. "The thought of that, the thought of the South losing the war, the thought of my grandparents losing everything, *me* losing everything that I was still set to inherit—I just couldn't handle it anymore. I wanted you expelled. I wanted you jailed. I believe I wanted you dead."

I made another attempt to move away from Gemma, but she blocked my path, yet again.

"And so, I lied." Gemma said, a sentence far too terse, too quick, I thought, and incongruous with the gravity of her confession. "I fabricated the story that you'd poisoned me and Sarah in the mere hopes that you would be locked away forever, unable to create your art, ever again. It was easy enough to get

Sarah to go along with the idea. She would have done anything I told her in those days. And I knew that all of the townspeople, and even the Keep family, would be suspicious of you. You were always such a strange and solitary figure, always to yourself, in your own head, that no one ever really knew what you were up to. And so I knew that my plan would be easily executed. You can't imagine my shock, my horror, when I learned that you'd been cleared of all charges."

I stared at Gemma, realizing then that she had completed her admission, and expected my response. I could hardly catch my breath or regain my composure, much less formulate any sort of response to all that she told me in that moment.

"Say something," Gemma demanded. "Tell me you forgive me, tell me you hate me, tell me you want me dead," she said, shaking her head, her hollow eyes growing wide. "Only say something to me."

"I don't hate you," I began slowly, knowing myself to be dealing with someone quite dangerous. "You were a child, then. We both were."

Gemma shook her head, seeming dissatisfied with my words, as if they were not sufficient punishment for all that she had confessed.

"I've never forgiven myself for what I did," she said. "If it's any consolation, I have felt such guilt about it for all of this time. I had to come here to apologize for my actions, lest I never find rest for the remainder of my life." Gemma looked up at my sculpture then and threw a defeated arm in its direction. "And now you've become the artist you were always meant to be," she said. "So, you've thrived, despite it all, despite what I did."

I took in my breath at such an assertion. I did not feel as if I were thriving, did not believe myself, just then, after the jeers and insults during my Centennial debut, to be a success. I wanted to tell her this, to tell her that she should send a letter to the newspapers, should admit to what she did, should clear my name definitively, and on the record, so that I might find more favorable audiences in the future. But I did not want to belabor the point, did not want to speak with Gemma Ennes any longer, and so I only nodded, and said, "I did, Gemma. I did make it, despite it all."

Gemma only slowly nodded her head at this, then looked down, and broke into silent tears. I watched as she cried, as her knees buckled, as she knelt to the ground and apologized to me, again and again, her voice growing weaker and quieter as she assured me that the cruelty of the years she had faced were sufficient retribution for all she had done. I made no move to comfort Gemma, too afraid to even extend a hand in her direction, and only stood silently as Gemma continued to cry for several moments, before finally drying her tears, collecting herself, and standing once again. Gemma left me then, her disappearance as sudden as her appearance had been. I felt a near-physical deflation once she left, once I confirmed that I was finally, truly, alone. I crumpled to the floor, heaving, trying and failing to catch my breath. A horrible pain shot through my side, and I cried out in pain, in anguish at the release of fourteen years of a lifetime of pent-up anxiety and torture. I cried so loud that it might have been reported in the papers, might have been news that was carried around for quite some time, but the exhibition hall was empty, and no one was there to witness my cries.

# Chapter 25

"Just move your head a bit to the left, please," I said to the sitter in my studio, some months after my Centennial debut, once I had finally returned to Rome.

"How is this?" the sitter asked, turning his head as requested.

"Perfect, Mr. President," I said, as Ulysses Grant shifted in his seat before me. He had visited my studio during his tour of the European Continent after an extended stay in Rome, declaring that he simply had to meet the sculptress who had made such a stir at the American Centennial. "I still can't believe I'm directing the former American president, Civil War hero, on how to sit while I sculpt him," I mused.

It was a dream opportunity for me, perhaps even more important than my exhibition at the Centennial, and I only wished that I felt better while I sculpted him, as the pain in my side I felt after speaking to Gemma at the Centennial had never dissipated, and its severity had only increased in the time since. I pushed past the pain for my meeting with President Grant, and indeed, pushed past the chance to visit Samuel and his family in Montana to do so.

*Please forgive me,* I had written to my brother, who had invited me to extend my stay in America and go with him to Montana to meet his family. *Surely, you understand that I cannot forgo the opportunity to sculpt our former president, who has been such a friend to our people.*

Samuel had written back that he understood my need to return to Rome, my need to continue my artistic career there, and of course, my desire to meet a figure as distinguished as President Grant. I comforted myself with the idea that such meetings were a testament to Samuel and all that he had done for me, were a justification for all of the pain and suffering I had endured after Samuel decided to send me to school.

"I couldn't miss the chance to visit your studio," President Grant replied, shifting in his seat a bit more as I continued to sculpt him, "to see the sort of artist our country can create."

I smiled and reminded him, "I had to come to Rome to become a true artist, President Grant."

"And yet you got your start on American soil," he said, "and returned to our own internal conflicts, our own national struggles, for much of your inspiration. It seems that our great and challenging nation was the stone on which you sharpened your artistic tools."

I nodded, as I could not dispute the point.

"And when can we expect to welcome you back?" he asked. "Surely you must want to return at some point, to spend at least some more years in the country of your birth."

I shook my head. "I have heard of the conditions my people live in there, now, during the Reconstruction efforts," I said. "It is to squalor, I should return?"

President Grant conceded the point. "You know that I did all I could in the service of Reconstruction during my time in office," he said. "I called in the National Guard to defend your people when they were persecuted throughout the South. Were I to do anything else to force the Southern states to respect the rights of freedmen, I would have been called a dictator."

I sighed and accepted the truth of his words. "I've done all that I can, as well, I do believe," I said, momentarily placing my hammer and chisel upon my lap. "My art, my career. I used to think that if I could just show the American citizens, through my art, that my people have humanity, have souls, that it would solve everything, that it would bring about true respect, true equality."

"And you learned that people are not so simple, our problems are not so easy to solve," President Grant said, "as I did, during my time in office."

"That is what I learned, indeed," I confirmed, taking up my hammer and chisel yet again, and unleashing a blow upon the marble before me. It had been a difficult truth for me to accept in the years after the Centennial, as I watched from Rome as the American Reconstruction efforts led to further suffering and degradation for many of the freedmen and freedwomen. Samuel would write to me throughout the years about the ongoing struggles our people faced, especially in the South, with the rise of the Klansmen who sought to murder any colored person who asserted their new rights. It made me feel as if my life's work had all been for naught, a thought I had to consistently, and with much assiduous effort, fight against. Moments like that one with President Grant, however, helped me to endure, as I knew that a life as fulfilling and unique as mine could not have begun in any other country, at any other time.

"And yet you continue to sculpt, Miss Lewis," President Grant said, watching me work, much awe and admiration on his visage.

I nodded. "Art is my everything, Mr. President," I told him. "I don't have anything else, and so I will continue to create, despite whatever struggles come my way."

Some months later, Frederick Douglass and his new bride, Helen Pitts Douglass, came to Rome during their own European tour. Mr. Douglass called on me especially to be a sort of tour guide to the two of them as they made their way through the sights and wonders of that historic city, and I gladly accepted his request, excited to host such a celebrity, to show him the city that had become my home, that I had grown to love with all that I had.

We walked through the famous Piazza di Trevi one day, and I observed Mr. Douglass as he watched Helen, as she ran up to the fountain and tossed coins behind her, closing her eyes and making wishes in childish glee. Mr. Douglass looked off at Helen lovingly, his admiration of his new wife so frank as to be almost embarrassing to me, as if I were impertinent to stand there and witness it. Theirs was an unconventional marriage, as she was a white woman, many years Mr. Douglass's junior, and might have been somewhat naïve as to how their matrimony would be received, and the hatred and disdain that even a famous writer and orator could receive after committing that act of miscegenation, as the detractors called it. But to see how free these two were in Rome, how happy and gleeful, giddy in their companionship, was to know that love could truly transcend all restrictions placed upon it.

"Maybe I could have had a love like that," I said to Mr. Douglass, as he looked yonder at his wife. "Or like what you had with Anna," I said, referencing his first wife, lately passed away. I paused and shook my head, growing somber. "I couldn't see it for myself. I had a vision for my art, my career, but not for my love."

Mr. Douglass nodded. "You might be forgiven for such singular focus on your work," he said. "Many an artist has made the same choice, has seen singledom as the only path for a thriving career."

I looked off into the distance, then finding it easier to speak my true thoughts if I didn't meet Mr. Douglass's eye.

"I can't help feeling like it was all for nothing," I said, "when I see the way that our people live, in America. My art didn't help to improve anyone's station, as I'd always hoped, in my naïveté, that it would."

"You remind me of myself at about your age," Mr. Douglass said, with a small, sorrowful laugh. "Working myself to the bone just to see my work, and my words, wasted, even used against me in some instances."

He took in a breath. "I, too, wondered if it was all worth it, Edmonia. The strain that fame put on my family . . ." He hesitated and looked off into the distance, then focused his gaze on Helen. "I sometimes wonder if my Anna would still be alive had I been home with her more, had I better shown her how much I loved her. I wonder if I would have lost my youngest child, my sweet little Annie, and so many grandchildren, if I had been there to help, to provide a patriarch's warmth and protection. But my work always beckoned. Perhaps you made the right decision remaining alone. You might have spared the feelings of someone who would be devastated every time you walked out of the door, as my Anna always was when I went away for my work."

I thought of Cade, and of Ronan, and Domenico, too, and despite my best efforts, I couldn't quiet the thought that perhaps, even seeing that devastation on one of their faces each time I left, each time I went to my work, instead of going to my husband, might have been better than seeing nothing at all each time I came and went out of my studio door.

Shortly after my time with Frederick and Helen Douglass in Rome, I received word that Samuel, my dear brother, had passed away. The news was sent to me in a short letter from his wife, Melissa, and I read it, completely bewildered, as I stood in my art studio, visitors and spectators all around me. Visions of all our memories together flashed before my eyes, from our youth together in northern New York, to all of the belief he'd had in me, the time and money he'd spent on me throughout the years, all in the hopes I'd achieve something great. I knew that my brother had been a special man, an ambitious man, and I could only hope, then, that I had made him proud while he was alive.

It had become increasingly difficult for me to sell my work in the years after the Centennial Exposition, with the neoclassical style rapidly falling out of fashion, and buyers not wanting pieces so closely fashioned after the Greco-Roman antiquity, and so I could not send the money that Samuel's family needed to help fund his funeral, and could not affort to go to Montana to see his body laid to rest. I felt at a loss as to how I should properly mourn my brother, and with no real friends then remaining in Rome, with no one to turn to, I could only tell the news of Samuel's death to a few locals then roaming through my studio after I read that wretched letter. In the only act of tribute I could at that moment give to my brother, who had given all he had to me, I announced to the visitors in my studio the terrible news I had received.

"My brother has died," I said, to no one and everyone at once. "He is gone from me, forever now."

One kind lady looked at me, and gave a quick but nervous smile. She answered me in Italian, seeming to offer some sort of condolences, then quickly left my studio, though I had heard her speaking in English only moments before. I understood myself to be truly alone in the world, then, without my parents, without my aunts, without any true friends I could call my own, and without my brother, who had always believed in me, and supported me, more than anyone else I had known.

# Epilogue

*1907*

No state of being invites reflection the way that illness does, in its stark refusal to be ignored, its ability to level, to bring even the highest achiever down to nothing more than destitution and pain. My ailment came on slowly, furtively stealing what little energy, what little optimism I had left. The pain in my side first experienced at the Centennial persisted. Headaches became more frequent and grew in intensity and duration; an insurmountable fatigue, unyielding to any stimulant or nutriment, began to overtake me by the day. I initially blamed this on inactivity, a stasis after the excitement of the Centennial, the triumph of my meetings with President Grant and Mr. Frederick Douglass, the shock of my brother's death. But then, I understood that my pain was not simply the result of inactivity or stasis, and that I should seek a professional diagnosis for my ailment, and so I set out for just such guidance.

The first few doctors I visited told me that I was simply suffering from an affliction of the mind, and nothing corporeal. They told me to take the fresh air, to bathe in the sea, and that this would heal all. But then I noticed a swelling of my limbs, an inability to move, a debilitating pain that would not be quelled by open skies or seas. I understood then that my illness was physical, not merely mental, and that I would need to receive greater care. There was nothing left to do then but seek admission to whatever infirmary I could afford, and so it was that I found myself in Hammersmith, London, in a small charity hospital near the Thames, where I received my ultimate diagnosis of Bright's disease, an ailment of the kidneys, incurable I was told.

I would lie in my bed with little else to divert me but my memories, that ever-diminishing store of remembrances of days when I saw some success. The neoclassical style of art had long since fallen out of style, with audiences and art patrons favoring a more modern and impressionistic approach, Parisian art nouveau, a style that I could not manage to perfect, no matter how hard I tried, traveling to Paris, and ultimately to London to try and find new inspiration, though none came. And so it was by the time that I found myself hospitalized, I had gone many years with no successful art pieces, with no sales, with no visits to any studio I might rent. I was quite unknown by the time of my diagnosis, similar to the isolated girl I had been as a child, and just as powerless as I had been in those days. I even returned to my previous identity, the simple Mary Lewis, not wanting to be called Edmonia, to constantly feel all of the weight and expectation that had been imbued in that name.

It was with much discomfort that I rearranged myself one day, sitting up straighter in my hospital bed, wincing against the pain. In shifting my position, I saw three nurses just outside of my hospital room door, in the hallway speaking together in hushed tones. I trained my ear to their voices, trying hard to discern their words, and realizing that they were discussing me.

"Hannah, I've assigned you to Mary's room, as you're the newest charge here," the lead nurse said, authoritatively.

"Mary never has any visitors," a second nurse said. "No family, the poor thing. Won't matter one bit if you make a little mistake, Hannah dear, as no one will stop by to notice."

"She's quiet, that Mary. Perfect training for you," the first nurse agreed, as they whispered together at their station.

"She'll need laudanum administered as needed for the pain, and surfeit water when requested, to settle her stomach. Is that all clear?" the lead nurse asked.

"Yes, ma'am," Hannah replied.

The lead nurse nodded and placed an encouraging hand on Hannah's shoulder. "Good, dear, then off you go."

Hannah took a deep breath, then turned in my direction, facing my doorway.

"Hello, ma'am," Hannah said, entering my room with a tentative knock. She looked down at her clipboard, flipped through a couple of pages, then placed it upon a table and picked up a stethoscope. "This may be a bit cold," she said, placing the stethoscope upon my back.

I grimaced and shifted in my bed.

"Heart rate seems to be normal," she said, then produced a tincture from her uniform pocket. "And here is your dose of laudanum."

She spilled a bit of the medicine on my hospital gown as she brought it toward me.

"I'm so sorry, miss," she said, fumbling to grab a handkerchief and clean me. "I'm new here."

"No need to apologize," I said. "I've endured worse."

I sat up straighter in bed and stared at Hannah, at her trembling, brown hands. "I'm sure you've endured worse, as well. Rest assured that your job will get easier, sweet girl. They all do."

Hannah sighed in relief as I said this. "Thank you for saying that," she said, then seeming to grow more comfortable, to view me as a place of safety, as she might a mother, or an aunt, she sat upon my bed, the sudden familiarity making me a bit wary.

"You and I are the only ones here," she said, raising an eyebrow so that I understood her meaning. "I was so grateful to get this job. They've only just started letting colored girls work as nurses here. But then, the other nurses have been so mean to me, Miss Lewis. You wouldn't believe the things they've said."

"I would believe it," I said, with a small laugh. "I can only hope that these days, it's somewhat better than what might have been said to me, when I was your age."

"Did you work as a nurse?" she asked, furrowing her eyebrows.

"No," I replied, hesitant before offering any more information. I had never divulged too much of my life since checking into this hospital, but there was something in this young girl's countenance, some part of her that I believed I could trust, and so I went on. "I worked as an artist, some years ago."

"An artist?" she repeated. "Any work I might have heard of?"

"Just a few pieces that gained any sort of attention," I said. "John Brown and Colonel Shaw, when I was younger. Hiawatha and Minnehaha. *Forever Free* and *Death of Cleopatra* were my greatest works, I suppose, if any of them can be considered great now."

Hannah stared at me for a moment, her mouth slightly open before she stood abruptly from my bed. She grabbed her hospital chart and looked over it, flipping through the pages on the clipboard. "Mary Lewis is your name?" she asked.

"Yes," I replied.

"I know of those works to be by a Miss Edmonia Lewis," she said.

"You know of those works?" I asked, incredulously. "You know of Edmonia Lewis?"

"Why, yes," she said, still seeming a bit confused. "I first read about her in the papers when I was a little girl. I couldn't believe that a colored girl could have such success. There was some scandal that happened when she went to school, I remember reading, but I didn't care about any of that. All I cared about was that a colored girl *could* go to school, and I resolved that I would do the very same."

Hannah stared at me for a moment then, as a thought seemed to occur to her. "Is that you?" she asked. "Are you the sculptress, Edmonia Lewis?"

"Mary Edmonia Lewis," I confirmed, nodding my head slowly.

Hannah clapped a hand over her mouth, looked at me, then glanced out at the hallway as if to surmise whether the other nurses knew whom they had in their midst.

"I am such an admirer of you, of your work," she said, shaking her head in disbelief. "And what are you doing here?"

"I'm sick, Hannah," I said, with a weak laugh. "I'm not here for my pleasure."

She shook her head and laughed, as well. "No, I mean here, in this sort of hospital. It is for paupers, for—"

"And so, it is for me," I replied. "It is what I can afford."

"But surely your art brought you a great fortune, Miss Lewis," she said. "A home, a staff, at least a personal nurse to look after you, and—"

"My art did not bring me such things," I replied, "though I wish it would have."

I shifted again in the bed, my pain becoming evident on my face, as Hannah helped to sit me up, and repositioned my pillow behind my back. She brushed my hair back on my head, then, a move as tender and loving as one I might expect from a child, or grandchild. She took a breath, then continued speaking.

"Well, what did your art bring you, Miss Lewis?" she asked.

I considered for a moment before answering her. "Much anguish, Hannah," I said, with another mirthless laugh. "Many sleepless nights and stress, but not much money."

"Well," Hannah said, sitting closer to me and taking my weak hands into hers. "I can tell you what it brought me, and perhaps you need to hear it. Your art brought me joy and inspiration. It challenged me, it made me think. It showed me that I shouldn't let anyone tell me what I could do. I could decide for myself, come what may."

I sat back in my hospital bed as Hannah continued on, telling me all about what my work had meant to her. I knew then, that with but one mind inspired, one fire ignited, everything that I had endured was worth all of the effort, and the struggle, and the pain. I knew that my art would live on long after my corporeal body had departed this earth, and that the world would always see the humanity that had once been mine.

# Discussion Questions

1. Edmonia initially views her enrollment at New York Central College as the end of her childhood, and in a way, the end of the relative freedom she knew while living with her aunts among the Ojibwe tribe. Do you view her enrollment at that school in the same way? Would she have been able to embark on an artistic career without this initial schooling?

2. While at New York Central College, Edmonia encounters, for the first time, many people who have formerly been enslaved, including many peers who are being pursued as fugitives. How do these encounters shape and transform Edmonia's thinking and understanding of the world? How does Edmonia's relationship with Clara, in particular, change her views regarding the purpose of her academic career, and her art?

3. On the day that Edmonia is to depart for Oberlin College, her brother, Samuel, is accosted at the train station and accused of being a fugitive slave. How does this event impact Edmonia's feelings about her departure from New York and separation from her brother? Do you think that she was right to leave him and continue on to her new life in Ohio? Would you have behaved similarly in the same position?

4. Edmonia is told that she will be wholeheartedly accepted at the progressive Oberlin College, but in many ways, she is still treated as an outsider there because of her race and gender. Have you ever experienced similar treatment as an outcast in a place where you thought you'd be welcomed? How did you handle that situation?

5. Edmonia and Ronan have an immediate connection through their passion for art, and feel a similar bond

through their status as outsiders in Oberlin society. How do you think their relationship would have progressed if Edmonia and Ronan began a life together in Rome? Do you think that love alone is sufficient to overcome societal strictures and prejudices?

6. After enduring much unfair treatment from her roommates, Edmonia is relieved to befriend Josephine, the housemaid at the Keep boarding home, but their relationship grows strained as the novel progresses. What do you think gets in the way of their friendship? How does Edmonia's own discomfort with her position in Oberlin seem to impede their relationship? What are the ways Edmonia could have been a better friend to Josephine?

7. When Edmonia first meets Cade, she feels a certain warmth and comfort unlike anything she's experienced before, but despite her feelings for him, she later refuses his marriage proposal, citing concerns about her art. Do you think the choice to start a life and family with Cade truly would have inhibited Edmonia's art, or aided it? In what ways do domestic responsibilities still affect a woman's career prospects?

8. In a shocking turn of events, Edmonia is accused of poisoning her roommates, Gemma Ennes and Sarah Miles. Were there any moments in the novel where you believed that Edmonia was guilty of these accusations?

9. John Mercer Langston, Edmonia's defense attorney, ultimately gets her court case thrown out by citing a lack of corpus delicti, or sufficient evidence to prove guilt. Do you think this was the best outcome for Edmonia? Might she have been able to remain in Oberlin and complete her education if the case had gone to trial and she had been fully exonerated by a jury?

10. Lydia Maria Child takes an immediate interest in Edmonia after her arrival in Boston, and offers to help Edmonia,

both in her career, and as a sort of guiding, maternal figure. Do you think that Lydia Child's intentions were genuine? Did Lydia truly view Edmonia as a daughter? Was Edmonia too rash in going against Lydia's wishes about her art and ultimately ending their acquaintance?

11. Anne Whitney offers to help Edmonia get settled in Europe, and serves as a sort of benefactress while Edmonia lives in Rome, with the expectation that she will ultimately be remunerated when Edmonia sells more of her art. Does this financial support seem to help, or hinder, Edmonia's artistic practice? Is it more important for an artist to work solely based on creative inspiration, or are financial imperatives just as important to consider?

12. When Edmonia and Harriet Hosmer first meet, they both seem to view each other as friends, but eventually their relationship grows tense and competitive, and Harriet accuses Edmonia of copying her work. What are the limits between creative inspiration and plagiarism? Can two people vying for the same career position ever truly be friends, or will there always be an underlying competitive element to their relationship?

13. Shortly after her move to Rome, Edmonia meets Domenico, a stone mason and studio assistant who invites Edmonia to create art for the Italian Risorgimento cause. Was Edmonia right to lend her artistic talents to this cause of Italian Unification? Should she have heeded Anne Whitney's warnings and not involved herself with such a controversial and contentious movement?

14. After learning about the death of her aunts, Edmonia decides to create a series of Ojibwe sculptures to pay tribute to their lives, and realizes that she has neglected this part of her identity for many years. Do you think that Edmonia could have brought more attention to the plight of Native Americans throughout her career, or did the expectations

of her time, and the imperatives of the Civil War and Reconstruction Era, require a more limited racial focus? Have you ever had to repress one part of your identity in favor of another?

15. Edmonia is filled with anxiety about traveling to America for the Centennial Exposition after being away for so many years, and after receiving threatening letters about her return. What was the significance of this return for Edmonia? Would you have returned to America to exhibit your art, despite the threats?

16. In the novel, as Edmonia ages, she begins to reflect on her life and career, and often feels that she has failed in her pursuits because of the financial difficulties she faces when her art falls out of favor. In real life, Edmonia Lewis did die in relative obscurity, with many of her works going unrecovered for decades. Do you think it's better for an artist to achieve fame and fortune while living and fall out of favor later, or is it better for an artist to be unknown while living, and have a positive and enduring legacy after death?

# ACKNOWLEDGMENTS

I extend my first acknowledgment and thanks to my son, who has transformed my life entirely, and to whom this novel, and all that I do, is dedicated. To my husband, Ian, who has believed in me wholeheartedly and supported my every idea, dream, and venture since the day that we met, I give an immense and eternal thanks. I owe a huge thank-you and debt of gratitude to my incredible parents, for inspiring me and raising me to believe that I was capable of anything, and to my sister, Kelly, for always being a stellar example of care and kindheartedness. And to all of my extended family, as well as the friends who have become like family, thank you all for your constant love and encouragement. I'm truly blessed, and forever grateful, to have such a supportive community behind me.

Thank you to my agent, Mark Gottlieb, for his belief in my writing dating back to my MFA program thesis anthology, and for his vast industry experience and expertise that has helped to guide me as I navigate the literary world. To his assistant, Madeleine Nystrom, as well as the whole team at Trident Media Group, I give my sincere gratitude for your untiring work and dedication. I extend a massive thank-you to my editor, Leticia Gomez, for her continued belief in both me and my novel, for her endless grace and patience as I revised, and for her keen and discerning eye while editing my work. I'd also like to thank the Kensington Books publisher Jackie Dinas, publicist Michelle Addo-Chajet, and the entire Kensington Books and Dafina imprint teams for taking a chance on me and my work. I couldn't ask for a better team to publish my debut.

I wouldn't be where I am as a writer were it not for the academic communities that have helped to shape and challenge me, and so I owe a huge acknowledgment to the professors and peers I had while in the Columbia University MFA program, as well as during my undergraduate creative writing courses at

NYU. I'd also like to thank the colleagues and students I had while teaching in Columbia's University Writing Program and NYU's Liberal Studies Program, whose writing and insightful conversations helped to sharpen my own thinking and approach to my craft.

I'm grateful, as well, to all of the writers and historians who have delved into the details of Edmonia Lewis's life, and whose works were invaluable to me as I completed my research. Among these writers are Kirsten Pai Buick, Marilyn Richardson, Martha Malamud, Margaret Malamud, Harry Henderson, Albert Henderson, and many others, including those historians who have recovered many of Edmonia Lewis's sculptures and restored her grave in London. And finally, I want to extend a special acknowledgment to Edmonia Lewis herself, as the creativity, courage, and resolve she showed throughout her life have served to inspire me throughout my writing of this novel.